TRUE LOVE'S
REWARD

A Sequel to *Mona*

MRS. GEORGIE SHELDON

1st WORLD
LIBRARY
Literary Society

True Love's Reward

Mrs. Georgie Sheldon

© 1st World Library, 2009
PO Box 2211
Fairfield, IA 52556
www.1stworldlibrary.com
First Edition

LCCN: 2009923387

Softcover ISBN: 978-1-4218-8838-5
Hardcover ISBN: 978-1-4218-8937-5
eBook ISBN: 978-1-4218-8739-5

Purchase *"True Love's Reward"*
as a traditional bound book at:
www.1stWorldLibrary.com/purchase.asp?ISBN=978-1-4218-8838-5

1st World Library is a literary, educational organization
dedicated to:

- Creating a free internet library of downloadable ebooks

- Hosting writing competitions and offering book publishing
scholarships.

Interested in more 1st World Library books? contact:
literacy@1stworldlibrary.com
Check us out at: www.1stworldlibrary.com

1ˢᵗ World Library Literary Society

Giving Back to the World

"If you want to work on the core problem, it's early school literacy."

- James Barksdale, former CEO of Netscape

"No skill is more crucial to the future of a child, or to a democratic and prosperous society, than literacy."

- Los Angeles Times

"Literacy... means far more than learning how to read and write... The aim is to transmit... knowledge and promote social participation."

- UNESCO

"Literacy is not a luxury, it is a right and a responsibility. If our world is to meet the challenges of the twenty-first century we must harness the energy and creativity of all our citizens."

- President Bill Clinton

"Parents should be encouraged to read to their children, and teachers should be equipped with all available techniques for teaching literacy, so the varying needs and capacities of individual kids can be taken into account."

- Hugh Mackay

CHAPTER I

A NEW DISCOVERY DEEPENS A MYSTERY

When Mrs. Montague entered her room, an hour after Mona went up stairs, there was a deep frown upon her brow.

She found Mona arrayed in a pretty white wrapper, and sitting before the glowing grate reading a new book, while she waited for her.

"What are you sitting up for, and arrayed in that style?" she ungraciously demanded.

"I thought you would need help in undressing, and I put on this loose wrapper because it was more comfortable than any other dress," Mona answered, as she regarded the lady with some surprise, for she had never before quite so curtly addressed her.

Mrs. Montague did not pursue the subject, and Mona patiently assisted her in taking off her finery, hanging the rich dress carefully over a form, folding her dainty laces, and arranging her jewels in their cases.

"Can I do anything more for you?" she asked, when this was done.

"No."

"At what time shall I come to you in the morning?" the fair girl inquired, without appearing to heed the uncivil monosyllable.

"Not before nine o'clock; but you can mend that rip in my traveling suit before that, as we shall go back to New York on the eleven o'clock express."

"Very well; good-night," Mona said, with gentle politeness, as she turned to leave the room.

"Stop a moment, Ruth," Mrs. Montague commanded.

Mona turned back, flushing slightly at the woman's imperiousness.

"I have not been at all pleased with your deportment this evening," the woman continued, "You have been exceedingly forward for a person in your position."

Mona's color deepened to a vivid scarlet at this unexpected charge.

"I do not quite understand you—" she began, when her companion turned angrily upon her, thus arresting her in the midst of her speech.

"I do not see how you can fail to do so," was her icy retort. "I refer to your acceptance of Mr. Palmer's attentions. One would have supposed that you regarded yourself as his equal by the way you paraded the drawing-room with him to-night."

Mona could hardly repress a smile at this attack, and she

Mrs. Georgie Sheldon

wondered what Ray would have thought if he could have heard it. Yet a thrill of indignation shot through her at this unreasonable abuse.

"You witnessed my introduction to Mr. Palmer this evening," she quietly replied; "you heard him offer to conduct me to Mr. Wellington, and so know how I happened to accept his attentions."

"You should have rejected his offer," was the quick retort.

"I could not do so without appearing rude—you yourself know that no young lady would have done so under the circumstances."

"No young *lady*—no, of course not," interposed Mrs. Montague, with significant emphasis; "but you must not forget that your position will not admit of your doing what might consistently be done by young ladies in society. You received Mr. Palmer's attentions as a matter of course—as if you considered yourself his equal."

"I do so consider myself," Mona returned, with quiet dignity, but with a dangerous sparkle in her usually mild eyes. The woman's arrogance was becoming unbearable, even to her sweet spirit.

"Really!" was the sarcastic rejoinder. "Your vanity, Ruth, would be odious if it were not so ridiculous. But you should not allow your complacency, over a merely pretty face, to lead you into such presumption as you have been guilty of to-night. I blame myself somewhat for what has occurred; if I had not accorded you permission to witness the dancing, you would not have been thrown into such temptation; but I did not dream that you would force yourself upon the notice of any of Mr. Wellington's guests."

"You are accusing me very unjustly, Mrs. Montague," Mona began, with blazing eyes, but the woman cut her short.

"I consider myself a competent judge in such matters," she insolently asserted. "At all events, however, you are to receive no more attentions from Mr. Palmer. He—is the son of the gentleman whom I expect to marry, and I have no intention of allowing my seamstress to angle for my future step-son."

"Madame—" began Mona, indignantly.

"We will not discuss the matter further," Mrs. Montague interposed, imperiously; "you can go now, but be sure to have my traveling dress ready by nine o'clock in the morning."

Mona went out, and forced herself to shut the door after her without making the slightest sound, although every nerve in her body was tingling with indignation and resentment, to which she longed to give some outward expression.

But for one thing, she would have faced the coarse, rude woman, and proclaimed that she was already the promised wife of Raymond Palmer, and had a perfect right to receive his attentions whenever and wherever she chose.

That secret of the desertion of her mother haunted her, however, and she was bound to curb herself and bear everything for three months longer, while she would diligently apply herself to the task before her.

She retired immediately, but she could not go to sleep until she had relieved her overcharged heart of its bitterness and passion in a burst of weeping.

The next morning early Ray and his father were on their way to New York, and ten o'clock found them seated in the private court-room, where Mrs. Vanderheck was to answer the charges against her.

Money will accomplish a great deal, and in this case it had secured the privilege of a private examination, before a police justice, who would decide whether the suspected culprit should be held for the grand jury.

Immediately upon the arrival of the Palmers, Detective Rider came to them, accompanied by a gentleman whom he introduced as Justin Cutler, Esq., of Chicago.

They all took seats together, and presently a door opened to admit Mrs. Vanderheck, who was attended by her husband and counsel, and who was richly attired in a close-fitting black velvet robe, and wore magnificent solitaires in her ears, besides a cluster of blazing stones at her throat.

If she was the adventuress whom the officials were searching for, she was certainly bringing a bold front to the contest in thus parading her booty before their very eyes.

Her husband was an elderly gentleman, who appeared to be in feeble health, but who conducted himself with dignity and self-possession.

The case was opened by Mr. Cutler's counsel, who told the story of the purchase of the spurious crescents in Chicago, and affirmed that they had been found upon the person of the party under arrest.

Mrs. Vanderheck listened with intense interest throughout the recital, while a look of astonishment overspread her face as the narrative proceeded.

The crescents were produced and Mr. Cutler brought forth the bogus ones, which he still had in his possession, and the two pairs appeared to be exact counterparts of each other.

The magistrate examined them with interest and care, after which he placed them on the desk before him.

Mrs. Vanderheck's counsel then said that his client would like to relate how the contested jewels came in her possession.

Permission being given for her to do so, the lady took the stand and began:

"Three years ago the coming month, which, according to the dates just given by the prosecuting counsel, was about three months after the gentleman in Chicago was defrauded, I was boarding at the Revere House, in Boston. While there I became acquainted with a lady—a widow who called herself Mrs. Bent, and her appearance corresponds with the description given of Mrs. Bently. I was very much pleased with her, for she seemed to be a lady of very amiable character, and we became quite intimate. She appeared to have abundant means, spent her money very freely, and wore several diamonds of great beauty and value—among them the crescents which were taken from me last Friday evening. About two months after becoming acquainted with her, she came to me one day in great distress and said that the bank, in which she was a large stockholder, had suspended payment, and all her available funds were locked up in it. She said she had considerable money invested in Western land, which she might be able to turn into cash later, but until she could do so she would be absolutely penniless—she had not even enough ready money to defray her hotel bill, which had been presented that day. Then with apparent reluctance and confusion she remarked that she had often heard me

Mrs. Georgie Sheldon

admire her diamond crescents, and so she had ventured to come and ask me if I would purchase them and thus relieve her in her present extremity, while she offered them at a price which I considered a great bargain. I said I would consult my husband.

"I have a weakness for diamonds—I confess that I am extravagantly fond of them," Mrs. Vanderheck here interposed, a slight smile curling her lips, "and my husband has generously gratified my whims in this respect. He approved of the purchase of the crescents, provided some reliable jeweler would warrant that they were all right. I reported this decision to Mrs. Bent, and we went together to an expert to submit the stones to his verdict.

"He pronounced them exceedingly fine, and valued them far above the price which my friend had put upon them, and I told her I would take them. We returned to our hotel and went directly to my rooms, where my husband drew up a check for a hundred dollars more than the stipulated price, Mrs. Bent giving a receipt for the amount, while she was profuse in her expressions of gratitude for our kindness in relieving her from pecuniary embarrassment. 'I shall go immediately to pay my bill,' she said, looking greatly pleased that she was able to do so, as she handed me the case containing the diamonds, and then she immediately left the room. Half an hour later she came to me again, her eyes red and swollen from weeping, an open telegram in her hand. Her mother was dying, and had sent for her, and she was going immediately to her. She took an affectionate leave of me and soon after left the hotel. This, your honor, is how I came to have the crescents and"—taking a folded paper from her elegant purse—"here is the receipt for the money paid for them."

The lady took her seat after giving this testimony, while the receipt was examined by the police justice and Mr. Cutler's counsel.

"I hope the lady has not been a victim to the same cunning scheme that served to defraud the gentleman from Chicago," he gravely observed.

"You do not mean to imply that my stones are not genuine!" exclaimed Mrs. Vanderheck, with sudden dismay.

"I am not able to say, madame," his honor courteously replied, "but I should like to have them examined by an expert and proved."

Mr. Palmer here stated that he could settle the question if he were allowed to examine them.

Both cases were passed to him, and after closely inspecting the crescents for a moment or two, he returned them, with the remark:

"The stones are *all* paste, but a remarkably good imitation. I should judge that they had been submitted to a certain solution or varnish, which has recently been discovered, and is used to simulate the brilliancy of diamonds, but which, if the stones are dropped in alcohol, will dissolve and vanish."

"Impossible!" Mrs. Vanderheck protested, with some warmth. "It *cannot* be that I have worn paste ornaments for more than three years, and never discovered the fact."

"It is not strange that you were deceived," the gentleman replied, glancing at the glittering gems, "for I think that only an expert could detect the fact, they are such a clever imitation of genuine gems."

Mrs. Georgie Sheldon

"I cannot believe it," the lady persisted, "for Mrs. Bent was not out of my sight a moment, from the time the expert in Boston pronounced his verdict, until they were delivered to roe in my room at the hotel."

"Nevertheless," Mr. Palmer positively affirmed, "the woman must have adroitly managed to change the crescents on the way back, substituting the bogus for the real ones, for these are certainly paste."

Mr. Cutler's counsel here stated that his client had an important statement to make, whereupon that gentleman related that Mr. Arnold, the Chicago expert to whom the real crescents had been submitted, had made a private mark upon the setting, with a steel-pointed instrument, and if such a mark could be discovered upon Mrs. Vanderheck's ornaments they were doubtless real.

He produced the card which Mr. Arnold had given him, and the crescents were carefully examined, but no mark of any kind could be found upon them, and the general conclusion was that they were but a skillful imitation of genuine diamonds, and that Mrs. Vanderheck had only been another victim of the clever adventuress, whose identity was still as much of a mystery as ever.

Mr. Palmer and Ray now began to feel quite uncomfortable regarding the cross which Mr. Rider had also taken in charge. They consulted a few moments with Mrs. Vanderheck's counsel, and then the cross was quietly submitted to Mr. Palmer's examination.

He at once said it did not belong to him, although it was very like the one that had been stolen, for he also was in the habit of putting a private mark upon his most expensive jewelry; and he further remarked that he very much regretted that

Mrs. Vanderheck should have been subjected to so much unpleasantness in connection with the unfounded suspicion.

The case was then dismissed without further discussion, and the lady behaved in the most generous and amiable manner toward both Mr. Cutler and Mr. Palmer.

She said it was not at all strange that she should have been suspected, under the circumstances, and she bore them no ill-will on account of the arrest. She was only annoyed that any publicity had been given to the matter. She even laughingly accused Ray of having suspected her on the evening of Mr. Merrill's reception, and then she explained the cause of her own strange behavior on that occasion. She had read of the Palmer robbery and the circumstances of his being kidnapped, and she realized at once, upon being introduced to him when he had mispronounced her name, that his suspicions had fastened upon her.

She shook hands cordially with Mr. Cutler, and remarked that, while she experienced some vexation and mortification over the discovery that the crescents were spurious, the imposition had taught her a lesson, and she should henceforth purchase her diamonds of a reliable dealer in such articles.

"But," she added, gayly, "I shall never see a diamond crescent after this without asking the owner to allow me to examine it. I believe I shall turn detective myself and try to ferret out the original ones if they are still in existence."

She bowed smilingly to the three gentlemen, and passed out of the room, leaning upon the arm of her husband.

"Well, Ray," Mr. Palmer remarked, as they wended their way to the store, "we may as well give up our diamonds once

Mrs. Georgie Sheldon

for all; I have not the slightest hope that we shall ever see them again. If we ever do find them," he added, with an arch glance, "I'll present them to your wife on her wedding day— that is, if they come to light before that event occurs."

"Then my wife is to have no diamonds unless the stolen ones are found?" Ray responded, in a tone of laughing inquiry.

"I did not mean to imply that, my boy," Mr. Palmer responded. "I will present your wife with diamonds, and fine ones, too, when I am introduced to her."

"Then I will give you three months in which to make your selection," Ray retorted, with animation.

"Whew! you are hopeful, my son, or else you have had good news of your lady-love," the elder gentleman exclaimed, with surprise. "You are a sly dog, and I thought you seemed happier than usual, when you came to Hazeldean. You must tell me more about it when you have time. But three days will be time enough for my selections for your wife, and she shall have the stolen ones also, if they are ever recovered."

Mr. Rider was the most disappointed one of the whole party, for he had been so sure of his game; while he had been doggedly persistent for over three years in trying to hunt down the tricky woman, who had imposed upon Justin Cutler, and it was a bitter pill for him to swallow, to discover, just as he believed himself to be on the verge of success, that he was only getting deeper into the mire.

"She is the keenest-witted thief I ever heard of," he muttered, moodily, when the case was dismissed, "but if I could only get track of some of the Palmer diamonds there might be some hope for me even now, for I firmly believe that the same woman is at the bottom of all three thefts."

He would not take anything from Mr. Cutler for what he had done or tried to do, although the gentleman offered to remunerate him handsomely for his labor.

"I've earned nothing, for I've accomplished nothing," he said, dejectedly. "I feel, rather, as if I ought to pay your expenses on from the West, for it's been only a wild-goose chase."

"I had other business, aside from this, which called me to New York, so don't feel down at the mouth about the trip," Mr. Cutler kindly replied. "I am going to remain in the city for a few weeks, then I go to Havana to meet my sister, who has been spending the winter in Cuba for her health."

The same week Mrs. Vanderheck appeared at a select ball, wearing more diamonds than any one had ever before seen upon her at once; but after that one brilliant appearance it was remarked that she was becoming more subdued in her tastes, for she was never again seen in New York with such an expensive display of gems.

CHAPTER II

A STORMY INTERVIEW

After their return from Hazeldean, Mrs. Montague seemed to forget her spite against Mona. Indeed, she was even kinder than she had ever been. Mona quietly resumed her usual duties, and was so faithful and obliging that the woman apparently regretted her harshness on the night of the ball, and was very considerate in her requirements, and verified what Mary, the waitress, had once said, that she was a kind mistress if she wasn't crossed.

On the morning after their arrival in New York, Mona wrote a note to Ray, related something of what had occurred, and suggested that it might be as well not to antagonize Mrs. Montague further by being seen together while she remained in her employ. She told him where she would attend church the following Sabbath, and asked him to meet her so that they could talk over some plan by which they might see each other from time to time without exciting suspicion regarding their relations.

Mr. Amos Palmer called by appointment upon Mrs. Montague on Wednesday evening, following the return from Hazeldean, when he formally proposed, and was accepted.

When, on Thursday morning, the triumphant widow announced the fact to her nephew, he flew into a towering passion, and a bitter quarrel ensued.

"You have promised me that you would never marry," he cried, angrily; "you have pledged your word that I should be your sole heir, and I swear that you shall not give me the go-by in any such shabby fashion."

"Hush, Louis; you are very unreasonable," said his aunt. "I believe that it will be for your interest as well as mine that I marry Mr. Palmer, and because I simply change my name, it does not follow that you will not be my heir. You know that I have no other relative, and I mean that you shall inherit my fortune. If *you* will marry Kitty McKenzie immediately. I will settle a hundred thousand upon you outright."

"But I don't like the idea of your marrying at all—I vow I won't stand it!" the young man reiterated, and ignoring the subject of his own marriage. "I suppose you have reasons for wishing to change your name," he added, with a sneer, "but you must not forget that I know something of your early history and subsequent experiences, and I have you some-what in my power."

"And you are no less in mine, young man," his companion sternly retorted. "It will not be well for you to make an enemy of me, Louis—it will be far better for you to yield to my plans gracefully, for my mind is fully set on this marriage. Can't you understand that as the wife of a man in Mr. Palmer's position, nothing that has ever been connected with my previous history will be liable to touch me. Mrs. Richmond Montague," with a sneering laugh, "will have vanished, or become a myth, and Mrs. Palmer will be unassailable by any enemies of the past."

Mrs. Georgie Sheldon

"Yes; I can fully understand that," her nephew thoughtfully replied, "and perhaps—Well, if I withdraw my objections, will you let me off from any supposed obligations to Kitty McKenzie? Truly, Aunt Marg," with unusual earnestness, "I don't want to marry the girl, and I do want to marry some one else; give me the hundred thousand and let me choose my own wife, and we will cry quits."

"Louis Hamblin, I believe you will drive me crazy!" cried Mrs. Montague, growing crimson with sudden anger, "What new freak has got into your head now? Who is this some one else whom you wish to marry?"

"That girl up stairs—Ruth Richards, she calls herself," the young man answered, flushing, but speaking with something of defiance in his tone.

"Good gracious, Louis! you cannot mean it!" she exclaimed, aghast. "I told you I would have no nonsense in that direction. Does she, Ruth, suspect your folly?"

"Only to toss her head and turn the cold shoulder on me. She is in no way responsible for my folly, as you call it, except by being so decidedly pretty. You'd better give in, Aunt Marg—it'll be for your interest not to make an enemy of me," he quoted, in a peculiar tone, "and it will make a man of me, too, for I vow I love the girl to distraction."

Mrs. Montague uttered a sigh of despair.

"I was afraid you'd make a fool of yourself over her, and now I shall have to send the girl away. It is too bad, for she is the only expert seamstress I have had for a year," she said, tears of vexation actually rushing to her eyes.

"No, you don't," the young man retorted, flaming up angrily;

"don't you dare to send her away, or I swear I will do something desperate. Besides, the girl doesn't care a rap for me, but she is dead gone on young Palmer; and if you drive her away, the next you'll know she will forestall you in the Palmer mansion."

Mrs. Montague grew pale at this shaft, and sat for several moments absorbed in thought.

"I thought that he was in love with Walter Dinsmore's *protegee*, Mona Montague," she at last remarked, with a bitter inflection.

A peculiar smile flitted over Louis Hamblin's lips at this remark. But he quickly repressed it, and replied:

"So I heard and thought at one time; but he was deeply smitten with Ruth the night of the Hazeldean ball, and never left her side after refreshments; they sat in the balcony, half concealed by the draperies, until after one o'clock."

"You don't mean it!" Mrs. Montague exclaimed, with a start and frown. "Then the girl is more artful than I thought; but, on the whole, I'm not sure but that I should prefer to have Ray Palmer marry Ruth Richards rather than Mona Montague—it might be better for me in the end. I wonder where she is. I am almost sorry—"

She broke off suddenly, but added, after a moment:

"I don't know, Louis—I am somewhat perplexed. If, as you say, Ray Palmer is so deeply smitten with Ruth he must have gotten over his penchant for the other girl. I will think over your proposition, and tell you my conclusion later."

An expression of triumph swept over Louis Hamblin's face,

Mrs. Georgie Sheldon

but quickly assuming a grateful look, he remarked:

"Thank you, Aunt Margie—if you'll bring that about I'll be your loyal slave for life."

Mrs. Montague's lips curled slightly at his extravagant language, but she made no reply to it.

Presently, however, she asked:

"When are you going to attend to that matter of business for me? I do not think it ought to be delayed any longer."

"Blast it! I am tired of business," responded her dutiful nephew impatiently, adding: "I suppose the sooner I go, though, the quicker it will be over."

"Yes, I want everything fixed secure before my marriage, for I intend to manage my own private affairs afterward, the same as before," his companion returned.

Louis laughed with some amusement.

"You ought to have been a man, Aunt Marg; your spirit is altogether too self-reliant and independent for a woman," he said.

"I know it; but being a woman, I must try to make the best of the situation in the future, as I have done all my life," she returned, with a self-conscious smile.

"Well, I will look after that matter right away—get your instructions ready and I will be off within an hour or two," said the young man, as he rose and went out, while Mrs. Montague proceeded directly to her own room.

CHAPTER III

MONA FORESTER

While Louis Hamblin and Mrs. Montague were engaged in the discussion mentioned in the preceding chapter, below stairs Mona sat in the sewing-room reading the paper of the previous evening. She was waiting for Mrs. Montague to come up to give her some directions about a dress which she was repairing before she could go on with it.

She had read the general news and was leisurely scanning the advertisement columns, as people often do without any special object in view, when her eye fell upon these lines:

WANTED—INFORMATION REGARDING A PERSON named Mona Forester, or her heirs, if any there be. Knowledge to her or their advantage is in the possession of CORBIN & RUSSEL, No.—Broadway, N. Y.

Mona lost all her color as she read this.

"Can it be possible that there is any connection between this Mona Forester and my history?" she murmured thoughtfully; "Mona is a very uncommon name—it cannot be that my mother's surname was Forester, since she was Uncle Walter's sister. Perhaps this Mona Forester may have been some relative for whom she was named—possibly an aunt, or even her mother, and thus I may be one of the heirs. But," she interrupted herself and smiled, "what a romantic creature I am, to be weaving such a story out of a mere advertisement! Still," she added, more thoughtfully, "this woman's heirs cannot be very numerous or it would not be necessary to advertise for them."

She carefully cut out the lines from the paper, slipped the clipping into her pocket-book, then took up her work just as Mrs. Montague entered the room.

She gave instructions regarding the alterations she wished made, and then left Mona by herself again. All day long Mona's mind kept recurring to the advertisement she had cut from the paper, while she had an instinctive feeling that she might be in some way connected with Mona Forester, although how she could not comprehend.

"It would be useless for me to go to Corbin & Russel to make inquiries, for I could give them no reliable information about myself," she said, while considering the matter. "Oh, why could not Uncle Walter have told me more? I could not even prove that I am Mona Montague, for I have no record of my parents' marriage or of my birth. Perhaps, if I could find that woman—Uncle Walter's wife—she might be able to tell me something; but I do not know where to find her. Possibly Mrs. Montague would know whether this Mona Forester is a relative, if I dare ask her; but I do not—I could not—without betraying myself and perhaps spoil all my other plans. Oh, dear, it is so dreadful to be alone in the world and not really know who you are!" she concluded, with a sigh.

About the middle of the next forenoon Mrs. Montague asked her if she would come with her to look over a trunk of clothing preparatory to beginning upon spring sewing.

Mona readily complied with her request, and together they went up to a room in the third story. There were a number of trunks in the room, and unlocking one of these, Mrs. Montague threw back the lid and began to lay out the contents upon the floor. Mona was astonished at the number and richness of the costumes thus displayed, and thought her income must be almost unlimited to admit of such extravagance.

She selected what she thought might do to be remodeled, and then she began to refold what was to be replaced in the trunk.

Among other things taken from it, there was a large, square pasteboard box, and Mrs. Montague had just lifted it upon her lap to examine its contents to see if there was anything in it which she would need, when Mary appeared at the door, saying that Mr. Palmer was below and wished to see her.

Mrs. Montague arose quickly, and in doing so, the box slipped from her hands to the floor and its contents, composed of laces, ribbons, and gloves, went sliding in all directions.

"Oh dear! what a mess!" she exclaimed, with a frown of annoyance, "You will have to gather them up and rearrange them, Ruth, for I must go down. Just lay the dresses nicely in the trunk, and I will lock it when I return."

She went out, leaving Mona alone, and the latter began to fold the ribbons and laces, laying them in the box in an orderly manner.

When this was done she turned her attention again to the trunk into which Mrs. Montague had hastily tumbled a few garments.

"She has disarranged everything," the girl murmured. "I believe I will repack everything from the bottom, as the dresses will be full of wrinkles if left like this."

She removed every article, and noticing that the cloth in the bottom was dusty, took it out and shook it.

As she was about to replace it, she was startled to find herself gazing down upon a large crayon picture of a beautiful girl.

A low, startled cry broke from her lips, for the face looking up into hers was so like her own that it almost seemed as if she were gazing at her own reflection in a mirror, only the hair was arranged differently from the way she wore hers, and the neck was dressed in the style of twenty years previous.

"Oh, I am sure that this is a picture of my mother," she murmured, with bated breath, as, with reverent touch, she lifted it and gazed long and earnestly upon it.

"If you could but *speak* and tell me all that sad story—what caused that man to desert you in the hour of your greatest need!" she continued, with starting tears, for the eyes, so life-like, looking into hers, seemed to be seeking for sympathy and comfort. "Oh, how cruel it all was, and why should those last few weeks of your life have been so shrouded in mystery?"

She fell to musing sadly, with the picture still in her hands, and became so absorbed in her thoughts that she was almost unconscious of everything about her, or that she was neglecting her duties, until she suddenly felt a heavy hand upon her shoulders, and Mrs. Montague suddenly inquired:

"Ha! where did you get that picture? Why don't you attend to your work, and not go prying about among my things?" and she searched the girl's face with a keen glance.

Mona was quick to think and act, for she felt that now was her opportunity, if ever.

"I was not prying," she quietly responded. "I thought I would pack everything nicely from the bottom of the trunk, and as I took out the cloth to shake and smooth it, I found this picture lying beneath it. I was very much startled to find how much it resembles me. Who can she be, Mrs. Montague?" and Mona lifted a pair of innocently wondering eyes to the frowning face above her.

For a moment the woman seemed to be trying to read her very soul; then she remarked, through her set teeth:

"It is more like you, or you are more like it than I thought. Did you never see a picture like it before?"

"No, never," Mona replied, so positively that Mrs. Montague could not doubt the truth of her statement. "Is it the likeness of some relative of yours?" she asked, determined if possible to sift the matter to the bottom.

"A *relative? No*, I *hope* not. The girl's name was Mona Forester, and—I *hated* her!"

"Mona Forester!" repeated Mona to herself, with a great inward start, though she made no outward sign, while a feeling of bitter disappointment swept over her heart.

It could not then have been a picture of her mother, she thought, for her name must have been Mona Dinsmore, unless—strange that she had not thought of it when she read that advertisement in the paper—unless she had been the half-sister of her Uncle Walter.

"You hated *her*?" Mona murmured aloud, with her tender, devouring glance fastened upon the beautiful face.

The tone and emphasis seemed to arouse all the passion of the woman's nature.

"Yes, with my whole soul!" she fiercely cried, and before Mona was aware of her intention, she had snatched the picture from her hands, and torn it into four pieces.

"There!" she continued, tossing the fragments upon the floor, "that is the last of that; I am sure! I don't know why I have kept the miserable thing all these years."

Mona could have cried aloud at this wanton destruction of what she would have regarded as priceless, but she dared make no sign, although she was trembling in every nerve.

"Is the lady living?" she ventured to inquire, as she turned away, apparently to fold a dress, but really to conceal the painful quivering of her lips.

"No. You can finish packing this trunk, then you may take these dresses to the sewing-room. You may begin ripping this brown one. And you may take the pieces of that picture down and tell Mary to burn them. I came up for a wrap; I am going for a drive."

Mrs. Montague secured her wrap, then swept from the room, walking fiercely over the torn portrait, looking as if she would have been glad to trample thus upon the living girl whom she had so hated.

Mona reverently gathered up the fragments, her lips quivering with pain and indignation.

She laid them carefully together, but a bitter sob burst from her at the sight of the great ragged tears across the beautiful face.

"Oh, mother, mother!" she murmured, "what an insult to you, and I was powerless to help it."

She finished her packing, then taking the dresses that were to be made over, and the torn picture, she went below.

She could not bear the thought of having that lovely face, marred though it was, consigned to the flames, yet she dare not disobey Mrs. Montague's command to give it to Mary to be burned.

She waited until the girl came up stairs, then she called her attention to the pieces, and told her what was to be done with them.

She at once exclaimed at the resemblance to Mona.

"Where could Mrs. Montague have got it?" she cried; "it's enough like you, miss, to be your own mother, and a beautiful lady she must have been, too. It's a pity to burn the picture, Miss Ruth; wouldn't you like to keep it?"

"Perhaps Mrs. Montague would prefer that no one should have it; she said it was to be destroyed, you know," Mona replied, but with a wistful look at the mutilated crayon.

"You shall have it if you want it, and I'll fix it all right with her," said the girl, in a confidential tone, as she put the pieces back into Mona's hands. She had become very fond of the gentle seamstress, and would have considered no favor too great to be conferred upon her.

That same afternoon, when Mona went out for her walk, she took the mutilated picture with her.

She made her way directly to the rooms of a first-class photographer, and asked if the portrait could be copied.

Yes, she was assured; there would be no difficulty about getting as good a picture as the original, only it would have to be all hand work.

Mona said she would give the order if it could be done immediately, and, upon being told she could have the copy in three days, she said she would call for it at the end of that time.

She did so, and found a perfect reproduction of her mother's face, and upon her return to Mrs. Montague's she gave the pieces of the other to Mary, telling her she believed she did not care to keep them—they had better be burned as her mistress had desired.

This relieved her mind, for she did not wish the girl to practice any deception for her sake, and she feared that Mrs. Montague might inquire if her orders had been obeyed.

The following day she took the fresh portrait with her when she went out, and proceeded directly to the office of Corbin & Russel, who had advertised for information regarding Mona Forester or her heirs.

A gentlemanly clerk came forward as she entered, and politely inquired her business.

She asked to see a member of the firm, and at the same time produced the slip which she had cut from the paper.

The clerk's face lighted as he saw it, and his manner at once betrayed deep interest in the matter.

"Ah, yes," he said, affably; "please walk this way. Mr. Corbin is in and will be glad to see you."

He led the way to a private office, and, throwing open the door, respectfully remarked to some one within:

"A lady to see you, sir, about the Forester business." Then turning to Mona, he added: "This is Mr. Corbin, miss."

A gentleman, who was sitting before a desk, at once arose and came eagerly forward, scanning Mona's face with great earnestness.

"Have a chair, if you please, Miss——. Be kind enough to tell me what I shall call you."

"My name is Mona Montague," the young girl replied, a slight flush suffusing her cheek beneath his keen glance.

The gentleman started as she spoke it, and regarded her more closely than before.

"Miss Mona Montague!" he repeated, with a slight emphasis on the last name; "and you have called to answer the advertisement which recently appeared in the papers. What can you tell me about Miss Mona Forester?"

"She was my mother, sir," Mona replied, as she seated herself in the chair offered her. "At least," she added, "my mother's name was Mona Forester before her marriage."

Mrs. Georgie Sheldon

"Well, then, young lady, if you can prove that the Mona Forester, for whom we have advertised, was your mother, there is a snug little sum of money awaiting your disposal," the gentleman smilingly remarked.

Mona looked astonished. She had scarcely given a thought to reaping any personal advantage, as had been hinted in the advertisement, from the fact of being Mona Forester's child. Her chief desire and hope had been to prove her mother's identity, and to learn something more, if possible, of her personal history.

She was somewhat excited by the information, but removing the wrapper from her picture, she arose and laid it before Mr. Corbin, remarking:

"This is a portrait of Mona Forester, and she was my mother."

Mr. Corbin took the crayon and studied the beautiful face intently for a few moments; then turning his glance again upon his visitor, he said, in a tone of conviction:

"There can be no doubt that you and the original of this picture are closely united by ties of consanguinity, for your resemblance to her is very striking. You spoke in the past tense, however, so I suppose the lady is not living."

"No, sir; she died at the time of my birth," Mona answered, sadly.

"Ah! that was very unfortunate for you," Mr. Corbin remarked, in a tone of sympathy. "You gave your name as Mona Montague, so, of course, Miss Forester must have married a gentleman by that name. May I ask—ah—is he living?"

"No, sir, he is not."

"Will you kindly give me his whole name?" Mr. Corbin now asked, while his eyes had a gleam of intense interest within their dark depths.

"Richmond Montague."

Again the lawyer started, and a look of astonishment passed over his features.

"Where have you lived, Miss Montague, since the death of your parents?" he inquired.

"Here in New York, with my uncle."

"Ah! and who was your uncle, if you please?" and the man seemed to await her reply with almost breathless interest.

"Mr. Dinsmore—Walter Dinsmore."

The lawyer sat suddenly erect, and drew in a long breath, while his keen eyes seemed to be trying to read the girl's very soul.

He did not speak for nearly a minute; then he said, with his usual composure:

"So, then, you are the niece of Walter Dinsmore, Esq., who died recently, and whose property was claimed by a—a wife who had lived separate from him for a good many years."

Mona flushed hotly at this remark. It seemed almost like a stain upon her uncle's fair name to have his domestic affairs spoken of in this way, and she had been very sore over the revelation that he had had a discarded wife living.

"Yes, sir," she briefly responded, but with an air of dignity that caused a gleam of amusement to leap to the lawyer's eyes.

"Well—it is very queer," he remarked, musingly, while his eyes traveled back and forth between the picture he held in his hands and the face of the beautiful girl before him.

Mona looked a trifle surprised—she could not understand what was "queer" in the fact that she was Walter Dinsmore's niece.

"I suppose," resumed Mr. Corbin, after another season of reflection, during which he looked both grave and perplexed, "that you have the *proofs* of all that you claim? You can prove that you are the daughter of Mona Forester and—Richmond Montague?"

Again Mona blushed, and hot tears of grief and shame rushed to her eyes, as, all at once, it flashed into her mind that her errand there would be a fruitless one, for she was utterly powerless to prove anything, while the peculiar emphasis which Mr. Corbin had almost unconsciously used in speaking of her father made her very uncomfortable. She had hoped to learn more than she had to reveal, and that her strong resemblance to her mother's picture would be sufficient to prove the relationship between them; but now she began to fear that it would not.

"What proofs do I need?" she asked, in a voice that was not quite steady.

"The marriage certificate of the contracting parties, or some witness of the ceremony, besides some reliable person who can identify you as their child," was the business-like response.

"Then I can prove nothing," Mona said, in a weary tone, "for I have no certificate, no letters, not even a scrap of writing penned by either my father or my mother."

A peculiar expression swept over Mr. Corbin's face at this statement, and Mona caught sight of it.

"What could it mean?" she asked herself, with a flash of anger that was quite foreign to her amiable disposition. "Did the man imagine her to be an impostor, or did he suspect that there might have been no legal bond between her parents?"

This latter thought made her tingle to her fingertips, and aroused all her proud spirit.

"I can at least prove that I am Walter Dinsmore's niece," she added, lifting her head with a haughty air, while her thoughts turned to Mr. Graves, her uncle's lawyer. He at least knew and could testify to the fact. "He took me," she continued, "three days after mother's death, and I lived with him from that time until he died."

"Ah! and your mother was Mr. Dinsmore's sister?" questioned Mr. Corbin.

"Yes. I always supposed, until within a few days, that she was his own sister," Mona said, thinking it best to be perfectly open in her dealings with the lawyer; "that her name was Mona Dinsmore; but only this week I learned that it was Mona Forester, so, of course, she must have been a half-sister."

"Well, if you can prove what you have stated it may lead to further developments," said Mr. Corbin, kindly. "Let me examine your proofs, and then I shall know what to do next."

Mrs. Georgie Sheldon

A sudden fear smote Mona—a great shock made her heart almost cease its beating at the lawyer's request.

What proofs had she for him to examine? How could she establish the absolute fact?

It was true that her uncle had authorized a will to be made leaving all his property to his "beloved niece," but he had not been able to sign it, and it of course amounted to nothing. Must even this relationship be denied her in law? Oh, why had he not been more careful in regard to her interests? It was very hard—it was very humiliating to have her identity thus doubted.

"Mr. Horace Graves was my uncle's lawyer; he will tell you that I am his niece," she faltered, with white lips.

"My dear young lady, I know Mr. Graves, and that he is a reliable man," Mr. Corbin observed; "but a hundred people might assert that you were Mr. Dinsmore's niece, and it would not prove anything. Don't you know that to satisfy the law upon any point there must be indisputable proof forthcoming; there must be some written record—something tangible to demonstrate it, or it amounts to nothing? You may be the niece of Mr. Dinsmore; you may be the daughter of Mr. and Mrs. Richmond Montague; this may be the portrait of Miss Mona Forester; but the facts would have to be established before your claim could be recognized and the property bequeathed to Miss Forester made over to you."

"Oh," cried Mona, in deep distress, "what, then, shall I do? I do not care so much about the property as I do about learning more about my mother. I will tell you frankly," she went on, with burning cheeks and quivering lips, "that I know there is some mystery connected with her married life; my uncle told me something, but I have reason to believe that he kept back much that I ought to know," and Mona proceeded to relate all that Mr. Dinsmore had revealed to her on her eighteenth birthday, while the lawyer listened with evident interest, his face expressing great sympathy for his fair young visitor.

"I am very glad to have you confide in me so freely," he remarked, when she concluded, "and I will deal with equal frankness with you so far as I may. Our reason for advertising for information regarding Miss Mona Forester was this: I received recently a communication from a lawyer in London, desiring me to look up a person so named, and stating that a certain Homer Forester—a wool merchant of Australia—had just died in London while on his way home to America, and had left in his lawyer's hands a will bequeathing all that he possessed to a niece, Miss Mona Forester, or her heirs, if she was not living. The date and place of her birth were given, but further than that Homer Forester could give no information regarding her."

"Where was she born?" Mona here interposed, eagerly, "Oh, sir, it is strange and dreadful that I should be so ignorant of my own mother's history, is it not?"

"Miss Forester, according to the information given in her uncle's will, was born in Trenton, New Jersey, March 10th, 1843, but that is all that I can tell you about her," bestowing a glance of sympathy upon the agitated girl. "You say that she died at the time of your birth. I wish you could bring me proof of this and that you are her daughter; but of course your mere assertion proves nothing, nor your possession of this picture, which may or may not be her. Believe me, I should be very glad to surrender this property to you if it rightly belongs to you."

"Of course I should like to have it, if I am the legal heir," Mona said, thoughtfully; "but," with a proud uplifting of her pretty head, "I can do without it, for I am able to earn my own living."

"Is there no one to whom you can appeal? How about Mr. Dinsmore's wife, who succeeded in getting all his property away from you—could she prove anything?" and Mr. Corbin regarded his companion with curious interest as he asked the question.

"I do not know—I have never even seen her," said Mona, thoughtfully; "or, at least, if I have, it must have been when I was too young to remember anything about her; besides, I should not know where to find her. There is only one person in the world, I believe, who really knows anything about me."

"And who is that?" interposed Mr. Corbin, eagerly.

"Mrs. Richmond Montague, my father's second wife."

Mr. Corbin suddenly arose from his chair, and began to pace the floor, while, if she had been watching him closely, Mona might have seen that his face was deeply-flushed.

"Hum! Mrs. Richmond Montague—is—Where is Mrs. Richmond Montague?" he questioned, somewhat incoherently.

"Here, in this city."

"Then why do you not appeal to her?" demanded the lawyer, studying the girl's face with some perplexity.

"Because—there are reasons why I do not wish to meet her just at present," Mona said, with some embarrassment, "and I do not know that she would be able to prove anything. To be frank," she continued, with increasing confusion, "the present Mrs. Montague entertained a strong dislike, even hatred, against my mother. Doubtless her animosity extends to me also, and she would not be likely to prove anything that would personally benefit me."

"You have not a very high opinion of Mrs. Richmond Montague, I perceive," Mr. Corbin remarked, with a curious smile.

"I have nothing special against her personally, any further than that I know she hated my mother, and I do not wish to meet her at present. Why," with sudden thought, "could not you try to ascertain from her some facts regarding my mother's marriage?"

"I might possibly," said Mr. Corbin, gravely, "but that would not benefit you; you would be obliged to meet her in order to be identified as Mona Forester's child."

"I had not thought of that," replied Mona, with a troubled look, "and," she added, "she could not even identify me to your satisfaction, for she never saw me to know me as Mona Montague."

"*As Mona Montague!*" repeated the quick-witted lawyer; "does she know you by any other name? Are you not keeping something back which it would be well for me to know?"

"Yes; I will tell you all about it," Mona said, flushing again, and resolving to disclose everything. She proceeded to relate the singular circumstances which led to her becoming an inmate of Mrs. Montague's home, together with the incident of finding her mother's picture in one of her trunks.

"Ah! I think this throws a little light upon the matter," Mr. Corbin said, when she concluded. "If you had told me these facts at first we should have saved time. And you never saw this woman until you met her in her own house?" he asked, in conclusion, and regarding Mona searchingly.

"No, never; and had it not been for the hope of learning something about my mother's history, I believe I should have gone away again immediately," she replied.

"I should suppose she would have recognized you at once, by your resemblance to this picture," remarked her companion.

"She did notice it, and questioned me quite closely; but I evaded her, and she finally thought that the resemblance was only a coincidence."

"Well, I must confess that the affair is very much mixed— *very* much mixed," said the lawyer, with peculiar emphasis, "but I believe, now that I know the whole story, that the truth can be ascertained if right measures are used; *and*," he continued, impressively, "if we can prove that you are what you assert, the only child of Richmond Montague and Mona Forester, you will not only inherit the money left by Homer Forester, but, being the child of the first union—provided we can prove it legal—you could also claim the bulk of the property which your father left. Mrs. Montague, if she should suspect our design, would, of course, use all her arts to conceal the truth; but I imagine, by using a little strategy, we may get at it. Yes, Miss Montague, if we can only work it up it will be a beautiful case—a *beautiful* case," he concluded, with singular enthusiasm.

Mona gave utterance to a sigh of relief. She was more hopeful than ever that the mystery, which had so troubled her, would be solved, and she was very grateful to the kind-hearted lawyer for the deep interest he manifested in the matter.

"You are very good," she said, as she arose to take her leave; "but really, as I have said before, I am not so anxious to secure property as I am to know more about my parents. Do you suppose," she questioned, with some anxiety, "that the enmity between my uncle and my father was so bitter that— that Uncle Walter was in any way responsible for his—my father's—death?"

"Poor child! have you had that terrible fear to contend against with all your other troubles?" asked Mr. Corbin, in a tone of compassion. "No, Miss Montague," he added, with grave positiveness, "I do not believe that Walter Dinsmore— and I knew him well—ever willfully committed a wrong against any human being. Now," he resumed, smiling, to see the look of trouble fade out of her eyes at his assurance, "I am going to try to ferret out the 'mystery' for you. Come to me again in a week, and I believe I shall have something definite to tell you."

Mona thanked him, after which he shook hands cordially with her, and she returned to West Forty-ninth street.

"Well, well!" muttered the lawyer, after his fair client had departed, "so that is Dinsmore's niece, who was to have had his fortune, if he could have had his way about it! I wonder what Madame Dinsmore would say if she knew that I had taken her husband's *protegee* as a client! It is a burning shame that she could not have had his money, if it was his wish—or at least a share of it. Poor little girl! after living in such luxury all her life, to have to come down to such a humdrum existence as sewing for a living! I will do my best for her—I will at least try to secure Homer Forester's money to her. It's strange, too, that I should happen to have dealings with the brilliant Mrs. Montague, also. It's a very queer case and there is a deep scheme behind it all! I believe—"

What he might have believed remained unsaid, for the office-boy entered at that moment and announced another client, and the astute lawyer was obliged to turn his attention, for the time, in another direction.

CHAPTER IV

MR. CORBIN MAKES A CALL

On the evening of the same day that Mona visited the office of Corbin & Russel, attorneys at law, and shortly after Mrs. Montague had finished her lonely dinner—for her nephew was away on business—there came a sharp ring at the door of No.—West Forty-ninth street.

Mary answered it, and, after ushering the gentleman into the reception-room, went to her mistress to inform her that a caller was waiting below.

"Erastus Corbin," Mrs. Montague read, as she took the neat card from the salver, and her face lighted with sudden interest.

"Perhaps he has sold that property for me," she murmured. "I hope so, for I wish to turn all my real estate into money, if possible, before my marriage."

She made some slight change in her costume, for she never allowed herself to go into the presence of gentlemen without looking her best, and then hastened below.

She greeted the lawyer with great cordiality, and remarked, smilingly:

"I hope you have good news for me. Is that property sold yet?"

"I cannot say that it is sold, madame," Mr. Corbin returned; "but I have had an offer for it, which, if you see fit to accept, will settle the matter very shortly."

"Tell me about it," said the lady, eagerly.

Mr. Corbin made a statement from a memorandum which he drew from his pocket, upon the conclusion of which Mrs. Montague authorized him to sell immediately, saying that she wished to dispose of all her real estate, even if she had to sacrifice something in doing so, remarking that a bank account was far less trouble than such property; and, having discussed and decided some other points, the lawyer arose as if to take his leave.

"Pray do not hasten," Mrs. Montague smilingly remarked.

She happened to have no engagement for the evening, and, being alone, was glad of even the companionship of a prosy attorney.

"Thank you," Mr. Corbin politely returned; "but I have other matters on hand which ought to be attended to."

"Surely you do not work evenings as well as during the day?" Mrs. Montague observed, with some surprise.

"Not always; but just now I seem to have some very knotty cases on hand—one, in particular, seems to baffle all my skill with its mystery. Indeed, it bids fair to develop quite a romance."

"Indeed! you pique my curiosity, and we women are dear

lovers of romance in real life, you know," said the charming widow, with an arch smile. "Would it be betraying confidence to tell me a little about it?" she added, persuasively.

"Oh no; the matter is no secret, that I know of, and really you are so cozy here," with an appreciative glance about the attractive room as he resumed his seat, "I am tempted to stay and chat a while. I recently received a communication from an English lawyer who desired to turn a case over to me, as it related to American parties, and he had no time to come here to look them up. A man who was on his way home from Australia, was taken ill in London and died there; but before his death he made his will, leaving all his property to a niece, although he did not know whether she was living or not. All the information he could give regarding her was her name, with the date and place of her birth. In case she should not be living, her heirs are to inherit the money. I have made every effort to find her—have been to the place where she was born—but can get no trace of her—no one remembered such a person, and I could not even learn whether she had ever married. I am afraid that the case will prove to be a very complicated and vexatious one."

"I should think so," responded Mrs. Montague, who appeared to be deeply interested in the story. "What was the girl's name?"

"Mona Forester."

"Mona Forester!" repeated the woman, in a startled tone, and growing as white as her handkerchief. "I didn't know she had a relative in the world, except—"

She abruptly paused, for she had been thrown entirely off her guard, and had committed herself, just as the wily lawyer intended and suspected.

A flash of triumph gleamed in his eyes for an instant at the success of his ruse.

"Ah! did you ever know of such a person?" he demanded, eagerly, and with well-feigned surprise.

"I—I knew of—a girl by that name before I was married," Mrs. Montague reluctantly admitted, and beginning to recover her composure.

"Where did she reside?"

"She was born in Trenton, New Jersey, I believe," was the evasive reply.

"Yes, my papers so state—and she must be the same person," said Mr. Corbin, in a tone of conviction. "But that is very meager information. Was Trenton your home also?"

"No, I lived in New York until my marriage."

"Was Miss Forester ever married?"

"Yes."

"Ah! how fortunate that I happened to mention this circumstance to you this evening!" exclaimed the lawyer, with great apparent satisfaction, but ignoring the evident reluctance of his companion to give him information. "Perhaps you can give more particulars. Whom did the lady marry?"

"Don't ask me anything about her, Mr. Corbin," Mrs. Montague cried, excitedly, and with an angry gesture. "The girl ruined my life—she loved the man I loved and—I hated her accordingly."

"But surely you can have no objection to telling me what you know of her history," returned Mr. Corbin, with assumed surprise. "I have this case to settle, and I simply wish to find the woman or her heirs, in order to do my duty and carry out the instructions of the will. It would assist me greatly if you could tell me where I might find her," he concluded, in an appealing tone.

"She is dead—she died more than eighteen years ago."

"Ah! where did she die?"

"Abroad—in London."

"Did she leave any heirs?"

"She died in giving birth to her only child."

"Did the child live?"

"I—believe so."

"Was it a son or a daughter?"

"The latter."

"What became of her—where is she now?"

"I do not know—I do not care!" were the vicious words which burst from the woman's white lips, and Mr. Corbin saw that she was greatly excited, while everything that she had said thus far went to corroborate the statements Mona had made to him regarding her mother.

"But, my dear madame," Mr. Corbin said, soothingly, "while I do not like to trouble you, or recall painful memories, cannot you see that it is my duty to sift this matter and avail myself of whatever information I can get? If Miss Forester was married and had a child, that child, if living, is Homer Forester's heir, and I must find her. Now, if you know anything about these people that will assist me in my search, it becomes your duty to reveal it to me."

"I cannot; I do not know of anything that will assist you," sullenly returned Mrs. Montague, who was mentally reproaching herself in the most bitter manner for having allowed herself to be taken so unawares and to betray so much.

"Whom did the lady marry?" persisted Mr. Corbin.

"I will not tell you!" passionately exclaimed his companion. "Oh, why have I told you anything? Why did I acknowledge that I even knew Mona Forester? I should not have done so, but you surprised the truth from me, and I will tell you nothing more. I hated the girl, and though I have never seen her, I hate the child on her account, and I would not lift even a finger to help her in any way."

"Are you not unreasonably vindictive, Mrs. Montague?" mildly asked Mr. Corbin.

"Unreasonable or not, I mean what I say, and Homer Forester's money may be scattered to the four winds of heaven for any effort that I will make for Mona Forester's child," was the dogged response.

"Do you not see that I must learn the truth?" the lawyer asked, with some sternness, "and though I am averse to using threats to a lady, if you will not tell me voluntarily I shall be obliged to use means to compel you to reveal what you know."

"Compel me!" repeated Mrs. Montague, confronting him with haughty mien. "You cannot do that."

"But I can, Mrs. Montague," Mr. Corbin positively asserted. "Since you have acknowledged so much, and it is evident that you could reveal more, you can be compelled, by law, to do so under oath."

"You would not dare to adopt such stringent measures with me, after all the business that I have thrown into your hands," the woman said, sharply, but growing white about the mouth.

"My duty is just as obligatory to one client as to another. I am under as much obligation to carry out the conditions of Homer Forester's will as I am to be faithful to your interests," the lawyer replied, with inflexible integrity.

"Then you will no longer be faithful to me—you will transact no more business for *me*," Mrs. Montague asserted, with angry brow and compressed lips.

"Very well, if that is your decision I must submit to it," was the imperturbable response. "And now, madame, I ask you, once for all, to tell me the name of the man whom Mona Forester married?"

"I will not."

"Then let *me* tell *you* what conclusion I have drawn from what I have learned during this interview," said Mr. Corbin, as he leaned forward and looked straight into the woman's flashing eyes. "You have said you hated her because she ruined your life—because she loved the man you loved. You have refused to tell me the name of that man. You can have but one reason in thus withholding this information—that motive is fear; therefore, I infer that Mona Forester was the

Mrs. Georgie Sheldon

first wife of your husband—her child was your husband's daughter."

"Prove it, then!" cried his companion, with a scornful, though nervous, laugh. "Find the marriage certificate—find the witnesses who saw them married, the clergyman who performed the ceremony, the church register where their names are recorded, if you can."

"I believe they will be found in good time," confidently asserted Mr. Corbin, as he arose the second time to leave; "and, madame, if such proofs are found do you comprehend what the result will be? Not only will Mona Forester's child inherit the fortune left by Homer Forester, but also the bulk of your deceased husband's property."

"Never! for no one in this world can prove that Mona Forester was ever legally married, and—I defy you to do your worst," hoarsely cried Mrs. Montague, with lips that were almost livid, while she trembled visibly with mingled excitement, fear, and anger.

But the gentleman had no desire to discuss the matter further. He simply bade her a courteous good-evening, and then quietly left the house.

"It is the strangest affair that I ever had anything to do with," he muttered, as he walked briskly down the street. "The girl's story must be true, for it tallies exactly with the woman's admissions this evening. There must be proof somewhere, too. Can it be possible," he went on, with a start, "that they are in Mrs. Montague's hands? If so, she is liable to destroy them, and thus plunge my pretty little client into endless trouble. It is strange that her uncle, Dinsmore, could not have been more sensible and left some definite information regarding the child. But I am going to do my best for her, and though I never had quite so mysterious a case before, I believe the very obscurity which invests it only adds interest to it."

Mrs. Montague was in a terrible passion after her lawyer had left. She sprang to her feet and paced the floor from end to end, with angry steps, her face almost convulsed with malice and hatred.

"Can it be possible that I am going to have that battle to fight over again, after all these years?" she muttered; "that the child is going to rise up to avenge the wrongs of her mother? What if she does? Why need I fear her? I have held my own so far, and I will make a tough fight to do so in the future. Possession is said to be nine points in law and I shall hold on to my money like grim death. I never could—I never will give up these luxuries," she cried, sweeping a covetous glance around the exquisitely furnished room. "I plotted for them—I sold my soul for them and him, now they are mine—mine, and no one shall take them from me! Mona Forester, how I hated you!—how I hate your daughter, even though I have never seen her!—how I almost hate that girl up stairs for her strange resemblance to you. I would have sent her out of the house long ago for it, if she had not been so good and faithful a seamstress, and needful to me in many ways. She, herself, saw the resemblance to that picture—By the way," she interposed, with a start, "I wonder if she obeyed me about that crayon the other day! If she didn't—if she kept it I shall be tempted to believe—I'll find out, anyhow."

With a somewhat anxious look on her face, the woman hurried up stairs to her room.

Upon reaching it she rang an imperative peal upon her bell.

Mrs. Georgie Sheldon

Mary presently made her appearance, and one quick glance told her that something had gone wrong with her mistress.

"Bring me a pitcher of ice-water," curtly commanded Mrs. Montague. "And, Mary—"

"Yes, marm."

"Did Miss Richards give you a torn picture the other day?"

"Yes, marm," answered the girl, flushing, "she said you wanted it burned."

"Did you burn it?"

"N-o, marm, somehow I couldn't make up my mind to put it in the fire; it was such a pretty face, and so like Miss Richards, and I've been wanting a picture of her ever since she came here, only I thought maybe she'd resent it if I asked her for one; and so I pasted it together as well as I could, and tacked it up in my room," the girl explained, volubly, and concluded by meekly adding: "I hope there was no harm in it, marm."

"You may bring it to me," was all the reply that Mrs. Montague vouchsafed her attendant; and Mary, looking rather crestfallen, withdrew to obey the command.

"It is a shame to burn it," she muttered, as she took down the defaced picture, and slowly returned down stairs; "but I'm glad Miss Ruth gave it to me before she asked for it."

Mrs. Montague sprang up the moment the girl entered the room, and snatching the portrait from her hands, dashed it upon the bed of glowing coals in the grate.

"When I give an order I want it obeyed," she said, imperiously. "Now go and bring me the water."

Mary withdrew again, wondering what could have happened to make her mistress so out of sorts, and finally came to the conclusion that the lawyer must have brought her bad news.

"There! that is the last of that!" Mrs. Montague said, as she watched the flames curl about the beautiful face in the grate. "I'm glad the girl didn't keep the picture herself; I believe that all my previous suspicions would have been aroused if she had. It *can't* be that *she* is Mona's child, for she has always been so indifferent when I have questioned her. Possibly she may be a descendant of some other branch of the family, and does not know it. My only regret is that I did not try to see that other girl before Walter Dinsmore died; then I should have been sure. I wonder where she can be? And to think that Mona Forester should have had an uncle to turn up just at this time! I didn't suppose she had a relative in the world besides the child."

Her musings were cut short at this point by the return of Mary with the water. She poured out a glassful for her mistress, and then was told that she might go.

The lady set down the glass without even tasting its contents; then rising, went to the door and locked it, after which she walked to a small table which stood in a bay-window, and removed the marble top, carefully laying it upon the floor.

This act revealed instead of the usual skeleton stand where a marble top is used a polished table of solid cherry, with what appeared to be a lid in the top, and in which there was a small brass-bound key-hole.

Mrs. Georgie Sheldon

Drawing a bunch of keys from her pocket, Mrs. Montague selected a tiny one from among the others, inserted it in the lock, and the next moment the lid in the table was lifted, thus revealing a secret compartment underneath.

This was filled with various things—paper boxes, packages of various forms and sizes, together with some documents and letters.

Drawing a chair before the table, the woman sat down and began to examine the letters.

There was an intensely bitter expression on her face—a frown on her brow, a sneer on her lips—which so disfigured it that scarcely any one would have recognized her as the brilliant and beautiful woman of the world who so charmed every one in society.

There were perhaps a dozen letters in the package which she took out of the table, and these, as she untied the ribbon that bound them together, and slipped them through her fingers, were all addressed in a delicate and beautiful style of penmanship.

She snatched one from the others, and passionately tore it across, envelope and all. Then she suddenly dropped them on her lap, a shiver running over her, her cheek paling with some inward emotion.

"Ugh! they give me a ghostly feeling! My flesh creeps! I feel almost as if Mona Forester herself were standing beside me, and had laid her dead hand upon me. I cannot look them over—I will tie them up again and burn them all at once," she muttered, in a hoarse tone.

She gathered them up, and hastily wound the ribbon about

them, laying them upon the table beside her, then proceeded with her examination of the other contents of the secret compartment.

CHAPTER V

MONA DECLINES A PROPOSAL

Mrs. Montague next took a square pasteboard box from the secret compartment in the table, and opened it.

On a bed of pure white cotton there lay some exquisite jewelry. A pearl and diamond cross, a pair of unusually large whole pearls for the ears, and two narrow but costly bands for the wrists, set with the same precious gems.

"Pearls!" sneered the woman, giving the box, with its contents, an angry shake. "He used to call her his 'pearl,' and so, forsooth, he had to represent his estimate of her in some tangible form. There is nothing of the pearl-like nature about me," she continued, with a short, bitter laugh. "I am more like the cold, glittering diamond, and give me pure crystallized carbon every time in preference to any other gem. He wasn't niggardly with her on that score, either," she concluded, lifting the upper layer of cotton, and revealing several diamond ornaments beneath.

"She was a proud little thing, though," she mused, after gazing upon them in silence for a moment, "to go off and leave all these trinkets behind her. I'd have taken them with me and made the most of them. They haven't done me much good, however, since they came into my possession. I never could wear them without feeling as I did just now about the letters. I might have sold them, I suppose, and I don't know why I haven't done so, unless it is because they are all marked."

She covered them and threw the box from her with a passionate gesture, and then searched for a moment in silence among the remaining contents of the table.

She finally found what she wanted, apparently, for a look of triumph swept over her face.

It was a folded document, evidently of parchment.

"Ha, ha! prove your shrewd inferences, my keen-witted lawyer, if you can," she muttered, exultantly, as she unfolded it, and ran her eyes over it. "Mona Forester's child the heir to the bulk of my husband's property, indeed! Perhaps, but she will have to prove it before she can get it. How fortunate that I helped myself to these precious keepsakes when he was off his guard; even he did not dream that I had this," and she shook the parchment until it rattled noisily through the room; then refolding it, she put it carelessly aside, and turned once more to what remained to be examined.

"Here is that exquisite point-lace fan," she said, lifting a long, narrow box, and removing the lid. "I never had a point-lace fan until I bought it for myself; and here is that picture; I never had his likeness painted on ivory and set in a frame of rubies! Ha! Miss Mona, you were a favored wench, but your triumph was of short duration."

It is impossible to convey any idea of the bitterness of the woman's tone, or the vindictiveness of her look, as she took from a velvet case the picture of a handsome young man, of perhaps twenty-five years, painted on ivory, and encircled with a costly frame of gold set with rubies.

"You loved her," she cried, fiercely, as she gazed with all her soul in her eyes upon that attractive face, while her whole frame shook with emotion. "Nothing was too costly or elegant for your petted darling; her slightest wish was your law, while for me you had scarcely a word or a look of affection; you were like ice upon which not even the lava-tide of my idolatry could make the slightest impression. Is it any wonder that I hated her for having absorbed all that I craved? Is it strange that I exulted when they drove her from her apartments in Paris, believing her to be a thing too vile to be tolerated by respectable people. Well, she had his love, but I had him—I vowed that I would win, and—I did."

But, evidently, the memory of her triumph was not a very comforting one, for she suddenly dropped her face upon the hands that still clasped the picture, and burst into a torrent of tears, while deep sobs shook her frame, and she seemed utterly overwhelmed by the tempest of her grief.

Surely in this woman's nature there were depths which no one, who had seen her the center of attraction in the thronged and brilliant drawing-rooms in high-life, would have believed possible to her.

Suddenly, in the midst of this unusual outburst, there came a knock upon the door.

The sound seemed to give her a terrible start in her nervous state.

She half sprang from her chair, a look of guilt and fear sweeping over her flushed and tear-stained face, the table before her gave a sudden lurch, and before she could put out her hand to save it, it went over and fell to the floor with a crash, spilling its contents, and snapping the lid to the secret compartment short off at its hinges.

"What is it?—who is there?" Mrs. Montague demanded, as she went toward the door, while she tried to control her trembling voice to speak naturally.

"What has happened?—I thought I heard a fall," came the response in the anxious tones of Mona's voice.

"Nothing very serious has happened," returned Mrs. Montague, frowning, for the girl, who so closely resembled the rival she hated, coming to her just at that moment, irritated her exceedingly. "I simply upset something just as you knocked. What do you want?"

"I only came to ask if I should finish your tea-gown in the morning, or do the mending, as usual;" Mona replied.

"Finish the tea-gown. I shall need it for the afternoon."

"Very well; I am sorry if I disturbed you, Mrs. Montague. Good-night," and Mona turned away from the door wondering what could have caused such a clatter within the woman's room.

Mrs. Montague went back to the bay-window, righted the table, rearranged its contents, and fitted the broken lid over them with hands that still trembled with her recent excitement.

"What a pity that the lid is broken," she muttered, impatiently, "for now it will do no good to lock it. I cannot help it, however, and perhaps no one will suspect that there is a secret compartment beneath the slab."

She carefully replaced the heavy marble, moved the table to its usual position, and then, worn out with the conflict she had experienced, retired for the night.

But she did not sleep well; she was nervous, and tossed uneasily upon her bed until far into the small hours of the morning, when she finally dropped into a fitful slumber.

She was aroused from this about eight o'clock the following day by Mary, who came as usual to bring her a cup of coffee, which she always drank before rising. There also lay upon the tray a yellow official-looking envelope.

"What is this?" Mrs. Montague demanded, as she seized it and regarded it with some anxiety.

"A telegram, marm. A messenger brought it just as I was coming up stairs," the girl replied.

Her mistress tore it open and devoured its contents with one sweeping glance.

Instantly her face flushed a deep crimson, and she crushed the message hastily within her hand, while she began to drink her coffee, but seemed to become deeply absorbed in her own thoughts while doing so.

A few moments later she arose and dressed herself rapidly, but all the time appeared preoccupied and troubled about something.

"I believe I shall let Louis marry her if he wants to. I could settle the hundred thousand on him, and stipulate that they go West, or somewhere out of the State, to live. I believe I'll do it," she murmured once, while thus engaged, "that is, if—"

She did not finish the sentence, but, with a resolute step and air, went down to her breakfast.

She had no appetite, however, and after dallying at the table for half an hour or so, she went up stairs again and entered the sewing-room.

She found Mona busy at work upon the tea-gown—a beautiful robe of old-rose cashmere, made up with a lighter shade of heavy armure silk.

"Can you finish it in season?" she inquired.

"Oh, yes, easily. I have about an hour's more work to do upon it," the young girl answered.

"That is well, for I want you to go down town to do some shopping for me. I cannot attend to it, as I wish to keep fresh for my high-tea this afternoon," Mrs. Montague returned, flushing slightly. Then she added: "I will make out a list of what I need, and you may go as soon as the dress is done."

Mona was pleased with the commission, for the morning was lovely, and she had felt unusually weak and weary ever since rising. The close application to which she had been subjected since her return from Hazeldean—for she had been hurried with spring sewing—had worn upon her.

A feeling of discouragement had also taken possession of her, for she seemed no nearer learning the truth about her mother than when she had first come there.

She was confident that Mrs. Montague had been her father's second wife, and she fully believed that she must have in her possession papers, letters, or some other documents that would reveal all that she wished to know regarding

Richmond Montague's first marriage, and give her some information regarding the great sorrow that had so blighted the life of his beautiful young wife.

She had promised that she would give herself to Ray at the end of three months; he still held her to that promise, and six weeks of the time had already elapsed, and she seemed to be no nearer the attainment of her desires than when she had made it.

True, she had found the picture of her mother, and learned that her name was Mona Forester. She had also discovered that a relative had been seeking for her with the desire of leaving her all that he possessed.

But all this was very unsatisfactory, for she had not gained the slightest clew by which to prove herself to be the child of Mona Forester, or any one else.

It was all a wearisome and harrowing tangle, and it wore both upon her spirits and her strength.

It was true, too, that she had found Ray, and learned that he loved her. This was a great comfort, and she knew she had but to tell him that she was ready to go to him, and he would at once make her his wife; but—a flush of shame flooded her face every time she thought of it—she was continually haunted by the fear that her mother might never have been Richmond Montague's wife—that possibly she might have no legal right to the name she bore, in spite of her uncle's assurance to the contrary, and she shrank from marrying Ray if any such stigma rested upon her.

She had never breathed these fears to him—she kept hoping that some accident, or some remark from Mrs. Montague, would throw light on the perplexing mystery.

But Mrs. Montague never referred in any way to her past life in her presence. She had never once mentioned her husband, and, of course, Mona had not dared to ask her any questions upon these subjects.

"I can never marry Ray until I know," she had told herself over and over in great distress, "for I love him too well ever to bring any blight upon his life."

She had had a dim hope that Mr. Corbin might in some way manage to unravel the mystery, and yet she could not see that he had anything more tangible to work upon than she herself had.

Mona finished the dress and carried it to Mrs. Montague, who seemed very much pleased with it.

"You are a lovely seamstress, Ruth, and a good, faithful girl," she said, as she carefully examined the neatly made garment. "But for one thing," she added, as she covertly searched the girl's fair face, "I believe I should grow really fond of you."

This remark put Mona on her guard in a moment, though it also set her heart to beating with a vague hope.

"Thank you for your praise of my work, Mrs. Montague," she quietly said, "but," lifting a wondering glance to her face, "what is the one thing that I lack to win your esteem? If I am at fault in any way I should be glad to know and correct it."

"You lack nothing. It is because you so much resemble a person whom I used to detest—I am unaccountably antagonized by it," said the woman, frowning, for the clear eyes, looking so frankly into hers, were wondrously like Mona Forester's.

Mrs. Georgie Sheldon

"Oh, I suppose you refer to the person whose picture I found up stairs a while ago," said Mona.

"Yes," and Mrs. Montague looked slightly ashamed of her confession; "I imagine you think I am somewhat unjust to allow my prejudice to extend to you on that account, and I know I am; but the power of association is very strong, and I did hate that girl with all my heart."

Mona was trying to acquire courage to ask what reason she could have for hating any one who looked so gentle and inoffensive, when the woman resumed, with some embarrassment:

"Louis scolded me for the feeling when I mentioned it to him—he is not tainted in any such way, I assure you. Do you know, Ruth," with a little laugh of assumed amusement, "that he is very fond of you?"

Mona's face was all ablaze in an instant—her eyes likewise, although she was greatly surprised to learn that the young man had betrayed his liking for her to his aunt.

"I trust that Mr. Hamblin has not led you to believe that I have ever encouraged any such feeling on his part," she coldly remarked.

"I know that you have been very modest and judicious, Ruth; but what if I should tell you that the knowledge of his preference does not displease me; that, on the whole, I rather approve of his regard for you?" questioned Mrs. Montague, observing her closely.

"From what you told me a moment ago, I should suppose you would feel anything but approval," Mona replied, without being able to conceal her scorn of this sanction to

Louis Hamblin's presumption.

"What do you mean?" demanded her companion, with some sharpness.

"I refer to the prejudice which you confessed to entertaining against me."

"But did I not acknowledge that it was unjust? And when one confesses wrong and is willing to correct it, credit should not be withheld," Mrs. Montague retorted, with some warmth. "But seriously, Ruth," she continued, with considerable eagerness, "Louis is very much in earnest about this matter. He has dutifully asked my permission to address you, and I believe it would be for his happiness and interest to have a good wife, such as I am confident you would make. I know that he has betrayed something of this feeling to you, or I should not presume to speak to you about it; but my reason for so doing is that I thought perhaps you might feel more free to accept his suit if you knew that I approved of the union."

Mona was trembling now with mingled excitement and indignation. Excitement over the discovery that Louis Hamblin had really been in earnest when he had made love to her at Hazeldean, and indignation that he should still presume to think that she would marry him after the decided rebuff she had given him at that time. She was also astonished that Mrs. Montague should propose such a thing after what she had said, on the night of the ball, about her "angling for Ray Palmer, and imagining herself to be his equal in any respect."

Then she grew very pale with a sudden suspicion. Perhaps Mrs. Montague had discovered who she was, possibly Mr. Corbin had been to her to question her, and had aroused her suspicions that she was Mona Montague, and she was plotting to marry her to her nephew in order to keep her fortune in the family, and thus tie Mona's hands to render her incapable of mischief.

These thoughts inspired her with fresh hope and courage, for she told herself that if this was the woman's object, there must be some proofs in existence that her mother's marriage with Richmond Montague had been legal.

But Mrs. Montague was waiting for some answer, and she could not stop to consider these points very fully now.

"I thank you," she said, trying hard to curb the scorn that was surging fiercely within her, "but I shall be obliged to decline a union with Mr. Hamblin—I could never become his wife."

"Why not, pray?" sharply demanded her companion.

"Because I believe that marriage should never be contracted without mutual love, and I do not love Mr. Hamblin," Mona returned, with cold positiveness.

"Really?" Mrs. Montague sneered, with a frowning brow, "one would suppose that a person in your position—a poor seamstress—would be only too glad to marry a handsome young man with Louis' prospects—for he will eventually inherit my fortune if he out-lives me."

"Then, perhaps, it will be a surprise to you to learn that there is one poor seamstress in the world who does not regard marriage with a rich young man as the most desirable end to be achieved in life," Mona responded, with quiet sarcasm.

Mrs. Montague grew crimson with anger.

"Then you would not marry my nephew if he should offer himself to you?" she indignantly inquired.

"No, madame; I could not. With all due appreciation of the honor intended me, I should be obliged to decline it."

The girl spoke with the utmost respect and courtesy, yet there was a slight inflection upon certain words which irritated Mrs. Montague almost beyond endurance.

"Perhaps you are already in love with some one else— perhaps you imagine that you may win young Palmer, upon whom you so indelicately forced your society at Hazeldean," she snapped.

Mona could not quite conceal all emotion at this unexpected attack, and a lovely color stole into her cheeks, at which the watchful woman opposite her was quick to draw her own conclusions, even though the fair girl made no reply to her rude speech.

"Let me disabuse your mind at once of any such hopes and aspirations," Mrs. Montague continued, with increased asperity, "for they will never be realized, since Ray Palmer is already engaged."

This statement was made upon the strength of what she had learned from Mr. Palmer regarding Ray's affection for Mr. Dinsmore's niece, and his own approval of the union if the young lady could be found.

Poor Mona's powers of endurance were tried to the utmost by this thrust, and she longed to proclaim, there and then, that she knew it—that she was the young man's promised wife.

But the time for such an avowal was not yet ripe; a few weeks longer, if she could have patience, and then she hoped there would be no occasion for further secrecy.

She put a strong curb upon herself, and simply bowed to show that she had heard and understood Mrs. Montague's statement.

The effort, however, drove every atom of color from her face, and seeing this, Mrs. Montague believed that she had planted a sharp thorn in her bosom.

She did not wish to antagonize her, however, and she was almost sorry that she had said so much; but she was a creature of impulse when her will was thwarted, and did not always stop to choose her words.

She had, for certain reasons, yielded her objections to Louis marrying her, and now this unexpected opposition on Mona's part only served to make her determined to carry the point, for the sake of conquering her, if for no other.

"Well, we will not quarrel over the matter, Ruth," she said, in a conciliatory tone. "Of course I have no right to coerce you in such a matter, and you are too useful to me to be driven away by contesting the point. So we will drop the subject; and now if you will take this memorandum and go about the shopping I shall be obliged to you. I shall need all my strength for this evening, because I am to have a large company to entertain, and—"

She abruptly paused, and seemed a trifle confused for a moment. Then she asked, with unusual consideration:

"Shall I send you in the carriage?"

"No, I should prefer to take a car down town and then walk about to the different stores. I sit so much I shall be glad of the exercise," Mona replied, as she turned to leave the room, but wondering what Mrs. Montague had been going to add when she stopped so suddenly.

Mrs. Georgie Sheldon

CHAPTER VI

RAY MAKES AN IMPORTANT DISCOVERY

Mona hastened to her own chamber, after leaving Mrs. Montague, where she hastily exchanged her house dress for a street costume, and then started out upon her errands.

She had a great deal to think of in connection with her recent conversation with Mrs. Montague, but, although much had been said that had annoyed her greatly, on the whole she had been inspired with fresh hope that the mystery enshrouding her mother's life would eventually be solved.

She therefore quickly recovered her spirits, and her face was bright and animated as she tripped away to catch the car at the corner of the street.

She had several errands to do, and she very much enjoyed the freedom of running about to the different stores, to buy the pretty things regarding which Mrs. Montague had discovered she possessed excellent taste and judgment.

She had nearly completed her purchases—all but some lace, which that lady wished to add to the ravishing tea-gown which was to be worn that evening, and to get this she would have to pass Mr. Palmer's jewelry store.

Her heart beat fast as she drew near it, for she had been hoping all the way down town that she might see Ray and have a few minutes' chat with him.

She glanced in at the large show-window, as she went slowly by, and, fortunately, Ray was standing quite near, behind the counter, talking with a customer.

He caught sight of her instantly, but indicated it only by a quick flash of the eyes, and a grave bow, and quietly continued his conversation.

Mona knew, however, that having seen her, he would seek her at the earliest possible moment, and so slowly sauntered on, looking in at the different windows which she passed.

It was not long until she caught the sound of a quick step behind her, and the next moment a firm, strong hand clasped hers, while a pair of fond, true eyes looked the delight which her lover experienced at the unexpected meeting.

"My darling!—I was thinking of you the very moment you passed, and wishing that I could see you. I have something very important to tell you," he said, eagerly, but his fine face clouded as he uttered these last words.

"It is something that troubles you, I am sure, Ray," said Mona, who was quick to interpret his every expression.

"Yes, it is—I am free to confess," he admitted, then added: "Come in here with me—there will not be many people about at this hour—where we can talk more freely, and I will tell you all about it."

They were passing the Hoffman House at that moment, and the young man led the way inside the *cafe*.

Mrs. Georgie Sheldon

They proceeded to a table in a quiet corner, where, behind some palms and tall ferns, they would not be likely to be observed, and then gave an order for a tempting lunch, the preparation of which would require some time.

While waiting for it, Ray confided his trouble to Mona.

"My father is really going to marry Mrs. Montague," was the somewhat abrupt communication which he made with pale lips and troubled brow.

"I have known it for some time, but did not like to speak of it to you," Mona quietly replied.

"You have known it for some time?" Ray exclaimed. "For how long, pray?"

"Ever since we were at Hazeldean."

"Impossible! for my father did not make his proposal until after our return to New York."

"But she certainly told me the night of the ball, when she came up stairs to retire, that she expected to marry Mr. Palmer," Mona returned, and flushing at the memory of that conversation, which, however, she had been too proud to repeat to her lover.

"Well, she may have expected to marry him, and I imagine that his own mind was pretty well made up at that time," said Ray, gloomily, "but the matter was not settled until after our return, as I said before, and the engagement is to be formally announced this afternoon at the high-tea given by Mrs. Montague."

Ah! this explained to Mona what had puzzled her just before

leaving home—why Mrs. Montague had once or twice appeared embarrassed during their conversation, why she had abruptly paused in the midst of that last sentence, and why, too, she had been so unusually particular about her personal appearance for a home-reception.

She mentioned these circumstances to Ray, and asked, in conclusion, if he were also invited to the high-tea.

"Yes; but, really, I am so heart-sick over the affair I feel as if I cannot go. I am utterly at a loss to understand this strange infatuation," he continued, with a heavy sigh. "My father, until this meeting with Mrs. Montague, has been one of the most quiet and domestic of men. He went occasionally into society, but never remained late at any reception, and never bestowed especial attention upon any lady. He has been a dear lover of his home and his books. We have seldom entertained since my mother's death, except in an informal way, and he has always appeared to have a strong antipathy to gay society women."

"How strange! for Mrs. Montague is an exaggerated type of such a woman; her life is one continual round of excitement, pleasure, and fashion," Mona remarked, "and I am sure," she added, with a glance of sympathy at her lover's downcast face, "that Mr. Palmer would soon grow very weary of such an existence."

"I am certain of it, also," Ray answered, "and more than that, from what I have learned of the woman through you—of her character and disposition—I fear that my father is doomed to a wretched future, if he marries her."

"I have similar forebodings," Mona said, thoughtfully, as her mind recurred to the conversation of the morning. "How would it do for you to tell your father what you know? It might influence him, and I shall not mind having my secret revealed if he can be saved from future unhappiness."

"I fear it is too late for that now. He is so thoroughly infatuated and has committed himself so far, I doubt the wisdom of seeking to undeceive him," Ray responded, with a sigh. "What powers of fascination that woman has!" he exclaimed, with some excitement. "She charms every one, young and old. I myself experienced something of it until you opened my eyes to her real character."

"Such women are capable of doing a great deal of harm. Oh, Ray, I believe that society ruins a great many people. Perhaps it was well that my career in it was so suddenly terminated," Mona remarked, gravely.

Ray smiled fondly down upon her.

"I do not believe it could ever have harmed you very much," he said, tenderly; "but I believe very many young people are unfitted for the higher duties of life where they give themselves up to society to such an extent as they do here in New York; it is such a shallow, unreal kind of life. We will be social—you and I, Mona, when we make a home for ourselves; we will be truly hospitable and entertain our friends for the good that we can get and give, but not merely for the sake of show and of being 'in the swim.'"

The smile and look which concluded these observations brought the quick blood to the cheeks of the fair girl, and made another pair of eyes, which were peering at them through the palms and ferns, flash with malicious anger and jealousy.

"I have so few friends now, Ray, I fear we shall not have many to entertain," Mona replied, a little sadly.

"I do not believe you know how many you really have, dear. You disappeared from social life so suddenly, leaving everybody in the dark regarding your whereabouts, that very few had an opportunity to prove their friendship," Ray said, soothingly. "However," he added, his fine lips curling a trifle, "we shall know how to treat those who have met and ignored you. But have you heard anything from Mr. Corbin since I saw you last?"

"No, and I fear that I shall not," Mona replied, with a sigh. "I do not see any possible way by which he can prove my identity. As you know, I have not a single item of reliable evidence in my possession, although I firmly believe that such evidence exists, and is at this moment in Mrs. Montague's keeping."

She then related how her suspicions had been freshly aroused by the conversation of that morning, and Ray was considerably excited over the matter.

"Why did you not tell me before that Louis Hamblin made himself obnoxious to you at Hazeldean?" he questioned, flushing with indignation, for Mona had also told him of her interview with the young man in the library, in connection with the story of Mrs. Montague's more recent proposal to her.

"Because I believed that I had myself thoroughly extinguished him," Mona answered, smiling; "and besides," she continued, with a modest blush, "I believe that no true, considerate woman will ever mention her rejection of a suitor to a third party, if she can avoid doing so."

Ray gave her an admiring glance.

"I wish there were more women in the world of the same

mind," he said. "But mind, dear, I will not have you annoyed about the matter further. If, after what you have told Mrs. Montague to-day, young Hamblin should presume to renew the subject again, you are to tell me and I will deal with him as he deserves. It certainly is rather suspicious her wanting you to become his wife. Why, it is in everybody's mouth that she has been trying for months to make a match between him and Kitty McKenzie," he concluded, thoughtfully.

"Kitty McKenzie is far too good a girl for such a fate; but I am afraid she is really quite fond of him," said Mona, with a regretful sigh. "But shall you come up to Forty-ninth street this afternoon, Ray?"

"I suppose I must, or people will talk," he replied, dejectedly. "If my father is determined to marry the woman it will create gossip, I suppose, if I appear to discountenance it; so all that remains for me to do is to put the best possible face upon the matter and treat my future step-mother with becoming deference."

"What do you suppose she will say when she learns the truth about us?" Mona inquired, with an amused smile. "I imagine there will be something of a breeze about my ears, for she informed me this morning that I need have no hopes or aspirations regarding you upon the strength of any attention that you bestowed upon me at Hazeldean, for—you were already engaged," and a little ripple of merry laughter concluded the sentence.

Ray smiled, delighted to see the sunshine upon his dear one's face, and to hear that musical sound. Yet he remarked, with some sternness:

"I think she is overstepping her jurisdiction to meddle in your affairs to such an extent. But here comes our lunch," he interposed, as the waiter appeared, bearing a well laden tray of tempting viands.

"Then let us drop all unpleasant topics, and give ourselves up to the enjoyment of it," said Mona, looking up brightly. "A light heart and a mind at ease greatly aid digestion, you know."

She would not allow him to refer to anything of a disagreeable nature after that, but strove, in her bright, sweet way, to banish the cloud from his face, and succeeded so well that before their meal was ended they had both apparently forgotten Louis Hamblin and his aunt, and the unsuitable engagement about to be announced, and were only conscious that they were there together, and all in all to each other.

But time was flying, and Mona knew that she must get back to assist Mrs. Montague with her toilet for the high-tea.

"It was very nice of you, Ray, to bring me here for this delightful lunch," she said, as they arose from the table, with a regretful sigh that they must separate, and began to draw on her gloves.

"We shall take all our lunches together before long, I hope, my darling," he whispered, fondly; "half the stipulated time is gone, Mona, and I shall certainly claim you at the end of another six weeks."

Mona flushed, but she did not reply, and her heart grew heavy, for she knew she should not be willing to become Ray's wife until she could prove the circumstances of her birth.

She longed to tell him how she felt about it—she longed to

　　　　Mrs. Georgie Sheldon

know how he would feel toward her if they should discover that any stain rested upon her.

But she dare not broach the subject—a feeling of shame and humiliation kept her silent, and she resolved to wait and hope until the six weeks should pass.

They went out together, but still followed by that pair of malignant eyes, which had, however, been cautiously veiled, as was also the face in which they were set.

Ray walked with his betrothed to a corner, where he helped her aboard a car, and then returned to his store.

Later, on that same day, a gay company of gentlemen and ladies filled Mrs. Montague's spacious and elegant rooms, where she, in her elaborate and becoming costume, entertained in her most charming manner.

Mr. Palmer had come very early and secured a private interview, previous to the arrival of the other guests, and it was noticeable that, as the lady received, a new and magnificent solitaire gleamed upon the third finger of her left hand.

People surmised, very generally, what this meant, even before it was whispered throughout the rooms that the engagement of Mr. Palmer and the beautiful widow was formally announced. It was not very much of a surprise, either, as such an event had been predicted for some time.

Ray did not arrive until late, for he had little heart for the gay scene, and less sympathy in its object. But for his respect and love for his father, he would not have set foot in the house at all.

"Gentlemen's dressing-room on the left of the hall above," said the polite colored man, who attended the door, and Ray slowly mounted the stairs, hoping that he might catch a glimpse, if not secure an opportunity for a word with Mona.

But there was no such treat in store for him, for she was at that moment assisting Mary, who had met with a mishap in running up stairs, having stepped upon her dress and torn it badly.

Ray found the room indicated, which proved to be Mrs. Montague's boudoir, deposited his hat, gloves, and cane where he could conveniently get them again—for he did not intend to remain long—and then descended to the drawing-room.

He made his way at once to where Mrs. Montague was standing with her captive beside her, for he desired to get through with the disagreeable duty of offering congratulations, with all possible dispatch.

Poor Mr. Palmer! Ray pitied him, in spite of his aversion to the engagement, for he looked heated and flushed, and somewhat sheepish as his son approached, although he tried to smile and look happy, as if he enjoyed the glitter and show and confusion reigning all about him.

Ray politely shook hands with his hostess, making some general remark upon the occasion and the brilliant assembly, as he did so.

"And—I hope I am to have your congratulations." Mrs. Montague archly remarked, as she glanced from him to his father.

"You certainly can have no doubt that I sincerely hope the

arrangement may be for your mutual happiness," the young man gravely replied, as he bowed before them both.

"Then show yourself a dutiful son by drinking a cup of tea with me," laughingly returned the lady, as she slipped her white hand within his arm, and led him toward the great silver urn, where several charming "buds" were dispensing the fragrant beverage to the numerous guests.

Ray had no alternative, and he well knew that the wily widow had adroitly taken this way to make it appear to her guests that the son heartily approved his father's choice.

She possessed infinite tact, and chatted away in the most brilliant manner, making him wait upon her so assiduously that Ray was sure, from the looks of those about them, that every one was admiring his devotion(?) to his future step-mother.

She released him at last, however, and returned to her position beside his father, and watching his opportunity he stole unobserved from the room, and up stairs, intending to get away from the house as soon as possible.

Reaching Mrs. Montague's boudoir, he walked to the bay-window, and looked out upon the street. He was nervous and excited, and wished to regain his accustomed composure before going down stairs again.

He stood there a moment absorbed in unpleasant reflections, then turned to get his coat and hat.

As he did so, one of his feet caught in the heavy damask draperies, and in trying to disengage it, something crackled sharply beneath it, and he stooped to ascertain what it was.

Sweeping aside the heavy curtains, he saw a long, narrow document lying upon the floor beneath its folds.

He picked it up, and saw that it was a piece of parchment with something apparently printed upon it.

Not supposing it to be anything of importance, he mechanically unfolded it and began to read.

"Why, it is a marriage certificate!" he exclaimed, in surprise, under his breath.

Not caring to read the whole form, he simply glanced at the places where the names of the contracting parties were written, and instantly a mighty shock seemed to shake him from head to foot.

"Ha! what can this mean?" he exclaimed, in a breathless voice.

His face grew deathly pale. A blur came before his eyes. He rubbed them to dispel it, and looked again.

"It cannot be possible!" he said, in a hoarse whisper, and actually panting as if he had been running hard. "I cannot believe my sight, and yet it is here in black and white! and Mona—Mona, my darling! the mystery will be solved, and you will be righted at last."

The certificate, as will be readily surmised, was the very one which Mrs. Montague had examined the previous evening.

When Mona had knocked upon the door, it will be remembered that she was greatly startled and had upset the table. The accident had caused the certificate to be thrown upon the floor, with the other things, and by some means it was pushed beneath the heavy damask curtain and had escaped Mrs. Montague's eye and memory, when she hastily gathered up the scattered treasures and rearranged them in the secret compartment of the table.

Thus it had come into Ray's possession just at a time when it was most needed and desired.

Regaining his composure somewhat, he read it carefully through from beginning to end.

"How could it have come to be in such a strange place, and to fall into my hands?" he said, the look of wonder still on his face. "She—that woman must have had it in her possession, even as Mona suspected, and by some mistake or oversight dropped and forgot it. Shall I tell her I have found it? Shall I return it and then demand it from her?" he questioned, his innate sense of honor recoiling from everything that seemed dishonorable. "No," he continued, sternly, "it is not hers—she has no right whatever to it; it belongs to Mona alone, for it is the proof of her birthright. I will take it directly to Mr. Corbin, and I will not even tell Mona until I have first confided in him."

With a resolute purpose written on his fine face, Ray carefully put the document away in an inner pocket; then donning his coat and hat, quietly left the house.

The last postal delivery of that same evening brought to Mrs. Richmond Montague the following anonymous letter:

"MADAME:—The girl in your employ, who calls herself Ruth Richards, is not what she pretends to be. Her true name is Mona Montague, and she is compromising herself by secret meetings with a gentleman in high life. She lunched this morning at the Hoffman House Cafe with Mr. Raymond

Palmer, the son of a worthy gentleman whom you intend to marry. You perhaps will best know whether she has any hidden purpose in figuring as a seamstress, and under the name of Ruth Richards, in your house."

Unfortunately for our young lovers, Miss Josephine Holt had also been taking an early lunch in the Hoffman House Cafe that morning, and had seen Ray and Mona the moment they had entered.

Ever since she had discovered Mona at Hazeldean she had been trying to think of some way by which she could separate them, and now, knowing that Mrs. Montague was bent upon marrying Mr. Palmer, and feeling sure that there was some secret which Mona wished to preserve by becoming a seamstress in the woman's house under an assumed name, she believed she could the best achieve her purpose by disclosing her identity and setting Mrs. Montague against her. How well she succeeded will be seen later on.

CHAPTER VII

MONA MAKES A SURPRISING DISCOVERY

It was now the third week in April, and the season was unusually early. The grass had become quite green, the trees were putting forth their leaves, and the weather was very warm for the time of the year.

On the morning after the high-tea and the announcement of the engagement, Mrs. Montague sought Mona and informed her that a party of friends had arranged for a pleasure trip through the South and down the Mississippi, and asked her if she would accompany her, since Louis had business to attend to, and could not act as her escort.

Mona did not exactly like to go, but there was really no good reason why she should refuse; the rush of sewing was nearly over, and if she were left behind, she would have to be idle the greater portion of the time; besides, she had worked very steadily, and she knew that she needed rest and relaxation.

She inquired how long Mrs. Montague intended to be gone, and the lady replied that she expected to return within two weeks.

"Of course you can please yourself about the matter, Ruth,"

she remarked. "I suppose I could take Mary, but she is not companionable—she would not appreciate the journey, and I really wish you would go. I should regard it as quite a favor," the woman concluded, appealingly.

If Mona had been more observing, she might have seen that she was being closely watched, and that her answer was anxiously awaited. Mona considered the subject a few moments before replying. Her greatest objection was leaving Ray for so long—two weeks would seem almost interminable without seeing him.

But, on the other hand, perhaps while in such close companionship with Mrs. Montague as there would have to be on such a journey, something might be dropped about her former life which would enlighten her regarding what she was so eager to ascertain. It would be a delightful trip, too, and Mona knew that she should enjoy seeing the country, as she had never been South.

"When do you start?" she inquired, before committing herself.

"I want to get off in the evening express," Mrs. Montague returned, watching every expression of the young girl's face.

"In *this* evening's express?" asked Mona, in surprise.

"Yes. It is short notice, I know," the woman said, smiling; "but I, myself, only knew of the plan yesterday, and, as you know, I was too busy to make any arrangements for it. Will you go, Ruth? We have nothing to do but to pack our trunks."

"I suppose there is no reason why I should not," the young girl returned, musingly, while she told herself that she could send a note to Ray, informing him of her intention. She was not quite sure that he would approve of it, and she wished that she could have known of it the previous day, so that she could have consulted him.

"That is nice of you," Mrs. Montague quickly responded, and assuming that her remark was intended as an assent to the trip; "and now we must at once go about our preparations. How long will it take you to pack?"

"Not long," Mona answered; "I have only my dresses to fold, and my toilet articles to gather up. I have not really unpacked since I came here," she said, smiling; "for I have needed so few things."

"Well, then, get yourself ready; then you may come to help me," Mrs. Montague said, as she arose to go to her own room, and breathing a sigh of relief that this vital point had been gained with so little trouble.

Mona was as expeditious as possible, but, somehow, now that she had given her consent to go, her heart grew unaccountably heavy, and she began to feel a deep aversion to leaving New York.

She wrote a hasty note to Ray, telling him of the intended journey, and how she regretted not being able to consult him, but could not, under the circumstances. She also wrote, as she did not know the route they were to take, she could not tell him where to address her, but would write to him again when she learned where they were to be.

Then she packed what she thought she would need to take with her, after which she went to assist Mrs. Montague. She found that she had been very expeditious, for she had one trunk already packed and locked, ready to be strapped, and was busily engaged filling another.

Their arrangements were all made and they were ready to start by the time dinner was served, and this meal Mrs. Montague insisted they should eat together, as they must leave immediately afterward.

She was very chatty and agreeable, treating Mona more as an equal than she had ever done before. She seemed in excellent spirits, and talked so gayly and enthusiastically about the trip that the young girl really began to anticipate it with considerable pleasure.

Mary and the cook were to have a holiday during their absence; the house was to be closed, and the coachman alone would remain about the premises to look after the horses and see that nothing happened to the place.

At seven o'clock they left the house, and an hour later were seated in a luxurious Wagner, and rolling rapidly Southward.

They arrived in St. Louis on the morning of the second day, and drove directly to the Southern Hotel, where Mrs. Montague said they would remain for a day or two, to rest, and where the friends who were going down the Mississippi to New Orleans with them would join them.

The following morning Mrs. Montague dressed herself with great care, and told Mona that she was going out to make some calls, adding that she might amuse herself as she chose, for there was nothing to be done, and she might get lonely to remain alone in the hotel.

The young girl resolved to improve the opportunity and look about the city a little on her own account.

She donned her hat and jacket, and running down to the street, hailed the first car that came along, with the intention of riding as far as it would take her.

She changed her purpose, however, as the car was about passing a street leading down to the great bridge across the Mississippi.

She had heard and read a great deal about the grand structure, and she determined to walk across and see how it would compare with the wonderful Brooklyn Bridge.

She was feeling very well, the morning was bright, and she enjoyed her walk immensely. By the time she returned her cheeks were like wild roses, and her whole face glowing from exercise.

She was a little weary, however, and glad to get seated again in a car going back toward her hotel.

The car had proceeded only about half a block, however, when it stopped again, and two people, a man and a woman, stepped aboard, and seated themselves next to her.

They seemed to be absorbed in earnest conversation, and did not appear to notice any one about them.

The woman was an elderly person, rather fine looking, with a good figure, and an erect, graceful bearing. Her hair was almost white, and there were deep wrinkles in her forehead, at the corners of her eyes, and about her mouth, although they were somewhat concealed, or softened, by the thickly spotted black lace veil which she wore; but on the whole she was an agreeable looking person, and her manner was full of energy and vitality.

Her companion was a rather rough-appearing personage and dressed like a Western farmer or miner, rather coarsely handsome, and with an easy, off-hand manner that was quite attractive, and he might have been thirty or thirty-five years of age.

"What a dark skin—what black hair and beard, with blue eyes!" was Mona's mental comment, as she observed this peculiarity about him. He also had very white teeth, which contrasted strikingly with the intense blackness of his mustache and beard.

He appeared to be quite disturbed about something, and talked to his companion rapidly and excitedly, but in low tones.

"You were very imprudent to try to dispose of so many at one place," Mona overheard his companion say, in reply to some observation which he had previously made, and then a great shock went tingling through all her nerves as her glance fell upon the dress which the woman wore.

It was a fine, heavy ladies' cloth, of a delicate shade of gray—just the color, Mona was confident, of that tiny piece of goods which Ray had shown her at Hazeldean, and which had been torn from the dress of the woman who had trapped him into Doctor Wesselhoff's residence, and stolen his diamonds.

She was very much excited for a few moments, and her heart beat with rapid throbs.

Could it be possible that this woman had been concerned in that robbery?

That woman had had red hair, and according to Ray's

Mrs. Georgie Sheldon

description, was much younger; but she might possibly be the other one, who had made arrangements with the physician for Ray's treatment. At all events, Mona was impressed that she had found the dress in which the fascinating Mrs. Vanderbeck had figured so conspicuously.

Her face flushed, her fingers tingled with the rapid coursing of her blood, and she felt as if she could hardly wait until the woman should rise, so that she might look for a place that had been mended in the skirt of her dress.

She resolved that she would ride as long as they remained in the car, and when they left it, she would follow them to ascertain their stopping place.

She could not catch anything more that they said, although she strained her ears to do so.

Those few words which she had overheard had also aroused her suspicions—"you were very imprudent to try to dispose of so many in one place," the woman had said, and Mona believed she had referred to diamonds; her vivid imagination pictured these people as belonging to the gang of robbers who had been concerned in the Palmer robbery, and now that the excitement attending it had somewhat subsided, they had doubtless come to St. Louis to dispose of their booty; while it was the strangest thing in the world, she thought, that she should have happened to run across them in the way she had.

They were drawing very near the Southern Hotel, where Mona and Mrs. Montague were stopping; but the excited girl resolved that she would not get out—she would ride hours rather than lose sight of these two strangers, and the chance to ascertain if that gray cloth dress was mended—"on the back of the skirt, near the right side, among the heavy folds." Ray had told her that was where the tear was.

But what if she should find it there? What should she do about the matter? were questions which arose at this point to trouble her. What could she, a weak girl, do to cause the arrest of the thieves? how was she to prove them guilty?

At that moment the man signaled the conductor to stop the car, and Mona's heart leaped into her throat, for they were exactly opposite her own hotel.

The couple arose to leave the car, and Mona slowly followed them.

As the woman was about to step to the ground she gathered up her skirts with her right hand, to prevent them from sweeping the steps of the car, and Mona looked with eager eyes, but she could detect no mended rent.

She kept a little behind them as they crossed the sidewalk and made straight for the entrance of the hotel, when, as they were mounting the steps, the woman suddenly tripped and almost fell.

In the act, her skirts were drawn closely about her, and Mona distinctly saw a place, where the plaits or folds were laid deeply over one another, that had been mended, and not nicely, either, but hastily sewed together on the wrong side. It would hardly have been noticed, however, unless one had been looking for it as Mona was, because it lay so deeply in among the folds.

The couple entered the hotel, and both gave Mona a quick, sharp glance as she followed; but she quietly passed them with averted eyes, and went into a reception-room on the left of the hall.

"Go and register, Jake, and I will wait here for you," Mona

heard the woman say, and the man immediately disappeared within the clerk's office opposite, while his companion walked slowly back and forth in the hall.

Presently the man rejoined her, remarking:

"It's all right; they had a room next yours which they could give me. Come," and both passed directly up stairs.

Mona waited a few minutes, to be sure they were well out of the way, then she quietly slipped across the hall to the office.

"Will you allow me to look at the register?" she asked of the gentlemanly clerk.

"Certainly," and with a bow and smile he placed it conveniently for her.

She thanked him, and glanced eagerly at the last name written on the page.

"J.R. Walton, Sydney, Australia," she read, in a coarse, irregular hand, as if the person writing it had been unaccustomed to the use of the pen.

Running her eye up the page, Mona also read, as if the name had been signed earlier in the day:

"Mrs. J.M. Walton, Brownsville, Mo."

"It would appear," mused Mona, as she left the office, "as if they are mother and son—that he had just returned from far Australia, and she had come here to meet him. But—I don't believe it! Walton—Walton! Where have I heard that name before?"

She could not place it, but she was so sure that these people were in some way connected with the Palmer robbery, she was determined to make an effort to establish the fact, and immediately leaving the hotel again, she sought the nearest telegraph office, and sent the following message to Ray:

"Send immediately piece of the ladies' cloth torn from dress."

This done she retraced her steps, and went directly up to her own room.

She found that Mrs. Montague had returned from making her calls, and was dressing for dinner.

She seemed a little disturbed about something, and finally it came out that the trip down the Mississippi would have to be delayed for a day or two longer than she had anticipated, as one of her friends was not quite well enough to start immediately.

Mona was very glad to learn this, for she was sure that she should hear from Ray and receive the piece of dress goods; her only fear was that the Waltons might not remain at the hotel long enough for her to find an opportunity to fit the piece into the rent, to ascertain if it belonged there.

The earnestly desired letter reached her the next evening. Ray had been very expeditious. Receiving Mona's dispatch just before the southward mail closed, he had hastily inclosed the piece of cloth, with a few words, in an envelope, and so there was no delay.

She was certain, as she examined it, that it was exactly the same color as the dress she had seen the day before, and reasonably sure regarding the texture; but the great question now to be answered was: Would it fit the rent?

"Now I must find the dress, if possible, when the woman is wearing something else," Mona mused, with a troubled face, and beginning to think she had undertaken a matter too difficult to be carried out. "Perhaps she has no other dress here; how, then, am I going to prove my suspicion true, or otherwise?"

She knew that she could go to the authorities, tell her story, and have the woman and dress forcibly examined; but she could not bear to do anything that would make herself conspicuous, and it would be very disagreeable to carry the affair so far and then find she had made a lamentable mistake.

"If Ray were only here he would know what to do," she murmured, "but he isn't, and I must do the best I can without him. I must find out where the woman rooms. I must examine that dress!"

Fortune favored her in an unexpected way the very next morning.

The chambermaid who had charge of the floor on which their rooms were located, came, as usual, to put them in order, but with a badly swollen face, around which she had bound a handkerchief.

"Are you sick?" Mona asked, in a tone of sympathy, for the girl's heavy eyes and languid manner appealed very strongly to her kind heart.

"I have a toothache, miss," the girl said, with a heavy sigh. "I never slept a wink last night, it pained me so."

"I am very sorry, and of course you cannot feel much like work to-day, if you had no sleep," Mona said, pityingly.

"Indeed I don't—I can hardly hold my head up; but the work's got to be done all the same," was the weary reply.

"Cannot you get some one to substitute for you while you have your tooth taken out and get a little rest?" Mona kindly inquired.

"No, miss; the girls are all busy—they have their own work to do, and I shall have to bear it as best I can."

"Then let me help you," Mona said, a sudden thought setting all her pulses bounding.

Perhaps she might come across that dress!

"You, miss!" the girl cried, in unfeigned astonishment. "A young lady like you help to make beds in a hotel where you are a guest!"

Mona laughed.

"I have often made beds, and—I am not regarded as a 'young lady' just now; I am only a kind of waiting-maid to the lady with whom I am traveling," she explained, thinking she might the more easily gain her point if the girl was led to think the difference in their positions was not as great as she had imagined. "Come now," she added, "I am going to help you, for I know you are not able to do all this work yourself," and she immediately began to assist in putting her own chamber to rights.

They went from room to room, Mona chatting pleasantly and trying to take the girl's mind from her pain; but she saw that it was almost more than she could do to keep about her work.

Finally she made her sit down and let her work alone.

"How many rooms are there yet to be cared for?" she asked, as she began to spread up the bed where they were.

"Only four more, miss—just what are left in this hall," said the girl, as her head fell wearily back against the high rocker which Mona had insisted upon her taking.

Mona went on with the work she had volunteered to perform, and when she returned to look at the girl again, she found that she was sleeping heavily.

"Exhausted nature has asserted itself, and I will let her rest," the young girl murmured; "there can be no possible harm in my doing this work for her, although I suppose it would not be thought just the thing for a stranger to have access to all these rooms."

She put everything there as it should be, then she went out, softly closing the door after her, that no one might see the girl sleeping.

She proceeded to do the four remaining apartments without finding what she sought until she came to the very last one.

As she entered it she picked up a card that had been dropped upon the floor, and a joyful thrill ran through her as she read the name, "Mrs. J.M. Walton."

She knew, then, that she had found the room occupied by the woman who had worn the gray dress.

Would she find the garment?

A trunk stood in one corner of the room, and her eyes rested covetously upon this. Then she went to the wardrobe and swung the door open.

Joy! the robe she sought was hanging on a peg within!

With trembling hands she sought for the rent which she had seen the day but one before.

She found it, and with fluctuating color and a rapidly beating heart, she took hold of the knot of the silk, which had been used to mend it, and deliberately pulled it out, when the ragged edges fell apart, revealing a triangular-shaped rent.

Mona drew her purse from her pocket, found the precious piece of cloth that Ray had sent to her, and laid it over the hole in the skirt.

It fitted perfectly into the tear, and she knew that the dress which the beautiful Mrs. Vanderbeck had worn, when she stole the Palmer diamonds, was found.

But the woman!

Mona was puzzled, for surely the woman whom she had seen wearing the dress was much older than the one whom Ray had described to her. She was wrinkled and gray; and then— the name! But stay! All at once light broke in upon her. Walton had been the name of the person who had so cleverly deceived Dr. Wesselhoff. She had been old and wrinkled, and now, without doubt, she had come to St. Louis to dispose of her share of the stolen diamonds, and had worn the other woman's dress, thinking, perhaps, it would be safe to do so, and would not be recognized under such different circumstances.

"But what shall I do?" seemed now to be the burden of her thought. At first she felt impelled to telegraph Ray to come and attend to the matter; then she feared the man and woman would both disappear before he could arrive, and she felt that some immediate action should be taken.

"I believe my best way will be to go directly to a detective, and tell him my story; he will know what ought to be done, and I can leave the matter in his hands," was her final conclusion.

She sped to her own room, secured a needleful of silk, then hastened back to Mrs. Walton's room and sewed the rent in the dress together once more, taking care not to fray the edges, lest the piece she had should not fit when it was examined again.

CHAPTER VIII

MR. RIDER BECOMES ACTIVE AGAIN

After hanging the dress again in its place, Mona quickly finished her work in the room, then went back to the girl whom she had left sleeping in one of the adjoining chambers, and awoke her.

She had slept nearly an hour, and, though Mona knew that she needed many hours more of rest, she was sure that she would be the better for what she had secured.

"You are very good, miss," she said, gratefully; "the pain is all gone from my tooth, and I feel ever so much better."

"Your sleep has quieted your nerves; but I advise you to see a dentist and have the tooth attended to," Mona returned; then hastened away to her room, where she dressed herself for the street and went out.

Mrs. Montague had been out for a long time driving with some friends.

Mona inquired of an elderly, respectable policeman, whom she found standing upon a corner, where she should go to find a detective.

Mrs. Georgie Sheldon

He directed her to the headquarters of the force, although he looked surprised at the question coming from such a source, and she repaired thither at once.

As she entered the office, a quiet-looking man, who was the only occupant at that time, arose and came forward, bowing respectfully; but he also appeared astonished to see a young and beautiful girl in such a place.

"I wish to see a detective," said Mona, flushing hotly beneath the man's curious glance.

"The men connected with this office are all out just at this moment, miss. I am a stranger, and only sitting here for a half-hour or so, just to oblige the officer in charge," the man courteously replied.

"I am very sorry," said the young girl, with a sigh, "for I have come upon business which ought to be attended to immediately."

"I am a detective, miss, although I do not belong here. I'm an officer from New York; but if you see fit to tell me your business, perhaps I might advise you," said the officer, kindly, for he saw that she was greatly troubled.

"You are from New York!" Mona exclaimed, eagerly; "then perhaps it will be better for me to tell you, rather than a St. Louis detective; for the robbery happened in New York."

The detective's eyes flashed with sudden interest at this.

"Ah!" was all he said, however, and this very quietly.

"Yes, it was a diamond robbery. A dress worn by one of the persons connected with it was torn; a small piece was entirely cut out of it. I have found the dress; I have fitted the piece into the rent, and now I want the woman who owns it to be arrested and examined," Mona explained, in low, excited tones, but very comprehensively.

"Ah!" said the detective again, in the same quiet tone; "you have reference to the Palmer robbery."

Mona lifted a pair of very astonished eyes to his face.

"Yes," she responded, breathlessly; "but how did you know?"

"Because I am looking after that case. I am in St. Louis upon that very business," replied the man, with a twinkle in his eyes.

"Are *you* Detective Rider?" questioned the young girl, wonderingly, and trembling with excitement.

Her companion smiled.

"What do you know about Detective Rider?" he inquired. Then, as she flushed and seemed somewhat embarrassed, he continued: "And who are *you*, if you please?"

"I am—I am acquainted with Raymond Palmer," Mona answered, evasively; "he has told me about the robbery and—"

"Ah! yes. I understand," interposed the quick-witted officer, as he comprehended the situation. "But sit down and tell me the whole story as briefly as possible, and I can then judge what will be best to do."

He moved a chair forward for her, then sat down himself,

Mrs. Georgie Sheldon

where he could watch her closely, as she talked, and Mona related all that we already know regarding the two people whom she had seen upon the street-car, together with all that followed in connection with the discovery of the rent in the gray cloth dress, the sending for the fragment that Ray had preserved, and which had fitted so exactly into the tear.

The detective listened with the closest attention, his small, keen eyes alone betraying the intense interest which her recital excited.

When she had concluded, he drew forth a set of tablets and made notes of several items, after which he said:

"Now, Miss—What shall I call you? Whom shall I ask for at the hotel, if I should wish to see you again upon this business?"

"Miss Richards. I am traveling with a Mrs. Montague, of New York," Mona replied.

"Well, then, Miss Richards, you go back to your hotel, and of course conduct yourself as if you had nothing unusual on your mind; but hold yourself in readiness to produce that important bit of cloth, if I should call upon you to do so within the next few hours. By the way," he added, with sudden thought, "if you have it with you, I might as well take a look at it."

Mona took the paper containing it from her purse and gave it to him.

"You are *sure* this matches the dress?" he asked, examining it closely. "We don't want to make any awkward mistakes, you know."

"It is identical. I believe that every thread in this piece can be matched by a corresponding thread in the garment," the fair girl asserted, so positively that he seemed to be entirely satisfied.

He returned the piece to her and then arose in a brisk, business-like way, which told that he was ready for action.

Mona also rose, and, bidding him a quiet good-day, went quickly out of the office, and hastened back to the hotel.

* * * * *

In order to understand more fully some of the incidents related, we shall have to go back a few days.

It was a bright, clear morning when a rather rough-looking, yet not unattractive person, entered a large jewelry establishment located on one of the principal streets of St. Louis.

He might have been thirty-five years of age, for there was a sprinkling of silver among his coarse, intensely black hair, which he wore quite long, and also in his huge mustache and beard. His face was bronzed from exposure; there were crow's feet about his eyes, and two deep wrinkles between his brows, and his general appearance indicated that he had seen a good deal of the rough side of life.

He wore a coarse though substantial suit of clothes, which hung rather loosely upon him; a gray flannel shirt with a turn-over collar, which was fastened at the throat by a flashy necktie, rather carelessly knotted; a red cotton handkerchief was just visible in one of his pockets; there were coarse, clumsy boots on his feet, and he wore a wide-brimmed, slouch hat.

Mrs. Georgie Sheldon

He inquired of the clerk, who came forward to wait upon him, if he could see the "boss of the consarn," as he had a little private business to transact with him.

The clerk smiled slightly at his broad vernacular, as he replied that he would speak to the proprietor, and presently an elderly gentleman appeared from an inner office, and inquired the nature of the man's business.

"I'm a miner," he said. "I'm just home from Australia, where I've been huntin' diamonds for the last ten years. I've made a pretty good haul, and sold most of 'em in London on my way home. I had a few dandy ones cut there, though, to bring back to my gal; but—but—well, to tell the plain truth," he said, with some confusion, "she's gone back on me; she couldn't wait for me, so married another fellar; and now I want to sell the stones. D'ye want to buy?"

There was something rather attractive, as well as amusing, in the man's frankness, and the merchant smiled, as he kindly remarked that he would examine the stones.

The miner thereupon pulled out a small leather bag from one of the pockets of his trousers, unwound the strong thong at its throat, and rattled out upon the counter several loose glittering diamonds of various sizes.

The merchant could hardly repress a cry of astonishment, for they were remarkable for their purity and brilliancy, while there were two among the collection of unusual size.

He examined them critically, and took plenty of time about it, while the miner leaned indifferently against the counter, his hands in his pockets, and gazed absently out of the window.

"What do you value these stones at?" the merchant finally inquired, as he removed the glass from his eye and turned to the man.

"Wall, I don't suppose it would make much difference what my price might be," he drawled; "I know they're about as good ones as anybody would care to see, and you know about what you'd be willin' to give."

"Yes; but I would like to know what value you put upon them before I make an offer," responded Mr. Cohen, shrewdly.

"Wall, before I found out about the gal, I wouldn't a' sold 'em at any price," was the rather gloomy response, "fur I'd promised 'em to her, ye know; but now—so's I get what's reasonable, I don't care much what becomes on 'em. What'll ye give? I'll trust to yer honor in the matter."

The jeweler had been watching the man closely while he was speaking, although he appeared to be thinking deeply of the purchase of the gems.

"I—do not think that I am prepared to set a price on them just at this moment," he at length thoughtfully remarked. "As far as I can judge, they are very fine stones and well cut; still, I am not an expert, although a dealer in such things, and I should like to submit them to one before making you an offer."

"All right," was the hearty and unhesitating reply, "that's fair, and I'm agreeable. Bring on your expert."

"Are you going to be in the city long?" asked the merchant.

"Wall, no; I didn't calkerlate on staying any longer'n I could

Mrs. Georgie Sheldon

turn the stones into money," the man said. "My old mother lives up to Brownsville, and I thought of goin' up to make her a little visit—han't seen her fur ten years. Then I'm going back to the mines, since I han't no reason to hang around these parts *now*," with a bitter emphasis on the last word.

"This is Tuesday," said Mr. Cohen, reflectively; "the expert to whom I wish to subject the stones is out of town, but will be here to-morrow evening; suppose you come in again on Thursday morning."

"All right," responded the miner, as he began to gather up his glittering pebbles, though there was a look of disappointment in his eyes. "I'd ruther have got rid of 'em, fur they're kind o' ticklish things to be carrying about. Wonder if I couldn't leave 'em in your safe till Thursday?"

"Certainly, if you are willing to trust them with me," said Mr. Cohen, looking rather surprised at the man's confidence in him: "still you would have to do so on your own responsibility. I should not be willing to be held accountable for them in case of a robbery."

"Wall, then, perhaps I'd better take them along," the miner returned, as he tied the mouth of his leather pouch, and shoved it into one of his pockets.

Then drawing forth a plug of tobacco from another, he bit off a generous quid, remarking, as he did so:

"I'll be on hand Thursday mornin', I reckon. Good-day."

The merchant politely returned his salutation, and watched him thoughtfully after he shut the door and went swaggering down the street, looking in at every window he passed, in regular country fashion.

A few moments after, the merchant took his hat and also went out.

A few hours later, Mr. Amos Palmer received the following dispatch:

"Send expert and detective at once to examine suspicious stones. EZRA COHEN."

Ezra Cohen had for years had business relations with Amos Palmer, going to New York several times every twelve months to purchase diamonds and other jewels, for the St. Louis trade.

On his last visit thither Mr. Palmer had mentioned the bold robbery, which had resulted in his losing such valuable diamonds, and had described some of the most costly stones, saying, that possibly they might some time fall into his hands.

Mr. Cohen was not sure, but he was impressed that the two larger stones of the collection which the miner had brought to sell him, on that morning, resembled, in some points, the ones described by Mr. Palmer; and so he thought it worth while to have the matter proved, if possible, although he felt some compunctions regarding his suspicions, because the miner had appeared so frank and ingenuous.

If he had only left the stones with him as he had proposed doing, the matter of testing them could have been attended to during his absence. He hoped that he had not acted too hastily in telegraphing to Mr. Palmer; but he had done as his best judgment had prompted, and could only await the result with patience.

It was with no little nervousness, however, that he awaited

Thursday morning, especially after receiving a reply to his message to the effect that "Tom Rider, the detective, and a diamond expert, would arrive on an early train of that day."

They did so, and presented themselves at Ezra Cohen's establishment soon after the store was opened for business that morning.

The merchant was already there, awaiting them, and received the two gentlemen in his private office, where they held a confidential conversation regarding the matter in hand.

The expert was quite confident, after listening to Mr. Cohen's description of the diamonds, that they would prove to be the ones they were seeking, but the detective was not quite so hopeful; he had been disappointed so many times of late that he looked upon the dark side, while he was somewhat skeptical about the supposed miner making his appearance again.

About nine o'clock, however, the man swaggered into the store, an enormous quid of tobacco inside his cheek.

"*He* has never been in Australia," said Detective Rider, in a low tone, but with sudden energy, as he and his companion watched him approach the counter, where Mr. Cohen was quietly examining a case of watches.

"Wall," he remarked, in his broad, drawling tone, "got yer expert on hand this mornin'? I'd like to close up this 'ere business before I go up to Brownsville."

"Yes, I think I can settle about the diamonds to-day," Mr. Cohen politely remarked. "James," to a clerk, "please ask Mr. Knowlton to step this way."

James disappeared, and presently an elderly gentleman in spectacles issued from the private office.

"Mr. Knowlton," said the merchant, "this is the man who wished to dispose of some diamonds. Will you examine them, and give your opinion of their value?"

The miner darted a quick, searching look at the new-comer; but apparently the man was intent only upon the business in hand.

Drawing forth his leather pouch, the miner untied it and emptied its contents upon the square of black velvet which had been laid upon the show-case to receive them.

Mr. Knowlton examined each stone with careful scrutiny through a powerful glass, never once speaking until he had looked the collection through.

"They are quite valuable," he remarked, as he laid the last one down. "These," indicating the two large ones, "are especially so; you have been very fortunate, sir, to make such a collection, for there is not one poor one in the lot."

The miner gave a slight start at this observation, and the color deepened on his face; but he replied, with his habitual frankness:

"Well, I've had poor ones—plenty on 'em; but these were saved for a special purpose," and he winked knowingly at Mr. Cohen. Then he added, as he shot a sweeping look around the store and out through the window upon the sidewalk: "Jest give us their value in round figgers, and well soon settle this matter."

The expert quietly made a memorandum upon a card and

Mrs. Georgie Sheldon

laid it before the jeweler, then immediately withdrew to the private office.

"Well?" demanded Tom Rider, his keen little eyes gleaming with repressed excitement, as Mr. Knowlton shut the door after him.

"The two large stones belong to Amos Palmer, the others I never saw before, and you'd better hook your man as soon as possible, because he is beginning to smell powder," said the gentleman, in a low tone.

"I'm ready for him," muttered the detective, as he grabbed his hat, crushed it upon his head, and vanished out of the back door with a good deal more of elasticity in his step than when he had entered.

Going around to the front entrance he sauntered into the store and up to the counter, where Mr. Cohen was apparently trying to drive a close bargain for the Australian(?) diamonds, but really waiting for some sign from the men closeted in his office.

He paused at the entrance of the new-comer, bowed gravely, and politely inquired:

"What can I do for you, sir?"

"I'm sorry to give you any trouble," the detective returned, in quick, sharp tones, "but it is my duty to arrest this man! You are my prisoner, sir," he concluded, laying his hand on the shoulder of the supposed miner.

A startled oath broke from the man's lips, and he made an agile spring for the door.

But the detective was too quick for him, and deftly placed a pair of twisters about his wrists, with such force as to wring a howl of agony from him.

"None of that, my fine fellow," Mr. Rider said, sternly, as he slyly tried to slip his other hand underneath his coat, and he gave the twisters another forcible turn. "Just you let that revolver alone."

"All right," said the miner, apparently yielding; "but what's the charge? Ye can't expect a fellar to submit very tamely to this kind o' thing without knowing what he's nabbed for."

"I arrest you for robbery. These diamonds are stolen property," was the brief reply of the detective.

"You don't say!" drawled the man, in a tone of sarcastic wonder. "Perhaps ye'll be good enough to prove what ye assert."

The detective could but admire the cool effrontery of the fellow, but he quietly responded:

"It has already been proved—those large diamonds have just been identified."

"Ah!"

The miner said no more, but quietly submitted to have a pair of handcuffs snapped on his wrists.

The diamonds were secured, and the prisoner was marched off to the station-house, while Ezra Cohen gave utterance to a sigh of relief over the fact that he had made no mistake.

CHAPTER IX

MR. RIDER RECEIVES ANOTHER SET-BACK

Jake Walton, as the supposed miner gave his name, was thoroughly searched by Detective Rider, after reaching the station-house, but nothing suspicious was found upon him except a revolver. He had considerable money, but nothing to indicate that he had ever been concerned in any robbery, or to confirm the belief that he was other than he pretended to be.

He submitted to being searched with the utmost indifference, but drawlingly remarked during the operation, he "supposed they'd take bail—he wasn't used to bein' shut up, and it would come pretty tough on him."

"Of course the magistrate will accept suitable bail," said Rider, not imagining that the prisoner could find any one to go security for him to the large sum likely to be asked.

The miner requested that a lawyer might be sent to him at once, after which he coolly sat down, drew out a morning paper, and began to read.

Later in the day a legal gentleman presented himself in his cell, and there followed a long consultation between the two, and toward evening the lawyer, after consulting with a police justice, called at the Southern Hotel and inquired for a lady by the name of Mrs. J.M. Walton.

Yes, there was such a person stopping there, the clerk informed him, whereupon the lawyer sent up his card to her with the request that she would grant him a private interview.

The messenger returned in about fifteen minutes, saying the lady would receive him in her private parlor. Upon being conducted thither, he found a handsome elderly woman awaiting him, and immediately explained his business, relating the circumstances of the arrest of Jake Walton, and concluded by telling her that he had been employed as counsel for the young man, who had sent him to her to arrange for bail.

Mrs. Walton appeared to be greatly disturbed by these disagreeable tidings. She said she had come there expecting to meet her son, who had just returned from Australia, and it was very trying to be told that he had been arrested for theft. Then she inquired what amount would be required for security.

The counsel named the sum fixed by the police justice, whereupon Mrs. Walton appeared to be considerably agitated for a moment.

"I am an entire stranger in the city," she remarked, recovering herself somewhat. "I know no one to whom I could appeal to become bound for so large a sum. What can I do?"

"Have you plenty of means at your disposal, madame?" her companion inquired.

Mrs. Georgie Sheldon

"Yes, I could give bail to almost any reasonable amount, only being a stranger here, I fear it would not be accepted from me," the lady returned, with a look of anxiety.

"No; but I think I can suggest a way out of that difficulty," said the lawyer, with a crafty smile.

"Then do so," said Mrs. Walton, quickly; "I am willing to pay handsomely to secure the release of my son from his uncomfortable position."

"Very well. Then if you can command the sum named you can deposit it in one of the city banks and I will attend to all other formalities for you. Of course, the money will be returned to you after the trial of your son."

"Could such arrangements be made?" Mrs. Walton eagerly inquired.

"Certainly. All that is required is sufficient security to insure the young man's appearance at his trial, and then he will be released."

"Then I can arrange it," the woman said, apparently greatly relieved; and after discussing ways and means a while longer, the lawyer took his leave.

A few hours served to arrange matters satisfactorily to all parties. The sum required was deposited in one of the city banks, and the cashier was empowered to pay it over to the city treasurer, if Jake Walton failed to appear at the time named to answer to the charge of complicity in the Palmer diamond robbery. He was then released, the lawyer was handsomely remunerated for his efficient services, and Mrs. Walton and her son returned to the Southern Hotel.

It was on their way thither that they entered the car in which Mona was also returning to the hotel, and when she made the discovery that the woman had on the very dress which the charming Mrs. Vanderbeck had worn on the day of the Palmer robbery.

We know what followed—how she immediately sent on to Ray for the scrap of cloth, and how, later, she found that it exactly fitted the rent in the dress.

We know, also, how, immediately following this discovery, she sought the headquarters of the detective force, where she opportunely encountered Mr. Rider, and related to him the discoveries which she had made.

Mrs. Walton had not appeared personally in connection with the formalities regarding the release of her son.

Everything had been conducted by the shrewd lawyer, so Detective Rider had not met her at all; but he felt confident, when Mona described her, together with her dress, that she was not the mother of Jake Walton at all, but one of the "gang" who had so successfully robbed different parties during the last two or three years.

The moment the young girl disappeared from the office, after her interview with him, the detective executed a number of antics which would have done credit to a practiced athlete.

"The girl is a cute little body," he muttered, with a chuckle, as he sat down to rest a moment, and plan his course of action, "and it is lucky for me that she happened to be in St. Louis just at this time and stopping at that very hotel. I wonder," he added, with a frown, "that I didn't think that the woman who gave bail, might be one of the gang. By Jove!" with a sudden start, "I believe that money, which she deposited in the bank as security, is only a blind after all, and *they both intend to skip*! What a wretched blunder it was to accept bail anyway! But I'll cage both birds this time, only what I do must be done quickly. They must have done a smashing big business in diamonds," he went on, musingly; "and there are evidently two women and one man associated. This Mrs. Walton is doubtless the old one who tricked Doctor Wesselhoff, and that red-headed Mrs. Vanderbeck, I am still confident, is none other than the Widow Bently, who did Justin Cutler and Mrs. Vander *heck* out of their money. I'd just like to get hold of all three! Tom Rider, if you only could, it would be a feather in your cap such as doesn't often wave over the head of an ordinary detective, not to mention the good round sum that would swell your pocket-book! But half a loaf is better than no bread, and so here goes! I'll arrest them both, and shall object to anybody going bail for them."

Highly elated over the prospect before him, the man brushed his neat suit until there wasn't an atom of dust upon it, polished his boots until he could see his own face reflected in them, rearranged his necktie in the last new style, then ran lightly down stairs, and hastened, with quick, elastic tread, toward the Southern Hotel, where he expected to accomplish such great results.

* * * * *

"Where have you been, Ruth?" exclaimed Mrs. Montague, in an irritated tone, as Mona entered that lady's parlor upon her return from the detective's office. "I wish you wouldn't go out without consulting me. I've been waiting here for a long time for you to mend these gloves."

"I am very sorry," Mona returned, flushing, "but after you went out to drive I assisted the chambermaid, who was nearly crazy with the toothache, to put some of the rooms in order; then, as you had not returned, I went out for a little walk."

"Well, I don't mind about the walk, but I didn't bring you with me to do chamber-work in every hotel we stop at," sharply retorted the much annoyed lady. "You can go at the gloves right away," she added; "then I shall want you to help me pack, for we are to leave on the first boat to-morrow morning. And," she concluded, thus explaining to Mona her unusual irritability, "we've got to make the trip alone, after all, for my friend is worse this morning, and so the whole family have given it up."

"I am sorry that you are to be disappointed. I should suppose you would wish to give it up yourself. I am afraid you will not enjoy it at all," Mona replied, wondering why she did not at once return to New York instead of keeping on.

"Of course, I shall not enjoy it," snapped the woman, but bestowing a searching glance upon her companion, "and I would not go on, only Louis was to join us at New Orleans, and it is too late now to change his plans."

Mona's face fell at this unexpected and disagreeable intelligence.

The last thing she desired was Louis Hamblin's companionship, and she would have been only too glad to return at once to New York.

"Could you not telegraph to him?" she suggested.

"No; for I suppose he has already left New York," Mrs. Montague curtly replied.

Mona was quite unhappy over the prospect before her; then

it suddenly occurred to her that perhaps Detective Rider would need her as a witness, if he should arrest the Waltons, and in that case she would be compelled to return to New York.

Still she felt very uncomfortable even with this hope to encourage her, and but for the discovery of that morning, she would have regretted having consented to accompany Mrs. Montague upon her trip.

She sat down to mend the gloves, with what composure she could assume, although her nerves were in a very unsettled state, for she was continually looking for a summons from Mr. Rider.

When they were finished she helped about the packing of Mrs. Montague's wardrobe, and then repaired to her chamber, to get her own in readiness to leave; but still no word from the detective, and she thought it very strange.

It might have been an hour after Mona's return to the hotel, when that official sauntered into the office, where he picked up a paper and looked it over for a few minutes. Then he went to the counter, pulled the register before him, and began to glance up and down its pages.

He finally found the names he was searching for, then turning to the clerk, he requested that a boy might take a note from him to Mrs. J.M. Walton's room.

"Mrs. Walton?" repeated the clerk, with some surprise.

"Yes; I have a little matter of business with her," said Mr. Rider, who intended to make his arrest very quietly.

"I am sorry you did not come earlier, then," regretfully

responded the clerk, "for Mrs. Walton and her son left the hotel about two hours ago,"

The detective's heart sank with a sudden shock.

Gone! his birds flown when he had them so nearly captured!

"Are you sure?" he sharply demanded, while in spite of his long and severe training, he turned very white, and his under lip twitched nervously.

"Certainly, or I should not have so stated," returned the clerk, with some dignity. "When young Mr. Walton settled his bill, he ordered a carriage to be in waiting at eleven o'clock, and both he and his mother left the house at that time. I regret your disappointment, sir, in missing them."

This was almost more than Mr. Rider could bear; but he could not doubt the man's word, and he feared the thieves had escaped him again. They must have left while Mona was telling him her story at the detective headquarters.

They had been very sharp. Finding themselves in a bad box, they had planned their movements with great cunning. He believed that Mrs. Walton had deposited the amount required for bail in the bank, with the deliberate intention of forfeiting it, rather than have her accomplice brought to trial; doubtless he was too useful to her to run any risk of his being found guilty, and imprisoned for a term of years, and thus put an end to their successful career.

The detective berated himself soundly again for not objecting to the acceptance of bail at all, but it was too late now to remedy the matter. Regrets were useless, and he must bestir himself, strike a fresh trail, if possible, and hope for better results.

Mrs. Georgie Sheldon

He wondered why they had not skipped immediately after Jake Walton's release, but finally concluded that they had remained in the city for a day or two to disarm suspicion.

"Where did they go?" he inquired, as soon as he could command his voice to speak calmly.

"To the Grand Union Station. I believe they were going North, for I heard the young man say something about purchasing tickets, at reduced rates, for Chicago," the clerk replied.

"Had they baggage with them?" Mr. Rider questioned.

"Yes, a trunk and a good-sized grip," said the man.

The detective thought a moment.

Then he called for writing materials, hastily wrote a few lines, which he sealed, and directed to "Miss Richards."

"There is a young lady by that name stopping here, I believe," he remarked, as he laid the envelope before the clerk.

"Yes; she is with a Mrs. Montague."

"That is the lady," said the detective. "Will you see that this letter is given into her own hands, and *privately*? It is a matter of importance."

"Yes, sir, I will myself attend to the matter," responded the obliging clerk.

Mr. Rider deposited a piece of silver upon the envelope, touched his hat, and walked briskly from the hotel.

He jumped into a carriage that was waiting before the door.

"To the Grand Union Station," he ordered. "Be quick about it, and you shall have double fare."

The man was quick about it, but the train for Chicago had been gone some time.

Mr. Rider had of course expected this, but he at once sought an interview with the ticket agent, and made earnest inquiries regarding those who had purchased tickets for Chicago that morning; but he could learn of no persons answering to the description of the miner and his supposed mother.

If he could have obtained any intelligence regarding them, he had intended to telegraph ahead, and order their arrest when they should arrive at the end of their journey. But of course it would be of no use to put this plan into execution now, as he doubted very much their having gone to Chicago at all.

He was very much disheartened, and retraced his steps to his hotel, with a sickening sense of total defeat.

"Tom Rider," he muttered, fiercely, as he packed his own grip to take the first train back to New York, "you might as well give up the business and take up some trade; you've been hoodwinked by these clever thieves often enough."

But there was a very dogged, resolute expression on his plain face, nevertheless, as he turned it northward, which betrayed that he did not mean to give up his search quite yet.

That afternoon when Mona went down to dinner, the clerk of the hotel waylaid her and quietly slipped an envelope into her hand.

Mrs. Georgie Sheldon

"Thank you," she said, in a low tone, and hastily concealed it in her pocket.

When she was alone again she broke it open and read, with almost as much disappointment as the detective himself had experienced, when he found that his birds had flown, these words:

"Gone! They gave us the slip about eleven o'clock. Save the scrap of cloth—it may be needed later. R."

"Oh, dear!" sighed Mona, regretfully; "and the Palmer robbery is still as much of a mystery as ever."

CHAPTER X

THE PLOT AGAINST MONA THICKENS

The next morning Mrs. Montague and her young companion left the Southern Hotel and proceeded directly on board one of the palatial steamers which ply between St. Louis and New Orleans.

Mrs. Montague secured one of the best staterooms for their use, and immediately made herself comfortable for the trip.

The weather was very fine, the season advanced, for the foliage was rapidly developing to perfection, and the sail down the broad tortuous river was delightful.

Mona enjoyed it, in spite of her dread of meeting Louis Hamblin at the end of it, and her anxiety to get back to New York and Ray.

Mrs. Montague had entirely recovered her good nature; indeed, she had never been so kind and gracious toward her seamstress as during this portion of their trip. She appeared to exert herself to make her enjoy it—was more free and companionable, and an observer would have regarded them as relatives and equals.

Mrs. Georgie Sheldon

Mrs. Montague made many acquaintances, as she always did everywhere, and entered most heartily into every plan for amusing and entertaining the party on board the steamer.

The days were mostly spent in delightful intercourse and promenades on deck, where Mona was put forward and made to join in the pleasures; while the evenings were devoted to tableaux, charades, music, and dancing, as the passengers desired.

It seemed almost like a return to her old life before her uncle's death, and could she have obliterated all sadness and painful memories, Mona would have enjoyed it thoroughly.

They had barely touched the levee at New Orleans when they espied Louis Hamblin, dressed with great care and in the height of style, awaiting their arrival.

Mrs. Montague signaled to him from the upper deck; and he, with an answering wave of his hand, sprang aboard, and quickly made his way to her side.

He greeted her with evident pleasure, remarking that it seemed an age since he had seen her, and then he turned to Mona, with outstretched hand and smiling eyes.

"How well you are looking, Miss Richards," he remarked; "your trip has done you a great deal of good."

Mona bowed, but without appearing to notice his extended hand, and then she turned away to gather their wraps and satchels, preparatory to going ashore.

Mr. Hamblin frowned at her coldness, but a peculiar smile curved his lips as he whispered in Mrs. Montague's ear:

"We'll soon bring your proud beauty to better terms."

"Don't be rash, Louis," she returned; "we must be very wary if we would accomplish our purpose. You say you love the girl, and I have consented to let you have your way, but, since she is not inclined to accept your advances, you will have to play your cards very shrewdly if you expect to win."

"All right; I will be circumspection personified, if you will only help me to make that girl my wife," the young man said earnestly. "I do love her with all my heart; and, Aunt Margie, I'll quit sowing wild oats, turn over a new leaf, and be a good man if I succeed in this."

Mrs. Montague regarded him somewhat skeptically, as he made this eager avowal, but it was almost immediately followed by a look of anxiety.

"I hope you will—you certainly owe me that much after all that I have done for you," she returned. "Mind you," she added, "I never would have yielded this point if I had not been driven to it."

"Driven to it! How?" inquired her nephew, regarding her searchingly.

"Driven to it, because I have found out that she is Mona Montague, and I'm afraid that she has an eye to her father's property. I believe she is very keen—doubtless she knows that she has a legal claim upon what he left, and means to assert it, or she never would have so cunningly wormed herself into my family. Of course it will be difficult for her to prove her position, since I have that certificate of marriage; still she may have some other proof that I know nothing about which she is secretly working. Of course I'd rather you would marry her," Mrs. Montague gloomily observed, "and thus make our interests mutual, than run any risk of losing the whole of my money. Still, I did want you to marry Kitty McKenzie: I wanted you to fortify yourself with additional wealth."

"I have suspected that the girl was Mona all along," Louis quietly remarked.

"Oh, have you?" sharply retorted his aunt, as she studied his face with suspicious eyes. "Perhaps you have been plotting to marry her for the sole purpose of getting this fortune wholly under your control."

"Pshaw! Aunt Margie, how foolish you are! Haven't I always worked for your interests? More than that, haven't you always assured me that the fortune would be mine eventually? Why, then, should I plot for it?" the young man replied, in soothing tones, but coloring beneath her glance. "I tell you," he went on, a note of passion in his voice, "I love the girl; I would even be willing to marry her without a dollar in prospect, and then go to work to support her. Now come, do not let us quarrel over imaginary troubles, but unite our forces for our mutual benefit. It will be far safer for you if she becomes my wife, for then you will have nothing to fear, and I shall have won the desire of my heart."

"Well, it will have to be, I suppose," said Mrs. Montague, moodily. "I wonder how I was ever so deceived though, when she looks so like Mona Forester. I can understand now why Ray Palmer was so attentive to her at Hazeldean. Strange it never occurred to me, when I saw him waiting upon her, that she was Mona Montague, and they must have had a quiet laugh by themselves over having so thoroughly hoodwinked us."

"They didn't hoodwink me," Mr. Hamblin affirmed, with a

sly smile; "I knew all the time who she was."

"I don't see how you knew it," Mrs. Montague retorted, impatiently.

"I will tell you. I was in Macy's one day when the girl ran across some acquaintances. She bowed and smiled to them, as I suppose she had always been in the habit of doing; but the petted darlings of *le bon ton* drew themselves up haughtily, stared rudely at her, and passed on, while the poor child flushed, then paled, and looked ready to drop. A moment later, the two proud misses shot by me, one of them remarking with curling lips and a toss of her head, 'Do you suppose that Mona Montague expects that we are going to recognize her now?'"

"Why didn't you tell me this before?" Mrs. Montague angrily demanded.

"Because I knew that, if you suspected her identity, you would turn her out of the house forthwith, and then I should have hard work getting into her good graces."

"You are a sly one, Louis."

"One must look out for one's own interests in some respects," he coolly responded.

"Does she know that you suspect her identity?"

"No, not yet; but I mean she soon shall."

"Ah!" said Mrs. Montague, with sudden thought, "maybe you can use this knowledge to aid your suit—only don't let her know that I am in the secret until you are sure of her."

"That has been my intention all along—for I have meant to marry her, by hook or crook," and the young man smiled complacently.

"Look out, Louis; don't overreach yourself," said his companion, bending forward, and looking warningly into his face. "If you make an enemy of me, I warn you, it will be the worse for you."

"My dear aunt, I have no intention of making an enemy of you—you and I have been chums too long for any ill-will to spring up between us now. But," he concluded, looking about him, "we must not remain here talking any longer; most of the passengers have already left the boat I will go for a carriage and we will drive directly to the St. Charles, where I have rooms engaged for you."

Mrs. Montague turned to call Mona, who was standing at some distance from them, watching the men unload the boat.

"Come," she said, "we must go ashore."

Mona followed her from the boat, and into the carriage, utterly ignoring Louis Hamblin's assistance as she entered. She shrank more and more from him, while a feeling of depression and foreboding suddenly changed her from the bright, care-free girl, which she had seemed ever since leaving St. Louis, into a proud, reticent, and suspicious woman.

Upon reaching the St. Charles Hotel, Mrs. Montague informed Mona that dinner would be served shortly, and she would need to be expeditious in making her toilet.

"I should prefer not to go to the dining-room," Mona began, flushing.

"But I wish you to, for we are going to drive afterward to some of the points of interest in the city," Mrs. Montague returned.

"If you will excuse me—"

"Nonsense," retorted her companion, again interrupting her; "don't be a goose, Ruth! I want you with me, and we will not discuss the point any further."

Mona hesitated a moment, then turned away, but with a dignity which warned Mrs. Montague that it might not be well to enforce her commands too rigorously, or she might rebel outright.

Mona went down to the dining-room, but to her great relief received no disagreeable attentions from Mr. Hamblin, who sat on the right, while her seat was on the left of his aunt. He did not address her during the meal, except to ascertain if she was properly waited upon by the servants.

Afterward they went for a drive out on the shell road, which proved to be really delightful, for the city was in its prime, while, rain having fallen early in the day, the streets were not in the least dusty.

Mrs. Montague and Louis monopolized the conversation, thus leaving Mona free to look around about her.

The only thing that occurred to annoy her was on their return to the hotel. Louis, in assisting her to alight, held her hand in a close, lingering clasp for a moment, and, looking admiringly into her eyes, remarked, in a low tone:

"I hope you have enjoyed your drive, Miss—Richards."

What could he mean, Mona asked herself, by that significant pause before and that emphasis on her name?

She forcibly wrenched her hand from his, and deigning him no reply, walked with uplifted head into the hotel, and up to her own room.

The next day she politely, but firmly, declined to go out driving, and remained by herself to write a long letter to Ray; thus she avoided the hated companionship of the man, who became more and more odious to her.

The third evening after their arrival Mrs. Montague went to a concert with some people whose acquaintance she had made while on the steamer, and Mona congratulated herself that she could have a long quiet evening in which to read a book in which she had become deeply interested.

She had not a thought of being interrupted, for she supposed that Louis had accompanied his aunt, and she was sitting contentedly by the table in Mrs. Montague's private parlor, when she heard the door behind her open and close.

She looked up surprised, but the expression was quickly succeeded by one of dismay when she saw Louis Hamblin advancing toward her.

She arose, regarding him with cold displeasure.

He bowed politely as he remarked:

"Do not rise. I simply came to get some letters that Aunt Margie wished me to mail for her."

Mona resumed her seat, greatly relieved at this assurance, and went on with her reading, while the young man took up his aunt's writing-pad, which lay upon the table, as if to search for the letters.

He took out a couple and slipped them into his pocket; then selecting a pen, began himself to write.

Mona felt very uncomfortable, sitting there alone with him, but she kept hoping that he would soon go out again, and so went on with her reading.

Presently, however, he laid down his pen, and, glancing across the table at her, asked:

"What book have you that is so interesting?"

"The Senator's Bride,'" Mona briefly responded.

"Ah! I have never read it. What do you think of it?"

"It is quite entertaining," was the brief, cold reply.

"Pray, do not be so cold and proud—so exceedingly laconic," the young man said, with a smile, which was intended to be persuasive.

Instantly the young girl arose again, stately and frigid as an iceberg.

She attempted to pass him and go to her own room, but he threw out his hand, seized her arm, and stopped her.

"*Please* do not go!" he urged, in an imploring tone. "I have something which I want very much to say to you."

Mona's blood began to boil, and her eyes flashed dangerously at his presumption in daring to touch her.

She was too proud to struggle with him, and she could not shake off his hold upon her arm.

"Release me, Mr. Hamblin!" she said, in ominously quiet tones.

"Nay, *do* not treat me so!" he pleaded. "Be kind to me for once, and let me open my heart to you."

Her red lips curled.

"*Will* you let me pass?" she icily demanded.

He colored hotly at her tone; a flash of anger gleamed in his eyes.

"*No*. Be seated, *Miss Mona Montague*; I have something important to say to you," he said, in a tone that struck terror to her heart, while the utterance of her real name so startled and unnerved her that, almost involuntarily, she sank back into her chair, her face as white as her handkerchief, and trembling in every limb.

"Ah! that surprises you, doesn't it?" he remarked, with a smile of triumph; "and now I imagine you will be more tractable."

"What do you mean?" demanded Mona, recovering her composure somewhat, and determined not to commit herself, if she could avoid it.

"What do I mean?" he repeated, with a light laugh. "I mean to have a little private and serious conversation with Miss Mona Montague; and when I have finished, I do not believe that she will treat me quite so cavalierly as she has been doing of late."

"I do not wish to hold any conversation with you, Mr. Hamblin," Mona began, haughtily.

"Perhaps not, but you will, nevertheless," he interposed; "and, let me tell you, to begin with, it will be useless for you to ignore the name by which I have addressed you. I have discovered your identity in spite of your clever efforts to represent some one else—or rather to conceal your personality. I know that you are Mona Montague, the daughter of my aunt's husband and a girl named Mona Forester—"

"Stay!" cried Mona, starting again to her feet, her eyes blazing. "I will not hear my mother spoken of with any disrespect."

"I beg your pardon; I had no intention of wounding you thus," said the young man, regretfully, and flushing. "I simply wished you to understand that I had discovered your identity; and since you have now virtually acknowledged it, by asserting that Mona Forester was your mother, I beg you will be reasonable, and talk the matter over calmly with me, and hear what I have to propose to you."

Mona sank weakly back.

She saw that it would be worse than useless to deny what he had asserted; she had indeed betrayed and acknowledged too much for that.

"Very well. I will listen to what you wish to say, but be kind enough to be brief, for I have no desire to prolong this interview beyond what is absolutely necessary for your purpose," she said, with freezing dignity.

"Well, then," Louis Hamblin began, "I have known who you

were ever since you came into Aunt Margie's house as a seamstress."

Then he went on to explain how he learned it, and Mona, remembering the incident but too well, saw that it would be best to quietly accept the fact of his knowledge.

"Does Mrs. Montague also know?" she asked, with breathless eagerness.

"She suspected you at first," he evasively answered, "but you so diplomatically replied to her questions—you were so self-possessed under all circumstances, and especially so when one day you found a picture of your mother, that she was forced to believe your strange resemblance to Mona Forester only a coincidence."

CHAPTER XI

MONA IN A TRYING POSITION

Mona breathed more freely, for she believed from his evasive reply that Mrs. Montague did not now believe her to be Mona Forester's child.

"I beg you will not tell her," she said, impulsively, and then instantly regretted having made the request.

The young man's face lighted.

If they could have a common secret he believed that he should make some headway in his wooing.

"That will depend upon how kind you are to me," he said, meaningly.

Mona's head went up haughtily again. His presumption, his assurance, both annoyed and angered her.

He affected not to notice her manner, and asked:

"What was your object, Miss Montague, in coming into my aunt's family under an assumed name?"

Mrs. Georgie Sheldon

Mona thought a moment before replying; then she felt that since he already knew so much, it would do no harm to tell him the truth.

"I had no intention at first of going anywhere under an assumed name," she said, gravely. "I applied at an employment bureau for a situation as seamstress, and this position was obtained for me. I did not even know the name of the woman who had engaged me, until I entered Mrs. Montague's house. When I learned the truth, I was tempted to leave at once; but the desire to learn more than I already knew regarding my parentage made me bold to brave discovery, and remain at least for a while, and so upon the spur of the moment I gave the name of Ruth Richards—Ruth is my middle name, and Richards very nearly like that of the man who married my mother—"

"Who married your mother?" questioned Louis Hamblin, in a mocking tone.

"Yes; they were legally married. I at least know that much," said Mona, positively, determined to make him think she fully believed it.

"How did you learn so much?"

"My uncle assured me of the fact only the day before he died."

"Your uncle? You mean Walter Dinsmore, I suppose?"

"Yes; of course."

"How much of your history did he reveal to you?" questioned the young man, eagerly.

"I do not feel under any obligation to tell you that," Mona coldly answered.

"Now, Miss Montague," Louis said, with well assumed frankness and friendliness, "why will you persist in treating me as an enemy? Why will you not have confidence in me, and allow me to help you? I know your whole history—I know, too, from what you have said, that you are ignorant of much that is vital to your interests, and which I could reveal to you, if I chose. Now forget any unpleasantness that may have arisen between us, tell me just what you hoped to learn by remaining in my aunt's family, and, believe me, I stand ready to help you."

Mona lifted her great liquid brown eyes, and searched his face.

Oh, how she longed to know the truth about her mother; but she distrusted him—she instinctively doubted his sincerity.

He read something of this in her glance, and continued, hoping to disarm her suspicions:

"Of course you know that Aunt Margie is, or was, Richmond Montague's second wife—"

"Ah! by that statement you yourself virtually acknowledge that my mother was his first wife," triumphantly interposed Mona. "As I said before, my uncle assured me of the fact, but your admission is worth something to me as corroborative evidence. All that I desire now is tangible proof of it; if you can and will obtain that for me, I shall have some faith in your assertion that you wish to help me."

"Are you so eager to claim, as your father, the man who deserted your mother?" Louis Hamblin asked, with a sneer, and wishing to sound her a little further.

"No; I simply want proof that my mother was a legal wife—I have only scorn and contempt for the man who wronged her," Mona replied, intense aversion vibrating in her tones. "I regard him, as my uncle did, as a knave—a brute."

"Did Walter Dinsmore represent him as such to you?" inquired her companion, in a mocking tone.

"He did; he expressed the utmost contempt and loathing for the man who had ruined his sister's life."

The young man gave vent to a short, derisive laugh.

"I cannot deny the justness of the epithets applied to him," he said, with a sneer, "but, that such terms should have fallen from the immaculate lips of the cultured and aristocratic Walter Dinsmore, rather amuses me, especially as the present Mrs. Dinsmore might, with some reason, perhaps, bring the same charges against him."

"Did you know my uncle?" Mona questioned, with some surprise.

"Not personally; but Mrs. Montague knew him very well years ago."

"Oh! I wonder if you could tell me—" Mona began, greatly agitated, as she recalled the dreadful suspicion that flashed into her mind regarding her uncle, in connection with her father's death.

"If I could tell you what?" Louis inquired, while he wondered what thought could have so suddenly blanched her face, and sent that look of terror into her beautiful eyes.

"Oh, I want to know—did he—how did my father die?" the young girl cried, in faltering, trembling tones.

Louis Hamblin regarded her with unfeigned astonishment at the question.

"How did your father die?" he repeated. "Why, like any other respectable gentleman—in his own house, and of an incurable disease."

"Oh! then he did die a natural death," breathed Mona, with a sigh of relief that was almost a sob.

"Certainly. Ah!" and her companion appeared suddenly to divine her thoughts, "so you imagined that Walter Dinsmore killed Richmond Montague for the wrong done your mother! Ha! ha! I have no doubt that he felt bitter enough to commit murder, or almost any other act of violence, to avenge her; but let me assure you, Miss Montague, that that high-toned gentleman never soiled his hands with blood; and if that was your thought—"

"It is no matter what I thought," Mona hastily, but coldly, interposed, for she had no intention of confessing any such suspicion; but she was greatly relieved to learn that it had no foundation, and she now bitterly reproached herself for having even momentarily entertained a thought of anything that had been so foreign to her uncle's noble nature.

"To go back to what we were speaking of before," she continued, gravely, "will you furnish me with tangible proof of my mother's marriage? I know that she eloped with Richmond Montague, that they lived together for several months, when he suddenly deserted her, and that there is some mystery connected with that event—something which my uncle hesitated or feared to tell me. I know, too, that he was very anxious to reveal something more to me when he lay dying, and could not, because he had been stricken speechless. But for that fact, I believe I should not now be obliged to ask this favor of you," she concluded, flushing.

"Does it gall you so much, to ask a favor of me?" he inquired, bitterly. "But why," he went on, without waiting for a reply, "are you so exceedingly anxious to obtain this proof? Do you expect by the use of it to secure to yourself the property left by your father? Was that your object in remaining in my aunt's family under an assumed name?"

"No!" Mona vehemently returned. "I would not touch one dollar of his money. I would scorn to profit by so much as a penny of the fortune left by the man who deserted his wife in her sad extremity, and then, when death freed him from the tie which bound him to her, married a woman whom he did not love; who possessed so little of fatherly instinct in his nature, that he never acknowledged his child, nor betrayed the slightest interest in or affection for her. I would never own him for such a purpose; while, were it not for the sake of establishing my mother's honor, I would even repudiate the name I bear," she concluded, looking so proud and beautiful in her righteous scorn that the young man gazed upon her with admiration.

"You are very proud-spirited," he remarked; then, with a sly smile, "but as for the name you affect to so despise, it would be an easy matter to change it."

Mona colored at this observation, not because she gave a thought to his meaning, but because she hoped it would not be so very long before she would change the hated name of Montague for the honored one of Palmer.

Her companion noticed the flush, and an eager look flashed

into his eyes, while his lips trembled with the torrent of burning words which he longed to pour into her ears. But he controlled himself for the moment, and continued:

"You ask me if I will give you the tangible proof of your mother's marriage. I have told you that I can do so; that I know the whole story of the elopement and the desertion. I can produce absolute proof that Mona Forester was a legal wife."

"Then give it to me—give it to me and I will believe that you are my friend," Mona cried, appealingly, and trembling with excitement at his statement.

"I will do so gladly," the young man said, a smile of triumph curling his lips, "but I can only do so conditionally."

"Conditionally?" repeated Mona, her great eyes flashing up to his face with a startled look.

"Yes. I can produce the certificate proving your father's and mother's honorable marriage. I can give you letters that will also prove it, and prove, too, that your father was not quite so disreputable and heartless as you have been led to believe. There is also a picture of him, painted on ivory, and set in a frame of gold, embellished with costly stones, which he had made for his wife, and there are valuable jewels and other keepsakes which he bestowed upon her with lavish hands, and which now rightly belong to you. All these I will give you if—if you will marry me—if you will be my wife, Mona."

The girl sprang to her feet, every atom of color now gone from her face, and confronted him with haughty mien.

"*Your wife!*" she began, pantingly. But he would not let her

　　　　　Mrs. Georgie Sheldon

go on—he meant at least to explain himself more fully before allowing her to reject him.

"Yes, why not?" he asked, throwing into his tone all the tenderness he could command, "for I love you, Mona, with all my heart. I have told you so once before, but you would not believe me. You taunted me with unworthy motives, and asserted that I would not dare to confess my affection to my aunt; but I have confessed it, and she is willing that I should win you. I know that I have paid devoted attention to Kitty McKenzie, as you also twitted me of doing, and Aunt Margie wanted me to marry her; but when she found that I had no love to give her, that my heart was set upon you, she yielded the point, and I now have her full and free consent to make you my wife. Do not scorn my suit, Mona; I cannot think of you as Ruth Richards any longer; do not curl your proud lips and flash your glorious eyes upon me with scorn, as you did that day at Hazeldean, for I offer you a warm and loyal heart. I know, that I am not worthy of you," he went on, flushing and speaking humbly for once, for he was terribly in earnest; "I have been guilty of a great many things which I have learned to regret, since I have known you; but I can conquer everything if you will give me your love as an incentive, and I will be a better man in the future. I will even *work* for you, if you so despise the fortune which your father left and which I have expected to inherit from my aunt. Oh, Mona, do not despise my love for you, for it is the purest attribute of my nature, and—"

"Pray cease," Mona here interposed, for she felt unable to hear any more of this passionate avowal, while she was greatly surprised and really moved by the depth of feeling which he evinced. "I would be the last one," she continued, in kind, grave tones, but with averted eyes and trembling lips, "to despise the true affection of any man. If I said anything to wound you that day at Hazeldean, I regret it now, although I felt at the time that you showed some disrespect in your manner of approaching me. But I cannot be your wife; if you make that the condition"—and her lips curled a trifle here—"of my learning the mystery regarding my father's desertion of my mother, and securing the proof of their marriage; then I must forever relinquish all such hopes, for I could never marry a man—"

"But," he interrupted, excitedly.

"Let me finish," she persisted, lifting her hand to stay his words. "No woman should ever become the wife of a man she cannot love. I do not love you, Mr. Hamblin, and knowing this, you would not respect me if I should yield to your suit. Let me assure you that I honor you for some things you said to-day—that you would be willing to work for one whom you loved; that you would even relinquish a fortune for her sake. Believe me, I respect you and appreciate such an avowal, and only regret that your regard could not have been bestowed upon some one who could return such devotion. I cannot, but, Mr. Hamblin, I feel more friendly toward you at this moment than I have ever felt before. I beg, however," she concluded, sadly, "that you will never address me thus again, for it gives me pain to know that any one's life should be marred through me; put this affection away from you—crush it in your heart, and seek some dear, good girl who will love you and make you happier than I possibly could, if I should yield to your suit without any heart to give you."

"Put this love out of my heart! crush it!" burst forth the young man, with pale lips. "Could you do that, Mona Montague, if the man you loved should stand coldly up before you and bid you to do so?"

Mona flushed, and hot tears sprang into her eyes. She knew,

Mrs. Georgie Sheldon

but too well, that she could never crush out of her heart her love for Raymond Palmer.

If Louis Hamblin had bestowed but a tithe of such affection upon her there was indeed a sad future in store for him, and the deepest sympathies of her nature were aroused for him.

"I am sorry—" she began, falteringly, as she lifted her swimming eyes to his face, and both look and tone stirred him to hot rebellion, for he knew well enough of what she had been thinking.

"How sorry are you?" he cried, in a low, intense tone; "sorry enough to try to do for me what you have bidden me do for another? Will you crush your love for Ray Palmer, and bestow it upon me?"

Mona recoiled beneath these fierce, hot words, while she inwardly resented the selfishness and rudeness of his question.

Still she tried to make some allowance for his bitter disappointment and evident suffering.

"I do not think you have any right to speak to me like that," she said, in tones of gentle reproof, though her face was crimson with conscious blushes.

"Have I no right to say to you what you have said to me?" he demanded. "You have said that no woman should marry a man whom she does not love, while, in the very next breath you bid me go 'seek for some dear, good girl,' and ask her to marry me, who can never love any woman but you. Are you considerate—are you consistent?"

"Perhaps not," she returned, sorrowfully, "but I did not mean to be inconsistent or to wound you—I could hardly believe that you cared so deeply! I hoped you might be mistaken in your assertion that no other affection could be rooted in your heart."

"There may be other natures besides your own that are capable of tenacious affection," he retorted, with exceeding bitterness.

"True," Mona said, sighing heavily, "but," driven to desperation, and facing him with sudden resolution, "I cannot respond to your suit as you wish; I can never be your wife, for—perhaps, under the circumstances, I ought to make the confession—I am already pledged to another."

Mrs. Georgie Sheldon

CHAPTER XII

THE SECRET OF THE ROYAL MIRROR

Mona's eyes were averted and she was greatly embarrassed as she made the acknowledgment of her engagement, therefore she could not see the look of anger and evil purpose which suddenly swept every expression of tenderness from Louis Hamblin's face.

He could not speak for a moment, he was so intensely agitated by her confession.

"Of course, I cannot fail to understand you," he remarked, at last. "You mean that you are engaged to Ray Palmer, and that accounts for the attentions which he bestowed upon Ruth Richards at Hazeldean. You two were very clever, but even then I had read between the lines and knew what you have just told me."

"You knew, and yet presumed to make this avowal? You dared to ask another man's promised wife to marry you!" Mona exclaimed, all her embarrassment now gone, her scornful eyes looking straight into his.

"Well, perhaps I should not say I knew, but I surmised," he confessed, his glance wavering beneath hers.

"That is but a poor apology," she retorted, in the same tone as before; "you certainly have betrayed but very little respect for me if you even 'surmised' the truth, and would ask me to regard my plighted troth so lightly as to break it simply to gratify your own selfishness."

"And your respect for me has waned accordingly, I suppose you would be glad to add," Louis Hamblin interposed, with a sneer.

Mona made him no answer. She began to think that she had overestimated the purity of his motives—that all her recent sympathy had been expended upon an unworthy object.

"You will not forget, however, that I made the promise to surrender certain proofs and keepsakes conditional upon your yielding to my suit," he added, with cold resoluteness.

"No honorable man would make such conditions with the woman he professed to love," retorted Mona, with curling lips.

"A man, when he is desperate, will adopt almost any measure to achieve his object," her companion responded, hotly.

"We will not argue the matter further, if you please," Mona said, frigidly, as she took up her book, which she had laid upon the table when she arose, and started to leave the room.

"Mona, do not go away like this—you shall not leave me in such a mood!" the young man cried, as he placed himself in her path. "Do you not see that I am filled with despair—that I am desperate?"

"I am sorry," she answered, gravely, "but I can tell you

nothing different—my answer is final, and your own sense of what is right should make you realize and submit to it."

"Then you do not care for the marriage certificate and other proofs?" he said.

Again the young girl's lips curled with infinite scorn.

"Did you suppose that my love and my hand were, like articles of merchandise, to be bought and sold?" she asked, with scathing sarcasm. "Yes, I do care for—I do want the proofs; but they are not to be mentioned in connection with such sacred subjects," she went on, with dignity. "If you were really my friend you would never have suggested anything of the kind; you would have been glad to help me to any proof that would relieve my mind and heart from the harassing doubts regarding the history of my parents. If such proofs exist, as you claim, they rightly *belong* to me, and you are uncourteous, not to say dishonorable, in keeping them from me."

"People are not in the habit of resigning important documents simply for the sake of preserving themselves from the charge of discourtesy," Louis laconically observed.

"I am to understand from that, I suppose, that you will not give them to me," Mona remarked. "Well, since I *know* that there was no blame or shame attached to my mother—since I know that she was only a victim to the wickedness of others—it will not matter so very much if I do not have the tangible proofs you possess, and I must try to be content without them."

She made another attempt to leave the room, but he still stood in her way.

"I cannot—I will not give you up," he said, between his tightly locked teeth.

"You will be kind enough to let me pass, Mr. Hamblin." Mona returned, and ignoring his excited assertion.

"No, I will not," he fiercely replied.

She lifted her eyes, and met his angry glance with one so proudly authoritative that he involuntarily averted his own gaze.

"I beg that you will not cause me to lose all faith in you," she quietly remarked.

A hot flush surged to his brow, and he instantly stepped aside, looking crestfallen and half-ashamed.

Without another word, Mona passed from the room and entered her own chamber.

As soon as she had closed and locked the door, she sat down, and tried to think over all that had been said about her mother; this one subject filled all her mind to the exclusion of everything else.

But for Louis Hamblin's last remarks, and the betrayal of his real nature, and his selfish, ignoble purpose, she would have been grieved on his account, but she saw that he unworthy of her regard, of even one sorrowful thought.

"These papers and keepsakes of which he has told me are mine," she said to herself; "they belong by right to me, and I must—I will have them. That certificate, oh! if I could get but that, I could give myself to Ray without a scruple, and besides I could secure this property which Homer Forester has left to my mother, and then I need not go to Ray quite penniless. These things must be in either Louis Hamblin's or Mrs. Montague's possession—doubtless they are even now somewhere in the house in West Forty-ninth street. I shall tell Mr. Corbin immediately upon my return, and perhaps he will know of some way by which they can be compelled to give them up."

She fell to musing over the matter, little suspecting that the most important treasure of all—the contested marriage certificate—had already fallen into her lover's hands, and was at that moment safely locked in Mr. Corbin's safe, only awaiting her own and Mrs. Montague's return from the South to set her right before the world, both as to parentage and inheritance.

Louis Hamblin remained in Mrs. Montague's parlor until her return from the concert, brooding over the failure of his purpose, and trying to devise some scheme by which he could attain the desire of his heart.

He then gave her a faithful account of his interview with Mona, and they sat far into the night and plotted how best to achieve their object.

Mrs. Montague was now as eager to have Louis marry Mona as she had previously been determined to oppose it.

"I am bound that she shall never go into the Palmer family, if I can prevent it," she said, with a frowning brow. "If I am to be mistress of Mr. Palmer's home, I have no intention of allowing Mona Forester's child to be a blot on my future happiness."

"You are complimentary, Aunt Marg, in your remarks regarding my future wife," Louis sarcastically observed.

"I can't help it, Louis. I bear the girl no good-will, as you have known from the first, and you must make up your mind to accept matters as they are. You are determined to have her and I have given my consent to the marriage from purely selfish motives," Mrs. Montague returned, in a straightforward, matter-of-fact tone. "I would never have consented," she added, with a frown "if I had not feared that there is proof—besides what we possess—of Mona Forester's legal marriage, and that through it we might some time lose our fortune. I should be in despair to be obliged to give it up—life without plenty of money is not worth living, and I consider that I was very shrewd and fortunate in getting possession of that certificate and those other things."

"Did you bring them with you when you left home?"

"No; I never thought of them," Mrs. Montague responded, with a start and a look of anxiety. "It is the first time I ever came away from home without them; but after I received that telegram and letter I had plenty on my mind, I assure you—my chief aim was to get that girl out of New York, and away to some safe place where we could work out our scheme."

"But you ought never to leave such valuables behind," said her nephew; "the house might take fire, and they would be all destroyed."

"That would be but a small loss," the woman retorted. "I have thought a hundred times that I would throw them all into the fire, and thus blot out of existence all that remained of the girl I so hated; but whenever I have attempted to do so I have been unaccountably restrained. But I will do it as soon as we get home again," she resolutely concluded.

Louis Hamblin's eyes gleamed with a strange expression at this threat; but he made no reply to it.

"But let us settle this matter of your marriage," she resumed, after a moment of thought. "The girl shall marry you—I have brought her here for that purpose, and if she will not be reasoned into compliance with our wishes, she shall be compelled or tricked into it. But how, is the question."

"I will agree to almost anything, so that I get her," remarked her nephew, with a grim smile.

The clock on the mantel-piece struck two before they separated, but they had decided on their plan of action, and only awaited the coming day to develop it.

Meanwhile strange things had been happening in Mona's room.

We left her musing over her recent interview with Louis, and deeply absorbed in making plans to obtain possession of the proofs of her mother's marriage, which he had asserted he could produce.

The more she thought of the matter the more determined she became to accomplish her purpose, and she began to grow very anxious to return to New York to consult with Ray and Mr. Corbin.

"I wonder how much longer Mrs. Montague intends to remain here," she murmured. "She said she should return within a fortnight, but nearly that time has expired already. I cannot understand her object in prolonging her stay, since she was disappointed about coming with the party. I believe I will ask her to-morrow how soon we are to go back."

Mona felt very weary after the unusual excitement of the evening; her nerves were also considerably unstrung, and she resolved not to wait for Mrs. Montague's return, but retire at once.

She arose and began to prepare for bed, but having sent some clothing away to be washed that morning, she found that her night-robe had gone with the other articles, and unlocking her trunk, she began to look for another.

"I thought I put an extra one in the tray," she mused, as she searched for but failed to find it.

This obliged her to remove the tray and to unpack some of the contents beneath.

While thus employed she took out a box, and without thinking what it contained, carelessly set it across a corner of the trunk.

She finally found the garment she needed, and then began to replace the clothing which she had been obliged to remove during her search.

While thus engaged she turned suddenly to reach for something that had slipped from her grasp, and in the act she hit her elbow against the box setting on the corner of her trunk, and knocked it to the floor.

"Oh! my mirror!" she cried, in a voice of terror, and hastily gathering up the box, uncovered it to see if the precious relic had been injured.

To her great joy she found that it had not been broken by the fall; but as she lifted it from the box, to examine it still further, the bottom of the frame dropped out, and with it the things which Mr. Dinsmore had concealed within it.

"Mercy!" Mona excitedly exclaimed; "it looks like a little

Mrs. Georgie Sheldon

drawer, and here are some letters and a box which some one has hidden in it! Can it be that these things once belonged to Marie Antoinette, and have been inclosed in this secret place all these long years?" she wonderingly questioned.

"No, surely not, for they would be yellow with age," she continued, as she began to examine them.

"Ah!" with a start, and growing pale, "here is a letter addressed to me—*For Mona*—and in Uncle Walter's handwriting! He must have known about the secret of this mirror, and put these letters here with some special object in view. What can it mean?"

She grew dizzy—almost faint with the excitement of her discovery, and the things dropped from her nerveless fingers upon her lap.

"There is some secret here!" she whispered, as she gazed down at them, an expression of dread in her startled eyes. "Perhaps it is the secret which I have so long wanted to know! Can it be that the mystery of my mother's sad fate is about to be solved—that Uncle Walter had not the courage to tell me all, that never-to-be-forgotten morning, but wrote it out and hid it here for me to find later? Ah!" and she lifted her head as if suddenly recalling something, "this was what he tried to make me understand the day he died! He sent me for the mirror, not to remind me to keep it always, as I thought at the time, but to explain the secret of it, so that I could find what he had hidden here. Oh, how he suffered because he could not show me! Why could I not have understood?" and her tears fell thick and fast, as she thus lived over again that painful experience.

She soon brushed them away, however, and lifting the mirror, examined it carefully.

She found that the tiny drawer would shove smoothly in and out, and she pushed it almost in, but took care not to quite close it.

"There must be a spring somewhere to hold it in place," she murmured, regarding it curiously. "Ah! now I feel it! But how is it operated? How can the drawer be opened again if I shut it entirely?"

She looked the mirror over most carefully, both on the back and front, but at first could detect nothing. But at length, as she still continued to work the drawer in and out, she noticed that the central pearl and gold point at the top of the frame moved slightly as she pressed the drawer close upon the spring, and she believed that she had discovered the Secret of the Royal Mirror.

With a resolute air she shut it entirely and heard the click of the spring as it shot into its socket. Her reason told her that pressure applied to that central point of pearl and gold would at once release the drawer again.

She tried it, and instantly it dropped out upon her lap.

"It is the strangest thing in the world. I feel almost as if I had opened a grave," she murmured, a shiver running along her nerves. "My heart almost fails me when I think of examining its contents—this letter addressed to me, this package of letters, and the tiny box. I wonder what there is in it?"

She looked strangely beautiful as she sat there upon the floor, her face startlingly pale, her eyes seeming larger than ever, with that wondering expression in their liquid depths, while she turned that little box over and over in her trembling hands, as if she tried to gather courage to untie the string that bound its cover on and look within it.

At last she threw up her head with a determined air, gathered up all the things she had found in the secret drawer, and rising, drew a chair to her table, where she sat down to solve the mystery.

CHAPTER XIII

"I SHOULD THINK WE WERE OUT AT SEA!"

Mona's curiosity prompted her to examine the contents of the little box first.

She untied the narrow ribbon that was bound about it, lifted the cover and a layer of cotton, and discovered the two rings which we already know about.

"My mother's wedding and engagement-ring!" Mona breathed, seeming to know by instinct what they were. "They must have been taken from her fingers after she was dead, and Uncle Walter has kept them all these years for me. Oh, why could he not have told me about them? I should have prized them so." She lifted them from their snowy bed with reverent touch, remarking, as she did so, the size and great beauty of the diamond in the engagement-ring.

"My dear, deeply wronged mother! how I should have loved you!" she murmured. "I wonder if you know how tenderly I feel toward you; if you can see me now and realize that I, the little, helpless baby, for whose life you gave up your own, am longing for you with all my heart and soul."

She touched the rings tenderly with her lips, tears raining

Mrs. Georgie Sheldon

over her cheeks, while sob after sob broke from her.

She wiped away her tears after a little, and tried the rings upon her own fingers, smiling sadly to see how perfectly they fitted.

"Mamma's hand must have been about the size of mine," she said. "I think I must be very like her in every way."

She slipped the heavy gold band off and bent nearer the light to examine the inside, hoping to find some inscription upon it.

She found only the date, "June 6th, 1861."

"The date of her marriage," she whispered, a little smile of triumph lighting her face, then removing the other ring from her hand, she laid them both back in the box and put it one side, "Now for the letters," she said, taking up the one addressed to herself and carefully cutting one end across the envelope with a little knife taken from her pocket.

She unfolded the closely written sheets, which she drew from it, with hands that trembled with nervous excitement.

The next moment she was absorbed in their contents, and as she read a strange change came over her.

At first there was a quick start, accompanied by a low exclamation of surprise, then a look of wonder shot into her great brown eyes. Suddenly, as she hungrily devoured the pages, her color fled, even her lips became white, and an expression of keen pain settled about her mouth, but she read on and on with breathless interest, turning page after page, until she came to the last one, where she found her uncle's name signed in full.

"Now I know!" burst from her trembling lips, as the sheets fell from her nerveless hands and her voice sounded hollow and unnatural. "How very, very strange! Oh! Uncle Walter, why didn't you tell me? why didn't you—tell me?"

Her lips only formed those last words as her head fell back against her chair, all the light fading out of her eyes, and then she slipped away into unconsciousness. When she came to herself again she was cold, and stiff, and deathly sick.

At first she could not seem to remember what had happened, for her mind was weak and confused. Then gradually all that had occurred came back to her.

She shivered and tried feebly to rub something of natural warmth into her chilled hands, then suddenly losing all self-control, she bowed her face upon them, and burst into a passion of tears.

"Oh, if I had only known before," she murmured over and over again, with unspeakable regret.

But she was worn out, and this excitement could not last.

She made an effort to regain her composure, gathered up the scattered sheets of her uncle's letter, restoring them to the envelope, and then took up the other package which was bound with a scarlet ribbon.

There were half a dozen or more letters and all superscribed in a bold, handsome hand.

"They are my father's letters to my mother," Mona murmured, "but I have no strength to read them to-night."

She put them back, with the other things, into the secret

drawer in the mirror, which she restored to its box, and then carefully packed it away in her trunk, with all her clothing except what she wished to put on in the morning.

"I shall go back to New York to-morrow," she said, with firmly compressed lips, as the last thing was laid in its place. "I cannot remain another day in the service of such a woman; and, since I have now learned everything, there is no need; I must go back to Ray and—happiness."

A tender smile wreathed her lips as she prepared to retire, but she could not sleep after she was in bed, even though she was weak and exhausted from the excitement of the last few hours, for her nerves throbbed and tingled with every beat of her pulses, and it was not until near morning that slumber came to her relief.

She was awake long before the gong for breakfast sounded, however, and rising immediately dressed herself for traveling, after which she finished packing, and then went down to breakfast with a grave, resolute face, which betrayed that she had some fixed purpose in her mind.

Mrs. Montague regarded her with some surprise as she noticed her dress, but she made no remark, although she looked troubled and anxious.

As soon as they arose from the table Mona went directly up stairs again, and waited at the door of Mrs. Montague's parlor until that lady made her appearance.

Louis was with her, but Mona ignored his presence, and quietly asked:

"Can I see you alone for a few moments, Mrs. Montague?"

"Certainly," she replied, giving the girl a sharp, curious glance, and immediately preceded her into the room. "Well?" she inquired, turning and facing her, the moment the door was closed, as if already she suspected what was coming.

"I simply wanted to tell you that I am going to return to New York to-day," Mona said, in a tone which plainly indicated that no argument would serve to change her determination.

"Aren't you somewhat premature in your movements? What is your reason for wanting to go home in such a hurry?" Mrs. Montague demanded, with some asperity.

"There are a number of reasons. I have some business to attend to, for one thing," Mona answered.

Mrs. Montague appeared startled by this unlooked-for reply. She had expected that she would complain of Louis' persecution of the previous evening.

"Do you think it just fair, Ruth, to leave me at such short notice?" she inquired, after thinking a moment.

"I am very sorry if my going will annoy you," Mona said, "but you will have Mr. Hamblin for an escort, and so you will not be left alone. I have made up my mind to go, and I would like to leave at as early an hour as possible."

Mrs. Montague saw that it would be useless to oppose her, but a look of cunning leaped into her eyes as she returned, with an assumption of graceful compliance:

"Then we will all go. A few days will not matter much with me; I have been disappointed in almost everything since leaving home, and I am about ready to go back myself. I am sure I do not wish to keep you if you are unhappy or discontented, and so

Mrs. Georgie Sheldon

we will take the afternoon boat if you like. I feel a certain responsibility regarding you, and could not think of allowing you to return alone and unprotected," she interposed, a curious smile curving her lips; then she added: "I will have Louis go to secure staterooms immediately, and you can do your packing as soon as you like."

"It is all done. I am ready to go at any hour, but," and Mona flushed, "I should prefer to go by rail, as we could reach New York much more quickly than by boat."

Mrs. Montague frowned at this remark.

"Pray do not be in such an unnecessary hurry, Ruth," she said, with some impatience. "It is much pleasanter traveling by boat than by rail at this season of the year, and I enjoy the water far more. I think you might oblige one by yielding that much," and the woman watched her anxiously as she awaited her reply.

"Very well," Mona said, gravely, though reluctantly. "I will do as you wish. At what hour does the steamer leave?"

"I don't know. I shall have to ask Louis, and I will tell you later. Now, I wish you would baste some fresh ruching on my traveling dress, then you may hem the new vail that you will find upon my dressing-case," and having given these directions, Mrs. Montague hurried from the room to find her nephew.

She met him in the hall, where he had been walking back and forth, for he surmised what the nature of Mona's interview would be, and knew that the time had come for him to act with boldness if he hoped to win the prize he coveted.

"Come into your room, where we shall not be overheard,"

Mrs. Montague whispered, and leading the way thither, they were soon holding an earnest consultation over this unexpected interruption of the scheme which they had arranged the night before.

They talked for half an hour, after which Mrs. Montague returned to her parlor and Louis at once left the hotel.

He did not return until nearly lunch time, when, in Mona's presence, he informed his aunt that the staterooms were secured, and the boat would leave at seven that evening.

"If you will get your trunks ready I will send them aboard early, and then I shall have no trouble about baggage at the last moment, and can look after your wraps and satchels," he remarked, as he glanced significantly at his aunt.

"Mine are ready to strap, and Ruth's was packed before breakfast, so they can be sent off as soon as you like," Mrs. Montague returned.

He attended to the strapping of them himself, and a little later they were taken away.

Mona wondered somewhat at this arrangement. She thought the trunks might just as well have gone with them, but concluded that Louis did not wish to be troubled with them at the last moment, as he had said.

At half-past six they left the hotel, and drove to the pier where the steamboat lay.

Louis hurried the ladies on board, and to their staterooms, telling them to make haste and get settled, as dinner would be served as soon as the boat left the landing.

He had secured three staterooms for their use, another circumstance which appeared strange to Mona, as she and Mrs. Montague had occupied one together in coming down the river.

"Perhaps," she said to herself, "she is angry because I insisted upon going home, and does not wish to have me with her. I believe, however, I shall like it best by myself."

She arranged everything to her satisfaction, and then sat down by her window to wait until the gong should sound for dinner, but a strange feeling of depression and of homesickness seemed to settle over her spirits, while her thoughts turned with wistful fondness to her lover so far away in New York, and she half regretted that she had not insisted upon returning by rail.

She wondered that she did not hear Mrs. Montague moving about in her stateroom, but concluded that she had completed, her arrangements for the night and gone on deck.

Presently the last signal was given, and the steamer swung slowly away from the levee. A few moments later the gong sounded for dinner, and Mona went out into the saloon to look for her companions.

She met Louis Hamblin at the door leading to the dining-saloon, but he was alone.

"Where is Mrs. Montague?" Mona inquired, and wondering if he was going to be sick, for he looked pale, and seemed ill at ease.

"Hasn't she been with you?" he asked, appearing surprised at her question. "I thought she was in her stateroom."

"No, I did not hear her moving about," Mona replied, "so supposed she had come out."

"Perhaps she is on deck; if you will wait here I will run up to look for her," Louis remarked, and Mona sat down as he walked away.

He presently returned, but alone.

"She is not up stairs," he said; "I will go to her stateroom; perhaps she has been lying down; she said she had a headache this afternoon."

Again he left Mona, but came back to her in a few minutes, saying:

"Yes, it is as I thought; she isn't feeling well, and doesn't care to go down to dinner. I am to send her a cup of tea, and then she will retire for the night. Shall we go down now? You must be hungry," he concluded, smiling.

Mona would have much preferred to go by herself, and have him do the same, but she did not wish to have any words with him about it, so quietly followed him to the table, and took her seat beside him.

He was very polite and attentive, supplying all her wants in a thoughtful but unobtrusive way, and did not once by word or look remind her of anything disagreeable.

The dinner was a lengthy affair, and it was after eight when they left the dining-saloon, when Mona at once retreated to her stateroom to rid herself of Louis Hamblin's companionship. On her way thither she rapped upon Mrs. Montague's door, and asked:

Mrs. Georgie Sheldon

"Cannot I do something for you, Mrs. Montague?"

There was no response from within, and thinking she must be asleep, Mona passed on to her own room.

It was growing quite dark, and Mona, feeling both weary and sleepy from the restlessness and wakefulness of the previous night, resolved to retire at once.

She felt really relieved, although a trifle lonely to be in a stateroom by herself, but she fell asleep almost immediately, and did not awake until the gong sounded for breakfast.

She felt much refreshed, and after dressing went and knocked upon Mrs. Montague's door to inquire if she had rested well, and if she could do anything for her.

There was no reply, and thinking perhaps she was still asleep, or had already arisen, she went up on deck to get a breath of air before going to breakfast.

"Why!" she exclaimed on looking around her, as she reached the deck, "how very wide the river must be just here; I did not observe it to be so when we came down; perhaps, though, we passed this point during the night, but I did not suppose we could get out of sight of land on the Mississippi."

A storm was evidently brewing; indeed, it was already beginning to rain, the wind blew, and the vessel rolled considerably.

Mona could see nothing of either Mrs. Montague or Louis, and found that she could not walk about to search for them, for all at once she began to feel strangely dizzy and faint.

"Can it be that I am going to be sick?" she murmured, "I was not coming down, for there was not much motion to the boat, but now it rolls and pitches as if it were out on the broad ocean."

She was growing rapidly worse, and, retreating to her stateroom, she crept again into her berth, and rang for the stewardess.

She was ill all that day—so ill that she could not think of much but her own feelings, although she did wonder now and then if Mrs. Montague was prostrated like herself. She must be, she thought, or she certainly would come to her.

Once she asked the stewardess if she was ill, and the woman had briefly replied that everybody was sick, and then hurried out to answer some other call.

But during the next day Mona began to rally, and the stewardess advised her to go up on deck, saying that the fresh air would do much toward improving her condition. She assisted her to dress, and helped her up stairs to a chair, covered her with a warm robe, and then left her alone.

Mona at first was so faint and weary from her exertions that she did not pay much attention to her surroundings. She lay with her eyes closed for a while, but finally the air made her feel better, and she began to look about her.

An expression of wonder and anxiety instantly overspread her white face.

Where were the banks of the river, so green and bright, which had made the southward trip so delightful?

The sun was shining brightly, for the storm had passed and

Mrs. Georgie Sheldon

the sky was cloudless, but, looking in every direction, she could discern no land—all about her was but a wide waste of deep blue water.

"Why!" she cried, "I should think we were out at sea!"

She looked greatly disturbed, but just at that moment she saw Louis Hamblin coming toward her, and she noticed that he also looked somewhat pale, as if he, too, had been suffering from sea-sickness.

"You are really better," he smilingly observed as he reached her side; "you have had a severe siege as well as I."

"Then you have been sick?" Mona observed, but turning away from the intense look which he bent upon her.

"Indeed, I have. I have but just ventured out of my berth," he returned, shrugging his shoulders over painful memories.

"How is Mrs. Montague? I have not seen her since we left New Orleans," Mona inquired.

A peculiar look came into Louis Hamblin's eyes.

"Well, she has been under the weather, too, and has not cared to see any one," he said. "She simply wants to be let alone, like most people who suffer from sea-sickness."

"That accounts for her absence and silence," thought Mona. Then she asked: "Is it not very strange that we do not see the banks of the river? One would almost imagine that we were far out at sea."

Again that peculiar look swept over the young man's face.

"And so we are," he quietly answered, after a momentary pause.

"What?" exclaimed Mona, in a startled tone, and turning her blanched face upon him with a look of terror.

"Do not be excited, Miss Montague," he coolly observed. "Aunt Margie simply took a sudden freak to go home by sea; she thought the voyage would be beneficial to her. She did not confide her plans to you, as she feared you would object and insist upon going home alone by rail."

Mona flushed hotly. She was very indignant that Mrs. Montague should have done such a thing without consulting her, and she deeply regretted that she had not insisted upon acting according to her own wishes.

She had no suspicion even now of the wretched deception that had been practiced upon her, but she did not now wonder so much that the woman had so persistently kept out of her way, and she felt so angry that she did not care to meet her again until they should land.

"When shall we get to New York?" she inquired, in a low, cold tone.

"We shall land some time this evening," Louis Hamblin evasively replied, but watching her with curious interest.

Mona gave utterance to a sigh of relief, but did not appear to notice how he had worded his sentence.

She believed that in a few hours more she would forever sever all connections with this bold, bad woman who had been guilty of so much wrong; that she would forever be freed from the society and attentions of her no less unprincipled and disagreeable nephew.

She resolved to go at once to Mr. Graves, then send word to Ray of her return, when she would reveal all that she had learned about herself, and all her troubles would be over. There was now no reason why she should not become his wife as soon as he desired.

She lay back in her chair and closed her eyes, thus signifying to Mr. Hamblin that she did not wish to continue their conversation.

He moved away from her, but continued to watch her covertly, smiling now and then to himself as he thought of the developments reserved for her.

When the sun began to decline Mona arose to return to her stateroom, but she was still so weak she could not walk steadily.

The young man sprang at once to her side.

"Let me help you," he cried, offering his arm to her.

She was obliged to take it, much as she disliked to do so, and he assisted her to the door of her stateroom, where, touching his hat politely, he left her.

She lay down to rest for a while before gathering up her things preparatory to going ashore, but the effort of coming down stairs had so wearied her that almost immediately she fell into a sound sleep.

CHAPTER XIV

MONA FINDS FRIENDS

When Mona awoke again it was dark.

The lamps were lighted in the saloon, however, and shone dimly into her stateroom through the glass in the door.

She at once became conscious that the steamer had stopped, while the confusion and bustle on deck told her that they had arrived in port and the vessel was being unloaded.

She hastily arose and dressed to go ashore, and she had hardly completed her toilet when some one rapped upon her door.

Opening it she found Louis Hamblin standing outside.

"We have arrived," he said. "How soon can you be ready to go ashore?"

"Immediately," Mona replied, then asked: "Where is Mrs. Montague?"

"Waiting for us in the carriage. I thought I would take one invalid at a time," he responded, smiling.

"What time is it, please?" the young girl asked, thoughtfully.

"Nearly ten o'clock. We are very late arriving to-night."

Mona looked blank at this reply, for she felt that it would be too late to go to Mr. Graves' that night. She would be obliged to go home with Mrs. Montague after all, and remain until morning. So she said nothing about her plans, but followed Louis above to the deck, out across the gangway to the pier, where a perfect babel prevailed, although at that moment, in the excitement of getting ashore, she did not notice anything peculiar about it.

The young man hurried her to the carriage, which proved to be simply a transportation coach belonging to some hotel, and was filled with people.

"We have concluded to go to a hotel for to-night, since it is so late and the servants did not know of our coming," Louis explained, as he assisted his companion to enter the vehicle, which, however, was more like a river barge than a city coach.

"I do not see Mrs. Montague," Mona said, as she anxiously tried to scan the faces of the passengers, and now noticed for the first time that most of them appeared to be foreigners, and were talking in a strange language.

"Can it be possible that I have made a mistake and got into the wrong carriage?" said Louis, with well-feigned surprise. "There were two going to the same hotel, and she must be in the other. She is safe enough, however, and it is too late for us to change now," he concluded, as the vehicle started.

Mona was very uncomfortable, but she could not well help herself, and so was obliged to curb her anxiety and impatience as best she could.

A ride of fifteen or twenty minutes brought them to the door of a large and handsome hotel, where they alighted, and Louis, giving her bag and wrap to the porter, who came bowing and smiling to receive them, told Mona to follow him into the house while he looked after the trunks.

Without suspecting the truth, although she was sure she had never been in that portion of the city before, the young girl obeyed, but as she stepped within the handsomely lighted entrance, she was both confused and alarmed by the fact that she could not understand a word of the language that was being spoken around her, while she now observed that the hotel had a strangely foreign air about it.

"There is something very wrong about this," she said to herself. "It does not seem like New York at all, and I do not like the idea of Mrs. Montague keeping herself so aloof from me. Even if she were sick, or angry with me, she might at least have shown some interest in me. I do not like Louis Hamblin's manner—he does not appear natural. I wish—oh, I wish I had gone home by rail. I am sure this is not New York. I am afraid there is something wrong."

She arose and walked about the room, into which the porter had shown her, feeling very anxious and trembling with nervousness. It was very strange, too, that Louis did not make his appearance.

Even while these thoughts occupied her mind he came into the room, and Mona sprang toward him.

"What does this mean?" she demanded, confronting him with blazing eyes and burning cheeks.

"What does what mean?" he asked, but his glance wavered before hers.

"This strange hotel—these foreign-looking, foreign-speaking people? Why does not Mrs. Montague come to me? Everything is very mysterious, and I want you to explain."

"Aunt Margie has gone to her room, and—" Louis began, ignoring every other question.

"I do not believe it!" Mona interrupted, with a sinking heart, as the truth began to dawn upon her. "I have not seen her since we left New Orleans. I have seen only you. There is some premeditated deception in all this. I do not believe that we are in New York at all. Where are we? I demand the truth."

Louis Hamblin saw that he could deceive her no longer; he had not supposed he could keep the truth from her as long as he had.

"We are in Havana, Cuba," he braced himself to reply, with some appearance of composure, which he was far from feeling.

"Havana!—Cuba!" cried Mona, breathlessly. "Ah! that explains the foreign language—and I do not know Spanish." Then facing him again with an air and look that made him cower, in spite of his bravado, she sternly asked: "Why are we here?"

"We are here in accordance with Mrs. Montague's plans," he answered.

"Mrs. Montague had no right to bring me here without consulting me," the young girl returned, passionately.

"Where is Mrs. Montague?"

"I expect that Aunt Marg is in New York by this time," Louis Hamblin now boldly asserted.

"What?" almost shrieked Mona, smitten to the heart with terror at this intelligence. "Oh! you cannot mean to tell me that you and I have come to Havana alone! That—that—"

A hot blush mounted to her forehead, and for a moment she was utterly overcome with shame and horror over the terrible situation.

"Yes, that is just what we have done," Louis returned, a desperate gleam coming into his eyes, for he began to realize that he had no weak spirit to deal with.

There was a prolonged and ominous silence after this admission, while Mona tried to rally her sinking spirits and think of some plan of escape from her dreadful position.

When she did speak again she was white to her lips, but in her eyes there shone a resolute purpose which plainly indicated that she would never tamely submit to the will of the man before her.

"How have you dared to do this thing?" she demanded, but so quietly that he regarded her in astonishment.

"I have dared because I was bound to win you, Mona, and there seemed no other way," he returned, in a passionate tone.

"And did you imagine for one moment that you could accomplish your purpose by decoying me into a strange country?"

Mrs. Georgie Sheldon

"Yes; but, Mona—"

"Then you have yet to learn that you have made a great mistake," was the haughty rejoinder. "It is true that I am comparatively helpless in not being able to understand the language here; but there are surely people in Havana—there must even be some one in this hotel—who can speak either French or German, if not English, and to whom I shall appeal for protection."

"That will do you little good," retorted Louis, flushing with anger at the threat, "and I may as well tell you the truth first as last. Mona, you will have to give yourself to me, you will have to be my wife. Mrs. Montague and I have both decided that it shall be so, and we have taken pains to prevent any failure of our plan. You may appeal as much as you wish to people here—they cannot understand you, and you will only lay yourself liable to scandal and abuse; for, Mona, you and I came to Havana, registered as man and wife, and our names stand upon the register of this hotel as Mr. and Mrs. Hamblin, of New York, where already the story of our elopement from New Orleans has become the talk of the town."

The deadly truth was out at last, and Mona, smitten with despair, overcome by the revelation of the dastardly plot of which she was the victim, sank helplessly upon the nearest chair, quivering with shame and horror in every nerve, and nearly fainting from the shock which the knowledge of her terrible danger had sent vibrating through her very soul.

She covered her face with her hands, and tried to think, but her temples throbbed like hammers, her brain seemed on fire, and her mind was in a perfect chaos.

She sat thus for many minutes, until Louis Hamblin, who

was hardly less excited than herself in view of his anxiety as to what would be the result of this critical interview, could endure the silence no longer, and quietly but kindly remarked:

"Mona, I think it is best that you should go to your room and rest; it is late, and you are both weary and excited. Tomorrow we will talk this matter over again, and I hope that you will then be more reasonable."

The sound of his voice aroused all her outraged womanhood, and springing to her feet again, she turned upon him with all the courage of a lioness at bay.

"I understand you," she cried. "I know why you and that unprincipled woman have so plotted against me. You were afraid, in spite of what I told you the other night, that I would demand your fortune, if I once learned the whole truth about myself. I have learned it, and I have the proof of it also. A message came to me, after my interview with you, telling me everything."

"I do not believe you," Louis Hamblin faltered, but growing very pale at this unexpected information.

"Do you not? Then let me rehearse a little for your benefit," Mona continued, gathering courage as she went on, and in low but rapid tones she related something of the secret which she had discovered in the royal mirror—enough to convince him that she knew the truth, and could, indeed, prove it.

"Now," she continued, as she concluded this recital, "do you think that I will allow you to conquer me? You have been guilty of a dastardly act. Mrs. Montague has shown herself to be lacking in humanity, honor, and every womanly sentiment; but I will not be crushed; even though you have sought to compromise me in this dreadful way I will not yield to you. Your wife I am not, and no writing me as such upon steamer and hotel registers can ever make me so. You may proclaim from one end of New York to the other that I eloped with you from New Orleans, but it will not serve your purpose, and the one for whom I care most will never lose faith in me. And, Louis Hamblin, hear me; the moment I find myself again among English-speaking people, both you and Mrs. Montague shall suffer for this outrage to the extent of the law. I will not spare you."

"That all sounds very brave, no doubt," Louis Hamblin sneered, but inwardly deeply chagrined by her dauntless words and bearing, "but you are in my power, Miss Montague, and I shall take measures to keep you so until I tame that haughty spirit somewhat. You will be only too glad to marry me yet, for I have gone too far in this matter to be balked now. When you leave Havana you will go as Mrs. Louis Hamblin, or you will never go."

"I would rather never go than as your wife, and I will defy you until I die!" was the spirited retort, and the man before her knew that she meant it.

He wondered at her strength of purpose and at her courage. Many girls, finding themselves in such a woeful strait, would have been entirely overcome—would have begged and pleaded in abject fear or weakly yielded to circumstances, and married him, but Mona only seemed to gather courage as difficulties closed around her.

She looked very lovely, too. She had lost a little flesh and color during her illness on shipboard, and her face was more delicate in its outlines than usual. She would have been very pale but for the spot of vivid scarlet that glowed on each cheek, and which was but the outward sign of the inextinguishable spirit that burned within her. Her eyes gleamed with a relentless fire and her slight but perfect form was erect and resolute in its bearing.

Louis Hamblin for the moment felt himself powerless to combat with such mental strength, and ignoring entirely what she had just avowed, again asked:

"Will you go to your room now?"

He did not wait for any reply, but touched a bell, and a waiter almost immediately appeared to answer the call.

Louis signified to him that his companion wished to retire, whereupon the man took her bag and wrap and motioned Mona to follow him.

With despair in her heart, but a dauntless mien, the fair girl obeyed, and crossing the wide entrance hall, mounted the great staircase to the second story.

As they were passing through a long upper hall a door suddenly opened, and a gentleman came out of one of the rooms.

Mona's heart gave a leap of joy as she saw him, for she was almost sure that he was an American, and she was on the point of speaking to him, but he passed her so quickly she had no opportunity.

She was rejoiced, however, to observe that her guide stopped before the door of a room next to the one which the stranger had just left, and she resolved that she would listen for his return, and manage to communicate with him in some way before morning.

Mrs. Georgie Sheldon

The porter threw open the door, and stood aside to allow her to pass in.

The room was lighted, and she saw that while it was not large, it was comfortably furnished, and her trunk stood unstrapped in one corner. The next moment the door closed upon her, and she heard the key turned in the lock.

A bitter sob burst from her as she dashed the hot tears from her eyes, and a low, eager cry broke from her lips as she noticed that a door connected her room with the one from which the gentleman had issued a few moments before.

She sprang toward it, and turned the handle.

It was locked, of course. She told herself she might have known it would be, but she had acted upon an uncontrollable impulse.

But as she released her hold upon the knob she thought she heard some one moving about within the other room.

Perhaps the gentleman had his wife with him, and impelled by a wild hope, Mona knocked upon a panel to attract attention, and the next moment she was sure she caught the rustle of skirts as some one glided toward her.

Putting her lips to the key-hole, she said, in a low, appealing tone:

"Oh! can you speak English, French, or German? Pray answer me."

She thought she had never heard sweeter music than when the clear, gentle voice of a woman replied:

"I can speak English, but no other language."

"Oh! I am so glad!" almost sobbed Mona. "Please put your ear close to the key-hole, and let me tell you something. I dare not talk loud for fear of being overheard. I am a young girl, a little more than eighteen years old, and I am in a fearful extremity. Will you help me?"

"Certainly, if you are in need of help," returned the other voice.

"Oh, thank you! thank you!" cried Mona, and then in low, rapid tones she briefly told her story to the listener on the other side of the door.

When she had concluded, the woman said, wonderingly:

"It is the most dreadful thing I ever heard of. My brother, with whom I am traveling, will soon be back. We are to leave early in the morning, and he has gone down to the office to settle our bill and make necessary arrangements. I will tell him your story, and we will see what can be done for you."

Mona again thanked her, but brokenly, and then overcome by this unexpected succor she sank prone upon the floor weeping passionately; the tension on her nerves had given way and her overwrought feelings had to have their way.

Presently a hand touched the key in her door.

Startled beyond measure, she sprang to it, feeling sure that Louis Hamblin stood without.

"Do not dare to open this door," she cried, authoritatively.

"Certainly not; I simply wished to ask if you have everything you wish for the night," the young man returned, in perfectly courteous tones.

"Yes."

"Very well, then; good-night. I hope you will rest well," he said, then drawing the key from the lock, he passed on, and the next moment Mona heard a door shut across the hall.

It was scarcely five minutes later when she heard some one enter the room next to hers, and her heart leaped again with hope.

Then she heard a gentleman and lady conversing in low tones, and knew that her story was being repeated to one who had the power, if he chose to use it, to save her from her persecutor.

A little later she heard the gentleman go to a window and open it.

Then there came a gentle tap upon the door, and the lady said to the eager ear at the key-hole:

"There is a little balcony outside our window and another outside yours with only a narrow space between. My brother says if you will go out upon yours he will help you across to us, then we can talk more freely together, and decide upon the best way to help you. Turn down your light first, however, so that no one outside will see you."

"Yes, yes," breathed Mona, eagerly, and then putting out her light, she sprang away to the window.

She raised it as cautiously as she could, crept out upon the narrow iron balcony, and found a tall, dark figure looming up before her upon the other.

"Give me your hands," said the gentleman, in a full, rich voice that won the girl's heart at once, "then step upon the railing, and trust yourself entirely to me; you will not fall."

Mona unhesitatingly reached out her hands to him; he grasped them firmly; she stepped upon the railing, and the next moment was swung safely over the space between the two balconies, and stood beside her unknown friend.

He went before her through the window, and assisted her into the darkened room; the curtain was then lowered, and the gas turned up, and Mona found herself in the presence of a tall, handsome man of about thirty-three years, and a gentle, attractive-looking woman a few years his senior.

Mrs. Georgie Sheldon

CHAPTER XV

MONA'S ESCAPE

The gentleman and lady both regarded the young girl with curious and searching interest as she stood, flushed and panting from excitement, in the center of the room beneath the blazing chandelier.

"Sit here, Miss Montague," said the gentleman, pulling forward a low rocker for her, "but first," he added, with a pleasant smile, "allow me to introduce myself. My name is Cutler—Justin Cutler, and this lady is my sister, Miss Marie Cutler. Now, it is late—we will waive all ceremony, so tell us at once about your trouble, and then we will see if we cannot help you out of it."

Mona sat down and briefly related all that had occurred in connection with her trip since she left New York, together with some of the circumstances which she believed had made Mrs. Montague and Louis Hamblin so resolute to force her into a marriage with the latter.

Her companions listened to her with deep interest, and it was plain to be seen that all their warmest sympathies were enlisted in her cause.

Mr. Cutler expressed great indignation, and declared that Louis Hamblin merited the severest sentence that the law could impose, but, of course, he knew that nothing could be done to bring him to justice in that strange country; so, after considering the matter for a while, he concluded that the best way to release Mona from her difficulties would be by the use of strategy.

"We are to leave on a steamer for New York to-morrow morning, and you shall go with us," Mr. Cutler remarked, "and if we can get you away from the hotel and on board the boat without young Hamblin's knowledge, you will be all right, and there will be no disagreeable disturbance or scandal to annoy you. Even should he discover your flight, and succeed in boarding the vessel before she sails, he will be helpless, for a quiet appeal to the captain will effectually baffle him. But how about your baggage?" he asked in conclusion.

"My trunk is in my room," Mona returned.

"Of course you must have that," said Mr. Cutler; "the only difficulty will be in getting it away without exciting suspicion. We must have this door between these rooms opened by some means. I wonder if the key to ours would fit the lock."

He arose immediately and went to try it, but it would not work.

"No. I did not expect our first effort would succeed," he smilingly remarked, as he saw Mona's face fall. "There is one way that we can do if all other plans fail," he added, after thinking a moment; "you can go back to the other room and unpack your trunk, when I could easily remove it through the window, and it could be repacked in here; but that plan would require considerable time and labor, and shall be adopted only as a last resort. But wait a minute."

He sprang to his feet, and disappeared through the window, and the next moment they heard him moving softly about in the other room.

Presently he returned, but looking grave and thoughtful.

"I hoped I might find a key somewhere in there," he explained, "but the door bolts on that side. There should, then, be a key to depend upon for this side. I wonder—"

He suddenly seized a chair, placed it before the door, stepped upon it, and reached up over the fanciful molding above it, slipping his hand along behind it.

"Aha!" he triumphantly exclaimed all at once, "I have it!" and he held up before their eager gaze a rusty and dusty iron key.

A moment later the door was unlocked, and swung open between the two rooms.

Five minutes after, all Mona's baggage was transferred to Miss Cutler's apartment, the door was relocked and bolted as before, and the fair girl felt as if her troubles were over.

Overcome by the sense of relief which this assurance afforded her, she impulsively threw her arms about Miss Cutler, laid her head on her shoulder, and burst into grateful tears.

"Oh, I am so glad—so thankful!" she sobbed.

"Hush, dear child," said the gentle lady, kindly, "you must

not allow yourself to become unnerved, for you will not sleep, and I am sure you need rest. I am going to send Justin away at once, then we will both retire."

"Yes, I will go directly," Mr. Cutler remarked, "but I shall call you early. I will have your breakfast sent up here, when your trunks can be removed. Then, Miss Montague, you are to put on a wrap belonging to my sister, and tie a thick veil over your face. I will come to take you to the carriage, and no one will suspect but that you are Marie. Meantime she will slip down another stairway, and out of the private entrance; then away we will speed to the steamer, and all will be well. Now, good-night, ladies, and a good sleep to you," he concluded, cheerfully, as he quietly left the room.

Miss Cutler and Mona proceeded to retire at once, but while disrobing the elder lady told her companion how it happened that she and her brother were in Havana so opportunely. She had been out of health, and had come to Cuba early in the fall to spend the winter. Her brother had come a few weeks earlier to take her home, and they had been making excursions to different points of interest on the island.

"I am so glad," she said, in conclusion, "that we decided to take rooms at this hotel during our sojourn in Havana. At first I thought I would like to go to some more quiet place, but Justin thought we would be better served here, and," with a gentle smile, "I believe it was wisely ordered so that we could help you."

Mona feared that she should not be able to sleep at all, her nerves had been so wrought upon, but her companion was so cheerful and reassuring in all that she said that before she was hardly aware that she was sleepy she had dropped off into a sound slumber.

Mrs. Georgie Sheldon

At six o'clock the next morning a sharp rap on their door awakened the two ladies.

They arose immediately, and had hardly finished dressing when an appetizing breakfast appeared. Miss Cutler received the tray at the door, so that the waiter need not enter the room, and then was so merry and entertaining as, with her own hands she served Mona, that the young girl forgot her nervousness, in a measure, and ate quite heartily.

By the time their meal was finished another rap warned them that the porters had come for their trunks.

"Step inside the closet, dear," said Miss Cutler, in a whisper, and Mona noiselessly obeyed her.

The door was then opened, and both trunks were removed, apparently without exciting any suspicion over the fact that there were two instead of one as when Miss Cutler arrived.

A few minutes later Mr. Cutler appeared, and Mona, clad in Miss Cutler's long ulster—which she had worn almost every day during her sojourn there—and with a thick veil over her face, took her tall protector's arm, and went tremblingly out.

Her heart almost failed her as she passed through the main entrance hall, which she had crossed in such despair only a few hours previously; but Mr. Cutler quietly bade her "be calm and have no fear," then led her down the steps, and assisted her to enter the carriage that was waiting at the door.

The next moment another figure stepped quickly in after her, Mr. Cutler followed, the door was closed, and they were driven rapidly away.

Arriving at the steamer-landing, they all went on board, and after attending to the baggage, Mr. Cutler conducted his ladies directly to their stateroom.

"I will get you a room by yourself, if you prefer;" he said to Mona, "but I thought perhaps you might feel less lonely if you should share my sister's."

"Thank you, but I should much prefer to remain with Miss Cutler if it will be agreeable to her," Mona returned, with a wistful glance at the lady.

"Indeed, I shall be very glad to have you with me," was the cordial reply, accompanied by a charming smile, for already the gentlewoman had become greatly interested in her fair companion.

"That is settled, then," said the gentleman, smiling, "and now you may feel perfectly safe; do not give yourself the least uneasiness, but try to enjoy the voyage—that is, if old Neptune will be quiet and allow you."

"You are very kind, Mr. Cutler, and I cannot tell you how grateful I am to both yourself and your sister," Mona said, feelingly. "But, truly," she added, flushing, "I shall not feel quite easy until we get off, for I am in constant fear that Mr. Hamblin will discover my flight, and come directly here to search for me."

"Well, even if he does, you need fear nothing," Mr. Cutler returned, reassuringly; "you shall have my protection, and should Mr. Hamblin make his appearance before we sail and try to create a disturbance, we will just hand the young man over to the authorities. The only thing I regret in connection with him," the gentleman concluded, with a twinkle in his eye, "is that I cannot have the pleasure of witnessing his astonishment and dismay when he makes the discovery that his bird has flown. Now, ladies, make yourselves comfortable, then come and join me on deck."

He left them together to get settled for their voyage, and went up stairs for a smoke and to keep his eye upon the shore, for he fully expected to see Louis Hamblin come tearing down to the boat at any moment. The reader has, of course, recognized in Justin Cutler the gentleman who, at the opening of our story, was made the victim of the accomplished sharper, Mrs. Bently, in the diamond crescent affair. It will be remembered also that he came on to New York at the time of the arrest of Mrs. Vanderheck, and that he informed Detective Rider of his intention of going to Cuba to meet his invalid sister and accompany her home, and thus we find him acting as Mona's escort and protector also.

While the three voyagers were settling themselves and waiting for the steamer to sail, we will see how Louis Hamblin bore the discovery of Mona's escape.

He did not rise until eight o'clock, and after having his bath and a cup of coffee in his own room, he went to Mona's door and knocked.

Receiving no answer, he thought she must be sleeping, and resolved that he would not arouse her just then.

He went down stairs, and had his breakfast, then strolled out to smoke his cigar, after which he went back, and again tapped upon Mona's door.

Still no answer.

He called her name, but receiving no response, he took the key from his pocket and coolly unlocking the door, threw it wide open.

The room was, of course, empty.

There were no signs that the bed had been occupied during the night, and both the girl and her trunk were gone.

With a fierce imprecation of rage, the astonished young man rushed down to the office to interview the proprietor as to the meaning of the girl's disappearance.

Although Mona had supposed there was no one in the house who could speak English, there was an interpreter, and through him Louis soon made his trouble known.

"Impossible!" the amazed proprietor asserted; "no trunk had been removed from Number Eleven, and no young lady had left the house that morning."

Louis angrily insisted that there had, and in company with the landlord and the interpreter, he returned to Mona's room to prove his statement.

At first the affair was a great mystery, and created considerable excitement, but it was finally remembered that Americans had occupied the adjoining rooms, and it was therefore concluded that the young girl had managed in some way to make her situation known to them, and they, having left that morning, had, doubtless, assisted her in her flight.

"Who were they, and where were they going?" Louis demanded, in great excitement.

"Cutler was the name, and they had left early to take the steamer for New York," they told him.

"What was her hour for sailing?" cried the young man.

Mrs. Georgie Sheldon

"Nine-thirty," he was informed.

Louis looked at his watch.

It lacked fifteen minutes of the time.

"A carriage! a carriage!" he cried, as he dashed out of the hotel and down the steps at a break-neck pace.

He sprang into the first vehicle he could find, made the driver understand that he wanted him to hasten with all possible speed to the New York steamer, and enforced his wishes by showing the man a piece of glittering gold.

He was terribly excited; his face was deathly white, and his eyes had the look of a baffled demon. But he was not destined to have the satisfaction of even seeing Mona, for he reached the pier just in season to see the noble steamer sailing with stately bearing slowly out into the harbor, and he knew that the fair girl was beyond his reach.

Meantime, as soon as she had seen Louis and Mona safely on board the steamer, bound for Havana, Mrs. Montague, instead of going into the stateroom that had been engaged for her only as a blind, slipped stealthily back upon deck, hastened off the boat, and into her carriage, which had been ordered to wait for her, and was driven directly to the railway station, where she took the express going northward.

She did not spare herself, but traveled day and night until she reached New York, when she immediately sent a note to Mr. Palmer, notifying him of her return and desire to see him.

He at once hastened to her, for she had intimated in her communication that she was in trouble, and upon inquiring the cause of it, she informed him, with many sighs and expressions of grief, that her nephew and prospective heir had eloped with her seamstress.

Mr. Palmer looked amazed.

"With that pretty, modest girl, whom you had at Hazeldean with you?" he exclaimed, incredulously.

"Yes, with that pretty, modest girl," sneered Mrs. Montague. "These sly, quiet things are just the ones to entrap a young man like Louis, and there is poor Kitty McKenzie who will break her heart over the affair."

The wily widow's acting was very good, and Mr. Palmer sympathized with her, and used his best efforts to comfort her. But all that Mrs. Montague had cared to do was to set the ball rolling so that Ray might get it, and gradually led the conversation into a more interesting channel, and they discussed at length the subject of their own approaching union.

Mr. Palmer urged an early date, and after a little strategic hesitation, Mrs. Montague finally consented to make him happy, and the wedding was set for just one month from that day. This matter settled, the sedate lover took his leave, and his *fiancee* with a triumphant look on her handsome face, went up stairs to look over her wardrobe to see what additions would be needed for the important event.

"Whether Louis succeeds in making the girl marry him or not, she will have been so compromised by this escapade that Ray Palmer will, of course, never think of making her his wife, and my purpose will be accomplished," she muttered, with an evil smile.

She did not give a thought to the wanderers after that, but

Mrs. Georgie Sheldon

went about the preparations for her approaching marriage with all the zeal and enthusiasm that might have been expected in a far younger bride-elect.

Mr. Palmer went home feeling a trifle anxious as to how Ray would receive the news that the day was set for making Mrs. Montague his wife.

To see that he dreaded revealing the fact expresses but little of what he felt, but he had never taken any important step of late years without consulting his son, and he did not feel at liberty to now ignore him upon a matter of such vital interest.

So, after tea that evening, when they sat down to read their papers, he thought the opportunity would be a favorable one to make his confession.

Ray seemed anxious and depressed, for he had not received his usual semi-weekly letter from Mona that day, and was wondering what could be the reason, when Mr. Palmer suddenly remarked:

"Mrs. Montague has returned."

"Ah!" said Ray, and instantly his face brightened, for his natural inference was that Mona had, of course, returned with Mrs. Montague, and that accounted for his having received no letter that day.

"Yes, she arrived this morning," said his father.

"She is well, I suppose?" Ray remarked, feeling that he must make some courteous inquiry regarding his stepmother-elect.

"Yes, physically; but that scapegrace of a nephew has been

giving her considerable trouble," Mr. Palmer observed.

"Trouble?" repeated his son.

"Yes, he eloped with a girl from New Orleans. They went on board a steamer bound for Havana, registered as man and wife, and that is the last she has heard of him, while she was obliged to return to New York alone," explained Mr. Palmer, wondering how he was going to introduce the subject of his approaching marriage.

"Is that possible? Who was the girl?" exclaimed Ray, astonished and utterly unsuspicious of the blow awaiting his fond heart.

"Mrs. Montague's seamstress—Ruth Richards."

CHAPTER XVI

MONA CALLS ON MRS. MONTAGUE

Mr. Palmer's unexpected announcement fairly stunned Ray for a moment. His heart gave a startled bound, and then sank like a lump of lead in his bosom, while a deadly faintness oppressed him.

Indeed the blow was so sharp and sudden that it seemed to benumb him to such an extent that he made no outward sign—he appeared to be incapable of either speech or motion. His face was turned away from his father, and partially concealed by his newspaper, so that Mr. Palmer, fortunately, did not observe the ghastly pallor that overspread it, and not knowing that Ruth Richards was Mona Montague, he was wholly ignorant of the awful import of his communication.

"Ruth Richards?" Ray finally repeated, in a hollow tone, which, however, sounded to his father as if he did not remember who the girl was.

"Yes, that pretty girl that Mrs. Montague had with her at Hazeldean—the one to whom you showed some attention the night of the ball—surely you cannot have forgotten her. It seems," the gentleman went on, "that young Hamblin has been smitten with her ever since she entered his aunt's service, but she has opposed his preference from the first. He followed them South, and met them at New Orleans, and it seems that the elopement was arranged there. They were very clever about it, planning to leave on the Havana steamer on the very day set for their return to New York. Mrs. Montague learned of it at almost the last moment, and that they had registered as Mr. and Mrs. Hamblin, although she did not ascertain that there had been any marriage beforehand, and, overcome by this unexpected calamity, she took the first express coming North."

It was well for Ray that his father made his explanation somewhat lengthy, for it gave him time to recover a little from the almost paralyzing shock which the dreadful announcement had caused.

He was as white as a ghost, and his face was covered with cold perspiration.

"This terrible thing cannot be true," he said to himself, with a sense of despair at his heart. "Mona false! the runaway wife of another! Never!"

Yet in spite of his instinctive faith in the girl he loved, he knew there must be some foundation for what had been told to his father. Mrs. Montague had come home alone. Louis and Mona had been left behind! What could it mean?

His heart felt as if it had been suddenly cleft in twain. He could not believe the dreadful story—he would not have it so—he would not submit to having his life and all his bright hopes ruined at one fell blow. And that, too, just as he had learned such good news for his darling—when he had been planning to give her, upon her return, the one thing which she had most desired above all others—the indisputable proof of her mother's honorable marriage; when it would also be proved that she was the heir to the property which Homer Forester had left, and could claim, if she chose, the greater portion of the fortune left by her father.

Ray had been very exultant over the finding of that certificate in Mrs. Montague's boudoir, and had anticipated much pleasure in beholding Mona's joy when he should tell her the glorious news.

But now—great heavens! what was he to think?

Then the suspicion came to him, with another great shock, and like a revelation, that it was all a plot; that Mrs. Montague had perhaps discovered Mona's identity and possibly the loss of the certificate, which, she might think, had fallen into the young girl's hands. He had felt sure, from the quizzing to which Louis Hamblin had subjected him at Hazeldean, that that young man's suspicions had been aroused, and possibly this sudden flitting to the South had been but a plot, from beginning to end, to entrap Mona into a marriage with the young man in order to secure the wealth they feared to lose.

"When did Mrs. Montague leave New Orleans?" he inquired, when his father had concluded, while he struggled to speak in his natural tone.

"On Tuesday evening."

"And you say that the Havana steamer sailed that same day?"

"Yes."

"What was the name of the steamer?"

"I do not know. I did not ask," Mr. Palmer replied. He was thinking more about his own affairs than of the alleged elopement of the young people, or he must have wondered somewhat at his son's eager questions. "And, Ray," he added, as the young man suddenly laid down his paper and arose, "there is one other thing I wanted to mention—Mrs. Montague has consented to become Mrs. Palmer on the thirtieth of next month. I—I hope, my dear boy, that you will be prepared to receive her cordially."

"You know, father, that I would never willfully wound you in any way, and when Mrs. Montague comes as your wife, I shall certainly accord her all due respect."

Ray had worded his reply very cautiously, but he could not prevent himself from laying a slight emphasis upon the adverb, for he had resolved that if Mrs. Montague had been concerned in any way in a plot against Mona's honor or happiness, he would not spare her, nor any effort to prove it to his father, and thus prevent him, if possible, from ruining his own life by a union with such a false and unscrupulous woman.

"Thank you, Ray," Mr. Palmer replied, but not in a remarkably hopeful tone, and then remarking that he had a little matter of business to attend to, Ray went out.

Late as it was, he hastened to a cable office, hoping to be able to send a night dispatch to Havana, but he found the place closed, therefore he was obliged to retrace his steps, and wait until morning.

There was not much sleep or rest for him that night. His faith in Mona's truth and constancy had all returned, but he was terribly anxious about her, for the more he thought over what he had heard, the more he was convinced that she was the victim of some cunning plot that might make her very wretched, even if it failed to accomplish its object. He knew that she was very spirited, and would not be likely to submit to the wrong that had been perpetrated against her, and this of itself might serve to make her situation all the more perilous.

He was at the cable office by the time it was opened the next morning, and dispatched the following message to the American Consul in Havana:

"Couple, registered as Mr. and Mrs. Louis Hamblin, sailed from New Orleans for Havana, April 28th. Search for them in Havana hotels. Succor young lady, who is not Mrs. Hamblin. Answer."

Ray felt that this was the very best thing that he could do.

He would gladly have gone himself to Havana, and longed to do so, but he was sure that if she should escape from her abductor—for so he regarded Louis Hamblin—Mona would be likely to return immediately to New York and to him. Thus he concluded it would be best to send the above message and await an answer from the consul, then if he could learn nothing about the couple he would go himself to search for Mona.

The day seemed interminable, and he was nearly distracted when night came, and he received no answer to his dispatch. He had not been able to apply himself to business all day, but wandered in and out of the store, looking wan and anxious, and almost ill.

This led his father to imagine that he was unhappy over his contemplated marriage—a conclusion which did not serve to make the groom-elect feel very comfortable.

On the next morning, however, Ray received the following cablegram:

"Young lady all right; sailed for New York yesterday, May 1st."

The relief which these few words afforded Ray's anxious heart can better be imagined than described.

Mona was true to herself and him, and he knew well enough that she never would have returned to New York if she had been guilty of any wrong. She would soon be with him, and then he would know all.

He ascertained what steamer left Havana on the first, and when it would be likely to arrive in New York, and as the hour drew near, he haunted the pier, that he might welcome his darling, and give her his care and protection the moment she arrived.

Meantime Mona, her mind relieved of all anxiety, was having a very pleasant passage home with Justin Cutler and his sister.

The weather was delightful, the sea was calm, and none of them was sick, so they spent most of their time together upon deck, and Mona was so attracted toward her new friends that she confided to them much more of her history than she had at first done that evening in the Havana hotel. In so doing she had mentioned the Palmer robbery and what she had discovered in connection with it while she was in St. Louis.

This led Mr. Cutler to relate his own experience with the crescents, and also the similar deception practiced upon Mrs. Vanderheck, and he mentioned that it was the opinion of the detective whom he had employed to work up the case, and

Mrs. Georgie Sheldon

whom Mona had met in St. Louis, that the same parties were concerned in all three operations.

"They are a very dexterous set of thieves, whoever they are," he remarked, while they were discussing the affair, "but though I never expect to see those crescents again, for I imagine that the stones have been unset and sold, it would afford me a great deal of satisfaction to see that woman brought to justice."

"I have the bogus crescents in my possession," Miss Cutler smilingly remarked to Mona. "Justin has given them to me to keep for him. Would you like to see them, dear?"

"Yes, indeed," Mona replied, "and I, too, hope that woman may yet be found. The affair is so like a romance, I am deeply interested in it."

Mr. Cutler colored slightly as she spoke of the romance of the experience, for he was still quite sensitive over the cruel deception that had been practiced upon him, although he had never confessed to any one how deeply and tenderly interested he had become in the captivating widow who had so successfully duped him.

When the steamer arrived in New York, almost the first person Mona saw was Ray, who stood upon the pier searching with anxious eyes among the passengers for the face of his dear one.

A cry of glad surprise broke from her, and, snatching her handkerchief from her pocket, she shook it vigorously to attract his attention, her lovely face all aglow with joy at his unexpected appearance.

He caught sight of the fluttering signal almost immediately, and his heart leaped within him as he looked into her beaming countenance. Truth and love and purity were stamped on every expressive feature.

He sprang across the gang-plank, and in less time than it takes to tell it he was beside her, while oblivious, in his great thankfulness for her safety, to the fact that others were observing them, he caught her close to him in a quick embrace.

"My darling!" he whispered. "Oh, you can never know how thankful I am to have you safe in my arms once more! What an escape you have had!"

"Why, Ray! how did you know?—who told you?" Mona exclaimed, astonished, as, with a blushing face, she gently freed herself from his embrace, although she still clung almost convulsively to his hand.

"I will tell you all about it later," he returned, in a low tone, and now recalled to the proprieties of life. "I can only say that I learned of the plot against you, and have been nearly distracted about you."

"Ah, Mrs. Montague told you that I had eloped with her nephew," the young girl said, and now losing some of her bright color, "but," lifting her clear, questioning eyes to her lover's face, "you did not believe it; you had faith in me?"

"All faith," he returned, his fingers closing more firmly over the small hand he held.

She thanked him with a radiant smile.

"But how did you know I would come home on this steamer?" she persisted, eager to know how he happened to be there to meet her.

"I cabled the American Consul to search for you, and render you assistance. He replied, telling me that you had already sailed for New York," Ray explained.

"That was thoughtful of you, dear," Mona said, giving him a grateful look, "but I found friends to help me. Come and let me introduce you to them."

She led him to Mr. Cutler and his sister, who had quietly withdrawn to a little distance—for, of course, they took in the situation at once—and performed the ceremony, when, to her surprise, Mr. Cutler cordially shook her lover by the hand, remarking, with his genial smile:

"Mr. Palmer and I have met before, but my sister has not had that pleasure, I believe."

Ray greeted them both with his habitual courtesy, and then in a frank, manly way, but with slightly heightened color, remarked:

"My appearance here perhaps needs some explanation, but it will be sufficient for me to explain that Miss Montague is my promised wife."

"I surmised as much, not long after making the young lady's acquaintance," Mr. Cutler remarked, with a roguish glance at Mona's pink cheeks and downcast eyes. "But," he added, with some curiosity, "it is a puzzle to me how you should know that she would arrive in New York on this steamer to-day."

Ray explained the matter to him, and then they all left the vessel together.

Mr. and Miss Cutler were to go to the Hoffman House, and invited Mona to be their guest during their stay in the city, but thanking them for their kindness, she said she thought it would be best for her to go directly to Mr. Graves, as she had business which she wished him to attend to immediately.

She also expressed again her gratitude to them for their exceeding kindness to her, and promised to call upon them very soon, then bidding them an affectionate good-by she left the wharf with her lover.

They went for a drive in Central Park before going to Mr. Graves, for Ray was anxious to learn all the story of the plot against her and to talk over their own plans for the future.

He found it very difficult to restrain his anger as she told him of her interview with Louis Hamblin in New Orleans, and how she had been decoyed upon the steamer for Havana, with the other circumstances of the voyage, and her arrival there.

"The villain will need to be careful how he comes in my way after this," he said, with sternly compressed lips and a face that was white with anger. "I will not spare him—I will not spare either of those two plotters; but you shall never meet them again, my darling," he concluded, with tender compassion in his tones, as he realized how much she must have suffered with them.

"I shall have to go to West Forty-ninth street once more, for I have a good many things there, and shall have to attend to their removal myself," Mona returned, but looking as if she did not anticipate much pleasure from the meeting with Mrs. Montague.

"Well, then, if you must go there, I will accompany you,"

Ray said, resolutely. "I will never trust you alone with that woman again. And now I have some good news to relate to you."

He told her then of his discovery of the marriage certificate, and what he had done with it, after which she gave him a graphic account of the discoveries which she had made in the secret drawer of the royal mirror.

"How very strange, my darling," he exclaimed, when she concluded; "how nicely your discovery fits in with mine, and now every difficulty will be smoothed out of your way, only," with an arch glance, "I am almost afraid that I shall be accused of being a fortune-hunter when it becomes known what a wealthy heiress I have won."

Mona smiled at his remark, but she was very glad that she was not to go to him empty-handed.

"And, dear," Ray continued, more gravely, "I am going to claim my wife immediately, for, in spite of the great wealth which will soon be yours, you are a homeless little body, and I feel that you ought to be under my protection."

"Ah, Ray, it will be very nice to have a home of our own," Mona breathed, as she slipped her hand confidingly into his, and then they began to plan for it as they drove down town.

Arriving at the house of Mr. Graves, they were fortunate in finding both that gentleman and his wife at home, and Mona received a most cordial welcome, while the kind-hearted lawyer became almost jubilant upon learning all the facts regarding her parentage and how comparatively easy it would now be to prove it.

It was arranged that Mona and Mr. Graves should meet Ray

and Mr. Corbin at the office of the latter on the next morning, when they would all thoroughly discuss these matters and decide upon what course to pursue in relation to them.

This plan was carried out; the certificate and contents of the royal mirror were carefully examined, and then the two lawyers proceeded to lay out their course of action, which was to be swift and sure.

The third day after Mona's arrival in New York, Ray went with her to Mrs. Montague's house to take away the remainder of her wardrobe and some keepsakes which had been saved from her old home.

Mary opened the door in answer to their ring, and her face lighted with pleasure the instant she caught sight of Mona, although it was evident from her greeting that Mrs. Montague had not told her servants the story of the elopement.

"Is Mrs. Montague in?" Mona asked, after she had returned the girl's greeting.

"No, miss, she went out as soon as she had her breakfast, and said she wouldn't be home until after lunch," was the reply.

Mona looked thoughtful. She did not exactly like to enter the house and remove her things during her absence, and yet it would be a relief not to be obliged to meet her.

Ray saw her hesitation, and understood it, but he had no scruples regarding the matter.

"It is perhaps better so," he said, in a low tone; "you will escape an unpleasant interview, and since she is not here to annoy or ill-use you, I will take the carriage and go to attend to a little matter, while you are packing. I will return for you in the course of an hour if that will give you time."

"Yes, that will be ample time, and I will be ready when you call," Mona responded.

Ray immediately drove away, while she, after chatting a few moments with Mary, went up stairs to gather up her clothing and what few treasures she had that had once helped to make her old home so dear.

She worked rapidly, and soon had everything ready. But suddenly she remembered that she had left a very nice pair of button-hole scissors in Mrs. Montague's boudoir on the day they left for the South.

She ran lightly down to get them, and just as she reached the second hall some one rang the bell a vigorous peal.

"That must be Ray," she said to herself, and stopped to listen for his voice.

But as Mary opened the door, she heard a gentleman's tones inquiring for Mrs. Montague.

"No," the girl said, "my mistress is not in."

"Then I will wait, for my errand is urgent," was the reply, and the person stepped within the hall.

Mona did not see who it was, but she heard Mary usher him into the parlor, after which she went to obey a summons from the cook, leaving the caller alone.

Mona went on into Mrs. Montague's room to get her scissors,

but she could not find them readily. She was sure that she had left them on the center-table, but thought that the woman had probably moved them since her return.

Just then she thought she heard some one moving about in Mrs. Montague's chamber adjoining, but the door was closed, and thinking it might be Mary, she continued her search, but still without success.

She was just on the point of going into the other room to ask Mary if she had seen them, when a slight sound attracted her attention, and looking up, she caught the gleam of a pair of vindictive eyes peering in at her from the hall, and the next moment the door was violently shut and the key turned in the lock.

CHAPTER XVII

THE WOMAN IN BLACK

For a moment Mona was too much astonished to even try to account for such a strange proceeding.

Then it occurred to her that Mrs. Montague must have returned before she was expected, let herself into the house with her latch-key, and coming quietly up stairs, had been taken by surprise to find her in her room, when she had supposed her to be safely out of her way in Havana, and so had made a prisoner of her by locking her in the boudoir.

At first Mona was somewhat appalled by her situation; then a calm smile of scorn for her enemy wreathed her lips, for she was sure that Ray would soon return. She had only to watch for him at the window, inform him of what had occurred the moment he drove to the door, and he would have her immediately released.

With this thought in her mind, she approached the window to see if he had not already arrived.

The curtain was down, and she attempted to raise it, when, the spring having been wound too tightly, it flew up with such a force as to throw the fixture from its socket, and the whole thing came crashing down upon her.

She sprang aside to avoid receiving it in her face, and in doing so nearly upset a small table that was standing before the window.

It was the table having in it the secret treasures which we have already seen. She managed to catch it, however, and saved the heavy marble top from falling to the floor by receiving it in her lap, and sinking down with it.

But while doing this, the broken lid to the secret compartment flew off, and some of its contents were scattered over her.

Mona was so startled by what she had done, that she was almost faint from fright, but she soon assured herself that no real damage had occurred—the most she had been guilty of was the discovery of some secret treasure which Mrs. Montague possessed.

She began to gather them up with the intention of replacing them in their hiding-place—the beautiful point-lace fan, which we have seen before, a box containing some lovely jewels of pearls and diamonds, and a package of letters.

"Ha!" Mona exclaimed, with a quick, in-drawn breath, as she picked these up, and read the superscription on the uppermost envelope, "'Miss Mona Forester!' Can it be that these things belonged to my mother? And this picture! Oh, yes, it must be the very one that Louis Hamblin told me about—a picture of my father painted on ivory and set in a costly frame embellished with rubies!"

She bent over the portrait, gazing long and earnestly upon it, studying every feature of the handsome face, as if to impress them indelibly upon her mind.

"So this represents my father as he looked when he married my mother," she said, with a sigh. "He was very handsome, but, oh, what a sad, sad story it all was!"

She laid it down with an expression of keen pain on her young face and began to look over the costly jewels, handling them with a tender and reverent touch, while she saw that every one was marked with the name of "Mona" on the setting.

"These also are mine, and I shall certainly claim them. How strange that I should have found them thus!" she said, as she laid them carefully back in the box. Then she arose and righting the table, replaced the various things in the compartment.

In so doing she stepped upon a small box, which, until then, she had not seen.

The cover was held in place by a narrow rubber band.

She removed it, lifted the lid, and instantly a startled cry burst from her lips.

"Oh, what can it mean? what can it mean?" she exclaimed, losing all her color, and trembling with excitement.

At that moment the hall-bell rang again, and Mona turned once more to the window, now fully expecting to find that Ray had come.

No, another carriage stood before the door, but she could not see who had rung the bell.

She wondered why Ray did not come; it was more than an hour since he went away, and she began to fear that her captor was planning some fresh wrong to her, and he might be detained until it would be too late to help her.

She was growing both anxious and nervous, and thought she would just slip into Mrs. Montague's bedroom and see if she could not get out in that way.

Suiting the action to the resolve, she hastened into the chamber, and tried the door.

No, that was locked on the outside, and she knew that the woman must have some evil purpose in thus making a prisoner of her.

She turned again to retrace her steps, that she might keep watch for Ray at the window, when her eyes encountered an object lying upon the bed which drove the color from her face, and held her rooted to the spot where she stood!

*　*　*　*　*

About nine o'clock of that same morning, a woman might have been seen walking swiftly down Murray street, in the direction of the Hudson River, to the wharf occupied by the Fall River steamers.

She was tall and quite stout, but had a finely proportioned figure, and she walked with a brisk, elastic tread, which betrayed great energy and resolution.

She was dressed in deep mourning, her clothing being made of the finest material, and fitting her perfectly.

A heavy crape vail covered her head and partially enveloped

　　　　Mrs. Georgie Sheldon

her figure, effectually concealing her features, and yet a close observer would have said that she had a lovely profile, and would have noticed, also, that her hair was a decided red.

She appeared to be in a hurry, looking neither to the right nor left, nor abating her pace in the least until she reached the dock where the Fall River boat, Puritan, had but a little while previous poured forth her freight of humanity and merchandise.

As she came opposite the gang-plank a low whistle caused her to look up.

A man stationed on the saloon deck, and evidently watching for some one, made a signal, and with a nod of recognition, the woman passed on board and up the stairs to the grand saloon, where a man met her and slipped a key into her hand, then turned and walked away without uttering a word.

"Two hundred and one," she muttered, and walked deliberately down the saloon glancing at the figures on the doors of the various staterooms until she came to No. 201, when she unlocked it and went in.

Ten minutes later the man who had stood on deck as she came aboard, followed her, entered the stateroom, and locked the door after him.

The two were closeted there for nearly an hour, when the woman in black came out.

"I shall look for you at three precisely; do not fail me," said a low voice from behind the door.

"I will not fail you; but keep yourself close," was the equally guarded response, and then the heavily draped figure glided quickly down stairs and off the boat.

She crossed West street, passed on to Chambers, and turned to walk toward Broadway, passing, as she did so, a group of three or four men who were standing at the corner.

One of them gave a slight start as her garments brushed by him, took a step forward for a second look at her, then he quietly broke away from the others, and followed her, about a dozen yards behind, up Chambers street.

The woman did not appear to notice that she was being followed, for she did not accelerate her speed in the least, nor seem to pay any heed to what was going on about her. She kept straight on, as if her mind was intent only upon her own business.

But all at once, as she reached the corner of Broadway, she slipped into a carriage that stood waiting there, and was driven rapidly up town.

An angry exclamation burst from the man following her, who was none other than Rider, the detective, and he hastened forward to catch another glimpse of the carriage, if possible, before it should get out of sight.

He saw it in the distance, and hailing another, he gave chase as fast as the crowded condition of the street would permit.

Some twenty minutes later he came upon the same carriage standing on another corner, the driver as quiet and unconcerned as if he had not been dodging vehicles at the risk of a smash-up, or urging his horses to a lawless pace in that busy thoroughfare.

Mrs. Georgie Sheldon

But the coach was empty.

Mr. Rider alighted and accosted the man.

"Where is the passenger that you had a few minutes ago?" he inquired.

The man pointed with his whip to a store near by, then relapsed into his indolent and indifferent attitude.

Mr. Rider shook his head emphatically, to indicate his disbelief of this pantomimic information, and muttered a few words not intended for polite ears as he turned on his heel and moved away.

"Fooled again," he added, "and I thought I had her sure this time. Of course she didn't go into that store any more than that other party went from St. Louis to Chicago. But it's worth something to know that she is in New York. I'll try to keep my eyes open this time."

In spite of his skepticism, however, he entered the store and sauntered slowly through it, but without encountering any woman in black, having red hair.

"She came off the Puritan," he mused, as he issued into the street again, and turned his face up town. "I imagine that she either came on from Fall River last night, or she is going back this afternoon. I'll hang round there about the time the Puritan leaves. Meantime I'll take a stroll in some of the upper tendom regions, for I'll bet she is a high-liver."

He boarded a car and was soon rolling up toward the more aristocratic portion of the city, and thus we must leave him for a while.

When Ray returned to Mrs. Montague's residence for Mona, he found another carriage waiting at the door, and it was just at this moment that Mona made her strange discovery in the woman's bedroom.

"Mr. Corbin's carriage," Ray murmured to himself as he alighted and went up the steps. "I wonder if Mr. Graves is with him, and if Mrs. Montague has returned. I hope she has not made matters unpleasant for Mona."

He rang the bell and was admitted by Mary, who wondered how many more times she would be obliged to run to the door that morning.

"Is Miss—Miss Richards through with her packing?" the young man inquired, but having almost betrayed Mona's identity, which, in accordance with the advice of the lawyers, they were not quite ready to do yet.

"She's still up stairs, sir," the girl replied. "I'll step up and tell her that you have come. Perhaps you'll wait in the reception-room, sir, as Mrs. Montague has just come in and has callers in the drawing-room."

"Certainly," Ray answered, and was about to follow her thither, when he heard his name spoken, and turning, saw Mr. Graves beckoning to him from the doorway of the drawing-room.

"Come in here," he said; "we shall need you in this business," and Ray knew that Mrs. Montague was about to be interviewed upon various matters of importance.

"Very well," he replied, then turning to Mary, he added: "You may tell Miss Richards that she need not hurry. I will call you again when I am ready to go."

Mrs. Georgie Sheldon

He then followed the lawyer into the drawing-room and the door was shut.

"There is something queer going on in there," she muttered. "Mrs. Montague seemed all worked up over something, and those two men looked as glum as parsons at a funeral. There is cook's bell again, and Miss Ruth must wait," she concluded, impatiently, as a ring came up from the lower regions, and then she went slowly and reluctantly down stairs again.

CHAPTER XVIII

SOME INTERESTING DISCOVERIES

Upon entering Mrs. Montague's beautiful drawing-room, Ray found, as he had expected, that Mr. Corbin was there also, and he at once surmised the nature of the lawyer's business.

Mrs. Montague gave a start of surprise as she saw him, and lost some of her color; then recovering herself, she arose with a charming smile, and went forward to greet him.

Ray thought she looked much older than when he had seen her before, for there were dark circles under her eyes, with crows' feet at their corners, and wrinkles on her forehead and about her mouth, which he had never noticed until then, and which, somehow, seemed to change the expression of her whole face.

"This is an unexpected pleasure," she remarked, with great cordiality, "but you perceive," with a glance at the lawyers, "that I am overrun with business. May I ask you to step into the library for a few moments until I am at liberty?"

"No, if you please, madame, it is at my request that Mr. Palmer is here," quietly but decidedly interposed Mr. Graves.

Mrs. Georgie Sheldon

Mrs. Montague flushed hotly at this interference, then seeing that she could not change the condition of affairs, and that Ray evidently understood matters, as he only bowed in the most frigid manner in response to her effusive greeting, she resigned herself to the inevitable and returned to her chair with an air of haughty defiance.

It was Mrs. Montague whom Mona had heard moving about in the chamber adjoining the boudoir.

The woman had come in just after Mary admitted that first caller below, and speeding swiftly and noiselessly up stairs, was making some changes in her toilet when the bell rang again. Mr. Corbin and Mr. Graves were at the door. She heard it, and gliding softly into the hall, leaned over the balustrade to ascertain who had called.

The moment she heard Mr. Corbin inquire for her, she grew white with passion, and her eyes flashed angrily, for she imagined that he had come to question her again regarding Mona Forester. She did not see his companion, however.

"I will give him a dose to remember this time," she muttered. Then she heard Mary inform the gentlemen that she was not at home.

"Yes, I am, Mary," she said, in a low tone, for she felt in a defiant mood, and not suspecting the fatal nature of the lawyer's visit, and feeling very secure in her own position, she rather courted an opportunity to defy him. "Invite the gentleman in, and I will be down presently."

She turned to go back to her chamber to complete her toilet, when she heard some one moving about in her boudoir.

She glided to the door, softly opened it, and looked in.

Instantly her face lighted with a smile of evil triumph, though she gave a great start of surprise as she saw Mona there, and evidently searching for something.

She had already learned that the girl had managed to escape from the power of Louis and returned to New York. Therefore she now imagined that she had but just arrived and had come directly there to secure her other trunk, when doubtless she would immediately seek Ray Palmer's protection, and denounce both herself and her nephew for their plot against her.

Such a proceeding she knew would ruin all her prospects of becoming Mr. Palmer's wife, and, actuated by a sudden impulse, she hastily drew the door to again and locked it. Then she sped back to her chamber door and turned the key in that also, to prevent escape that way, and entirely forgetting in her excitement that she had intended to make still further changes in her toilet before going below.

This done, she sped swiftly down stairs, and encountered Mary in the hall.

"Lor', marm! I didn't know you had come in till you spoke," the girl remarked, with a curious stare at her.

"I have a latch-key, you know," Mrs. Montague returned, as she swept on toward the drawing-room, and the girl wondered why she "looked so strange and so flustered."

Mrs. Montague entered the room with haughty mien, intending to dispose of Mr. Corbin with short ceremony, but she was somewhat taken aback when she found that he was accompanied by another legal-looking gentleman.

She had but just exchanged formal greetings with them when Ray made his appearance; but she did not suspect that he was aware of Mona's presence in the house. Mr. Graves' remark had led her to suppose that he was there by his appointment.

Mr. Corbin bowed to the young man, and remarked:

"I was about to explain to Mrs. Montague that some proofs regarding the identity of Miss Montague have recently come into my possession."

"Do you mean to assert that you have proofs that will establish the theory which you advanced to me during your last call here?" Mrs. Montague demanded, with a derisive smile.

"That is exactly what I mean, madame," Mr. Corbin replied.

Mrs. Montague tossed her head scornfully.

She was sure that the only proof in existence of Mona Forester's legal marriage was at that moment safely lying in the secret compartment of that little table up stairs. She had not seen it since her return, for she had been too busy to look over those things again and destroy such as would be dangerous, if they should fall into other hands; but she had seen them so recently she felt very secure, and did not dream that she had been guilty of any carelessness regarding them.

She knew, also, that up to the evening of Louis' last declaration to her, Mona had no proof to produce, and, supposing that she had but just returned from Havana, she did not imagine that either of the lawyers or Ray had seen her to learn anything new from her, even if she had discovered anything.

"Well, I should like to see them," she responded, contemptuously, but with a confident air that would have been very irritating to one less assured than Mr. Corbin.

He quietly drew a folded paper from his breast-pocket, opened and smoothed it out, and going to the woman's side, held it before her for examination.

She was wholly unprepared for the appalling revelation that met her eyes, and the instant that she realized that the paper was the identical certificate, which she believed to be in her own possession, she lost every atom of her color. A cry of anger and dismay broke from her, and snatching the parchment from the lawyer's hand, she sprang to her feet, crying, hoarsely:

"Where did you get it? how did it come into your possession?"

"Pray, madame, do not be so excited," Mr. Corbin calmly returned, "and be careful of that document, if you please, for it is worth a great deal to my young client. Mr. Raymond Palmer supplied me with this very necessary link in the evidence required to prove Miss Montague's identity."

"And how came Raymond Palmer to have a paper that belonged to me?" demanded Mrs. Montague, turning to him with an angry gleam in her eyes. "I have supposed him to be a gentleman—he must be a thief, else he never could have had it."

"You are mistaken in both assertions, Mrs. Montague," Ray responded, with cold dignity. "In the first place, the paper does not belong to you; it rightly belongs to your husband's daughter. In the second place, it came into my possession in a perfectly legitimate manner. On the day of your high-tea I

Mrs. Georgie Sheldon

came here a little late, if you remember. Your private parlor above was used as the gentleman's dressing-room, and I found that document lying underneath the draperies of the bay-window. I accidentally stepped upon it. It crackled beneath my feet, and it was but natural that I should wish to ascertain what was there. When I discovered the nature of the paper I felt perfectly justified in taking charge of it, in the interests of my promised wife, and so gave it into Mr. Corbin's hands."

Mrs. Montague sat like one half stunned during this explanation, for she readily comprehended how this terrible calamity had happened to overtake her. She realized that the certificate must have slipped from her lap to the floor while she was examining the other contents of that secret compartment; and, when she had been so startled by Mona's rap and upset the table, it had been pushed underneath the draperies, while, during her hurry in replacing the various articles, she had not noticed that it was missing.

"Yes, I understand," she said, in a low, constrained, despairing tone. "You have balked me at last, but," throwing back her head like some animal suddenly brought to bay, "what are you going to do about it?"

"Only what is right and just, Mrs. Montague," courteously responded Mr. Corbin.

"Right and just!" she repeated, with bitter emphasis. "That means, I suppose, that you are going to compel me to give up my fortune."

"The law decrees that children shall have their father's property, excepting, of course, a certain portion," said the lawyer.

"A paltry one-third," retorted Mrs. Montague, angrily.

"Yes, unless the heirs choose to allow something more to the widow. Perhaps my client—"

Mrs. Montague sprang to her feet, her face flaming with sudden passion.

"Do you suppose I would ever humiliate myself enough to accept any favor from Mona Forester's child?" she cried, as she paced the floor excitedly back and forth, "Never! I will never be triumphed over. I will defy you all! Oh, to be beaten thus!—it is more than I can bear."

Mrs. Montague's fury was something startling in its bitterness and intensity, and the three gentlemen, witnessing it, could not help feeling something of pity for the proud woman in her humiliation, even though they were disgusted with her vindictiveness and selfishness.

"Defiance will avail you nothing, Mrs. Montague; an amicable spirit would conduce far more to your advantage," Mr. Corbin remarked. "And now I advise you," he added, "to quietly relinquish all right and title to this fortune excepting, of course, your third, and trust to your husband's daughter and her counsel to make you such allowance as they may consider right. If you refuse to do this we shall be obliged to resort to the courts to settle the question of inheritance."

"Take the matter into the courts, then," was the passionate retort. "I will defy you all to the bitter end. And you," turning with blazing eyes and crimson cheeks to Ray, "I suppose you imagined that you were to win a princely inheritance with your promised wife; that when you found this piece of parchment you would thus enable Mona Forester's child to triumph over the woman who hated her with a deadly hatred.

Not so, I assure you, for my vengeance is even more complete than I ever dared to hope, and your 'promised wife,' my fine young man, will never flaunt her colors in triumph over me here in New York, for her reputation has been irretrievably ruined, and the city shall ring with the vile story ere another twenty-four hours shall pass."

"Don't be too sure, madame; don't be too sure that you're going to down that clever little lady just yet," were the words which suddenly startled every one in the room, and the next instant the door swung wide open to admit a new actor in the drama.

A brisk, energetic little man entered the room, and going directly to Mrs. Montague's side, he laid his hand upon her shoulder.

"Madame, you are my prisoner," he added, in a more quiet but intensely satisfied tone.

"What do you mean, sir?" haughtily demanded the woman, as she shook herself free from his touch. "Who are you, and how came you here?"

"Well, we'll take one question at a time, if you please, madame," the new-comer returned. "First, what do I mean? Just what I say—you are my prisoner. I arrest you for obtaining money under false pretenses—for theft, for abduction. The proof of the first charge is right here in my hand. Look!"

He opened his palm and disclosed to the horrified woman's gaze and to the amazement of the other occupants of the room two beautiful crescents of blazing diamonds.

"Heavens! where did you get them? Oh, I know—I know!"

shrieked the unhappy creature, cowering and shrinking from the sight as if blinded by it, and sinking upon the nearest chair.

"Yes, I reckon you do," grimly remarked Detective Rider, for it was he, "and this clears up the Bently affair of Chicago, for here, on the back of the settings, is the very mark which Mr. Arnold of that city put upon them more than three years ago. Well, so much for that charge. Now, if Mr. Palmer will just step this way, maybe he'll recognize some of his property, and we'll explain the second and third charges."

Ray looked astonished as he went forward, but he was even more so when Mr. Rider held up before him an elegant diamond cross, which he instantly identified as one of the ornaments which the beautiful Mrs. Vanderbeck had selected on that never-to-be-forgotten day when he was decoyed into Doctor Wesselhoff's establishment and left there a prisoner, while the woman made off with her booty.

"Where did you get it?" he exclaimed, while Mrs. Montague fell back among the cushions of her chair and covered her face with her trembling hands, utterly unnerved.

"That remains to be explained, together with some other things which are no less interesting and startling," the detective returned, with an air of triumph. "And now," raising his voice a trifle, "if a certain little lady will show herself, I imagine we can entertain you with another act in this strange comedy."

As he spoke the drawing-room door, which the man had left slightly ajar when he entered, was pushed open, and Mona made her appearance with her arms full of clothing.

She glided straight to the detective's side, and handed him

Mrs. Georgie Sheldon

something which, with a dextrous movement, he clapped upon Mrs. Montague's bowed head.

It was a wig of rich, dark-red hair, which fell in lovely rings about the woman's fair forehead and white neck.

She lifted her face with a cry of terror at Mr. Rider's act, and behold! the beautiful Mrs. Vanderbeck was before them!

Ray knew at once why Mrs. Montague had looked so strangely to him as she arose to greet him when he entered.

Her face had been artistically made up, with certain applications of pencil and paint, to give her the appearance of being considerably older than she was. But he wondered how she happened to be so made up that morning.

"That is not all," Mr. Rider resumed, as he took a costly tailor-made dress from Mona's arm and held it up before his speechless auditors. "Here is the robe which was so badly rent at the time that Mrs. Vanderbeck escorted Mr. Raymond Palmer to the great Doctor Wesselhoff for treatment, while the fragment that was torn from it will fit into the hole. And here," taking another garment from Mona, "is a widow's costume in which the fascinating Mrs. Bently figured in Chicago, when she so skillfully duped a certain Mr. Cutler, swindling him out of a handsome sum of money, and giving him paste ornaments in exchange. No one would ever imagine the elegant Mrs. Richmond Montague and the lovely widow to be one and the same person, for they were entirely different in figure as well as face, the former being very slight, while the latter was inclined to be decidedly portly, as was also Mrs. Vanderbeck.

"But, gentlemen, that is also easily explained, as you will see if you examine these costumes, for there must be five pounds, more or less, of cotton wadding used about each to pad it out to the required dimensions. Clever, very clever!" interposed Mr. Rider, bestowing a glance of admiration upon the bowed and shivering figure before him. "I think, during all my experience, I have never had so complicated and interesting a case. I do not wonder that you look dazed, gentlemen," he went on, with a satisfied glance at his wide-eyed and wondering listeners, "and I imagine I could have surprised you still more if I had had time to examine a certain trunk which stands open up stairs in the lady's chamber. I think I could find among its contents a gray wig and other garments belonging to a certain Mrs. Walton, so called, and perhaps a miner's suit that would fit Mr. Louis Hamblin, alias Jake Walton, who in St. Louis recently tried to dispose of costly diamonds which he had brought all the way from Australia, for his rustic sweetheart—eh? Ha, ha, ha!" and the jubilant man burst into a laugh of infinite amusement.

"Truly, Mr. Rider, your discoveries are somewhat remarkable; but will you allow me to examine that cross?" a new voice here remarked, and Mr. Amos Palmer arose from a mammoth chair at the other end of the drawing-room, where he had been an unseen witness of and listener to all that had occurred during the last half hour.

It was he who had rung the bell just as Mona was about to enter Mrs. Montague's boudoir in search of her scissors, and who, upon being told that the lady was out, had said he would wait for her. He had called to ask his *fiancee* to go with him to select the hangings for the private parlor which he was fitting up for her in his own house.

His face, at this moment, was as colorless as marble; his eyes gleamed with a relentless purpose, and his manner was frigid from the strong curb that he had put upon himself.

At the sound of his voice Mrs. Montague lifted a face upon which utter despair, mingled with abject terror, was written. She bent one brief, searching glance upon the man, and then shrank back again into the depths of her chair, shivering as with a chill.

CHAPTER XIX

HOW IT HAPPENED

Mr. Rider passed Mr. Palmer the diamond cross, which he took without a word, and carefully examined, turning it over and over and scrutinizing both the stones and the setting with the closest attention, though Ray could see that his hands were trembling with excitement, and knew that his heart was undergoing the severest torture.

"Yes," he said, after an oppressive silence, during which every eye, except Mrs. Montague's, was fixed upon him, "the cross is ours—my own private mark is on the back of the setting. And so," turning sternly to the wretched woman near him, "you were the thief; you were the unprincipled character who decoyed my son to that retreat for maniacs, and nearly made one of me! Then, oh! what treachery! what duplicity! When you feared that the net was closing about you and you would be brought to justice, you sought to make a double dupe of me by a marriage with me, imagining, I suppose, that I would suffer in silence, if the theft was ever discovered, rather than have my name tarnished by a public scandal. So you have sailed under many characters!" he went on, in a tone of biting scorn. "You are the Mrs. Bently, of Chicago! the Mrs. Bent, of Boston; Mrs. Vanderbeck and Mrs. Walton, of New York; and the woman in St. Louis, who

Mrs. Georgie Sheldon

gave bail for the rascally miner, who tried to dispose of the unset solitaires. Fortunately those have been proven to be mine and returned to me; but where are the rest of the stones? I will have them, every one," he concluded, in a tone so stern and menacing that the woman shivered afresh.

"They were all together—they were all yours except two; but the cross, we—we—"

Mrs. Montague proceeded thus far in a muffled, trembling tone, and then her voice utterly failed her.

"You did not dare to try to sell too many at one time, and so you reserved the cross for future use," Mr. Palmer supplemented. "Perhaps you even intended to wear it under my very eyes, among your wedding finery. I verily believe you are audacious enough to do so; but, madame, it will be safe to say that there will be no wedding now, at least between you and me."

The man turned abruptly, as he ceased speaking, and left the room, looking fully a dozen years older than when, an hour previous, he had come there, with hope in his heart, to plan with his bride-elect how they could make their future home most attractive for her reception.

Ray felt a profound pity for his father, in this mortifying trial and disappointment, and he longed to follow him and express his sympathy; but his judgment told him that it would be better to leave him alone for a time; that his wounded pride could ill-brook any reference to his blighted hopes just then.

It may as well be related just here how Detective Rider happened to appear so opportunely, and how Mona found the robes in which Mrs. Montague had so successfully masqueraded to carry out her various swindling operations.

It will be remembered that Mona, after she had gathered up the keepsakes belonging to her mother and returned them to the table, had found another box upon the floor of Mrs. Montague's boudoir.

When she had removed the rubber band that held the cover in its place, her astonished eyes fell upon a pair of exquisite diamond crescents for the ears, and a cross, which, from the description which Ray had given her, she knew must have been among the articles stolen from Mr. Palmer.

Instantly it flashed across her what this discovery meant.

She felt very sure that Mrs. Montague must have been concerned in the swindling of Mr. Cutler, more than three years previous, and also of Mrs. Vanderbeck in Boston, besides in the more recent so-called Palmer robbery.

Still, there were circumstances connected with these operations that puzzled her.

Mrs. Bently, the crafty widow of Chicago, had been described to her as a stout woman with red hair. Mrs. Vanderbeck had also been somewhat portly, likewise Mrs. Walton, whom she had seen in St. Louis, and these latter were somewhat advanced in years also.

Mrs. Montague, on the contrary, was slight and sylph-like in figure; a blonde of the purest type, with light golden hair, a lovely complexion, with hardly the sign of a wrinkle on her handsome face.

But she did not speculate long upon these matters, for, having made this discovery, she was more anxious than before to be released from her place of confinement. So she had gone into the adjoining room, and tried the door leading into the hall.

That, too, as we know, she had found locked, and then, as she turned to retrace her steps, she was stricken spellbound by something which she saw upon the bed.

It was nothing less than a widow's costume, comprising a dress, bonnet, and vail, together with a wig of short, curling red hair!

Yes, Mrs. Montague was the "widow!" or woman in black whom Detective Rider had observed and followed only a little while previous. When she found that the man was on her track she had slipped into the carriage and ordered the driver to take her with all possible speed to a certain store on Broadway. Arriving there, she had simply passed in at one door and out of one opposite leading upon a side street, where she hailed a car, and, thoroughly alarmed, went directly home instead of going to the room where she usually made these changes in her costume.

Upon reaching her own door, she quietly let herself in with her latch-key, and going directly to her chamber, tore off her widow's weeds, and wig, and threw them hastily upon the bed. She hurriedly donned another dress, and was about to remove the cleverly simulated signs of age from her face, when she heard the bell ring, and went into the hall to ascertain who had called. We know the rest, how she recognized the lawyer, and imagined he had come again to annoy her further upon the subject of Mona Forester's child; how, almost at the same moment, she discovered Mona's presence in the house, and instantly resolved to lock her up until she could decide what further to do with her. And thus, laboring under so much excitement, she entirely forgot about the wrinkles and crow's-feet upon her face, and which so changed its expression.

The moment Mona saw the costume upon the bed everything was made plain to her mind. Mrs. Bently, of the Chicago and Boston crescent swindle, was no other than Mrs. Montague in a most ingenious disguise.

Glancing about the room for further evidences of the woman's cunning, she espied a trunk standing open at the foot of the bed, as if some one had been hastily examining the contents and forgotten to shut it afterward.

She approached it, and on top of the tray there lay the very dress of gray ladies' cloth which she had seen hanging in the closet of a certain room in the Southern Hotel in St. Louis. Then she knew, beyond a doubt, that Mrs. Montague had also figured as Mrs. Walton, the mother of the miner, in that city.

But who was the miner?

Louis Hamblin, in all probability, although she had not dreamed of such a thing until that moment.

"It is very strange that I should not have recognized Mrs. Montague, in spite of the white hair and the spotted lace vail," she murmured, thoughtfully. But after reflecting and recalling the fact that even the woman's eyebrows had been whitened and the whole expression of the face changed by pencil lines, to simulate wrinkles and furrows, and then covered with a thickly spotted vail, she did not wonder so much.

She was amazed and appalled by these discoveries, and trembling with excitement, she resolved to learn more, if possible.

Mrs. Georgie Sheldon

She lifted the lid of the hat-box, at one end of the tray, and there lay the very bonnet and vail that the woman had worn in St. Louis, and also the wig of white hair.

"What a wretched creature!" she exclaimed, in a horrified tone. Then wondering if Ray might not have come, while she had been there, she flew back to the window in the other room to look for him.

Yes, his carriage was standing before the door, and he would soon find means to release her, she thought.

But moment after moment went by, and no one came, while the continuous murmur of voices in the room below made her wonder what was going on there.

Presently, however, her attention was attracted to a man who was sauntering slowly along the opposite sidewalk, and she was sure she had seen him somewhere before, although, just at first, she could not place him.

"Why!" she exclaimed, after studying his face and figure a moment, "it is Mr. Rider. Can it be possible that he suspects anything of the mystery concealed in this house? At any rate, he is just the man that is needed here at this time."

She tapped lightly on the pane to attract his attention.

He stopped, glanced up, and instantly recognized Mona, nodding and lifting his hat to indicate that he did so.

She beckoned him to cross the street, and then cautiously raised the window. He was beneath it in a moment.

"Come in, Mr. Rider, and come directly up stairs to me," she said, in a low tone. "I have been locked in this room, and I have made an important discovery which you ought to know immediately."

He nodded again, his keen eyes full of fire, turned, ascended the steps, and pulled the bell.

Mary sighed heavily as she bent her weary steps, for the fifth time, up the basement stairs to answer his imperative summons.

"Is your mistress at home?" Mr. Rider inquired, in a quick, business-like tone.

"Yes, sir; but she is engaged with callers," the girl replied.

"So much the better," returned the detective; then, bending a stern look on her, he continued: "I am an officer; I have business in this house; you are to let me in and say nothing to any one. Do you understand?"

Mary grew pale at this, and fell back a step or two from the door, frightened at the term "officer."

Mr. Rider took instant advantage of the situation and stepped within the hall.

"Don't dare to mention that I am here until I give you leave," he commanded, authoritatively, and then ran nimbly and quietly up stairs.

It was the work of but a moment to find the room where Mona was confined, turn the key, and enter.

"What does this mean, Miss Richards?" he asked, regarding her curiously. "How do you happen to be locked up like a naughty child?"

Mrs. Georgie Sheldon

"I will explain that to you by and by; but first let me show you these."

She uncovered the box which contained the crescents and cross, and held the gleaming diamonds before his astonished eyes.

The man was so utterly confounded by the unexpected sight that for a moment he gazed at them with a look of wonder on his face.

"Zounds! where did you get them?" he cried, breathlessly.

Mona briefly explained regarding the accident to the table, which had resulted in her discovering the secret compartment with its treasures.

"Clever! clever!" the man muttered, as his eyes fastened upon the table and he comprehended the truth. "Well, well, young lady, you've done a fine stroke of business this day, and no mistake! These are the real articles, no paste or sham to fool me this time," he added, as he lifted the crescents from the box. "But—when—Mrs. Richmond Montague!—who'd have thought it?"

"This isn't all, Mr. Rider," Mona continued, in a whisper, for she feared Mrs. Montague might catch the sound of their voices.

"What! more discoveries!" the man exclaimed, all alert again, as he shut the box and slipped it into his pocket.

"Yes, step this way, if you please," and leading him to the door of Mrs. Montague's chamber, she pointed at the costume lying upon the bed.

The quick eyes took it all in at a glance, and his face lighted with a swift flash of triumph.

"The Bently affair—the Vanderbeck swindle—the Palmer robbery! Clever! clever!" he muttered, as he seized the costume, shook out its folds, discovered the thick layers of padding about the waist and hips, and eyed it with intense satisfaction. Then he revealed two rows of firm, white teeth in a broad smile, as he snatched up and twirled that dainty red wig upon his hand, examining it with a critical and admiring eye.

"And this, also," continued Mona, going to the trunk and lifting from it the tailor-made costume of gray ladies' cloth.

"Aha! ha!" chuckled Mr. Rider. "Really, Miss Richards, if you were only a man we might make a right smart detective of you. This is the very dress we have been wanting, and here is the rent. Have you still the fragment that you showed me in St. Louis?"

"Yes, it is here in my purse," Mona answered, drawing it from her pocket, and, taking the piece of cloth from it, she handed it to him.

"Here, too, is the gray wig worn by Mrs. Walton," she went on, as she lifted the lid of the hat-box and revealed its contents.

"Yes; true enough! and I'll wager that this trunk contains some other disguises which we should recognize," he responded. "But," he added, "we have enough for our purpose just now, and we will defer further examination until later. Now, Miss Richards, I am going down stairs to confront that woman with this stolen property. You follow me, but remain in the hall until I give you a signal, then come forward with these disguises. Have you any idea who is below calling on her ladyship?" he asked, in conclusion.

"No; but I am very sure that Mr. Raymond Palmer is somewhere in the house, for he was to call for me, and his carriage is at the door."

"I am glad to know that," the man cried, "and now I will make quick work of this business."

He turned and left the room with a quick step, and going directly below entered the drawing-room, just as Mrs. Montague was rudely taunting Ray about Mona.

The young girl gathered up the various articles of clothing and followed him, and we know what occurred after that.

CHAPTER XX

MRS. MONTAGUE EXPLAINS

It would be difficult to describe the abject distress of the wretched woman, whose career of duplicity and crime had been so unexpectedly revealed and cut short.

She was the picture of despair, as she sat crouching in the depths of her luxurious chair, her figure bowed and trembling, her face hidden in her hands.

There was a silence for a moment after Mr. Amos Palmer left the room; then Mr. Rider, who had been curiously studying his prisoner while the gentleman was speaking, remarked:

"It is the greatest mystery to me, madame, how, with the large fortune which you have had at your disposal, you could have wished to carry on such a dangerous business. What could have been your object? Surely not the need of money, nor yet the desire for jewels, since you have means enough to purchase all you might wish, and you tried to sell those you stole. One would almost suppose that it was a sort of monomania with you."

"No, it was not monomania," Mrs. Montague cried, as she

Mrs. Georgie Sheldon

started up with sudden anger and defiance; "it was absolute need."

"Really, now," Mr. Rider remarked, regarding her with a peculiar smile, "I should just like to know, as a matter of curiosity, how much it takes to relieve you from absolute need. I have supposed that you were one of the richest women in New York."

Mrs. Montague flushed a sudden crimson, and darted a quick, half-guilty look at Mr. Corbin. Then she turned again to the detective.

"Did you?—and so did others, I suppose!" she cried, with a short, scornful laugh. "Well, then, let me tell you that until I set my wits at work my income was only about twenty-five hundred dollars a year; and what was that paltry sum to a woman with my tastes?

"I do not care who knows now," she went on, with increasing excitement; "I have been humiliated to the lowest degree, and I shall glory in telling you how a woman has managed to outwit keen business men, sharp detectives, and clever police. In the first place, those crescents were presented to me at the time of my marriage. They are, as you have doubtless observed, wonderful jewels—as nearly flawless as it is possible to find diamonds. When I went to Chicago I was poor, for I had been extravagant that year and overdrawn my income. Money I must have—money I would have; and then it was that I attempted, for the first time, to carry out a scheme which I had planned while I was abroad the previous year. I had ordered a widow's outfit to be made, and padded in a way to entirely change my figure. I also purchased that red wig. While in Paris I learned the art of changing the expression of my face, by the skillful use of pencils and paint, and thus, dressed in my mourning costume with my eyebrows and lashes tinged to match my false hair, no one would ever have recognized me as Mrs. Montague.

"I had also provided myself, while in Paris, with several pairs of crescents, the exact counterparts, in everything save value, of the costly ones in my possession. I need not repeat the story of my success in getting money from Justin Cutler—you already know it; but I was so elated over the fact that I immediately went on to Boston, where I won even a larger sum from Mrs. Vanderheck."

"Yes; but how did you manage to change the jewels in that case, since you were with Mrs. Vanderheck from the time you left the expert until she paid you the money for them?" inquired Mr. Rider, who was deeply interested in this cunningly devised scheme.

"That was easily done," Mrs. Montague returned. "I had the case in my lap, and the duplicate crescents in my pocket. It required very little ingenuity on my part to so engage Mrs. Vanderheck's attention that I could abstract the real stones from the case and replace them with the others. Regarding the Palmer affair," she continued, with a glance of defiance at Ray, "it only required a few lines and touches to my face to apparently add several years to my age and change its expression; and, with my red hair and the change in my figure, my disguise was complete."

"And the name," interposed Ray, regarding her sternly; "you had a purpose in using that."

"Certainly, and the invalid husband also," she retorted, with a short, reckless laugh. "I had a purpose, too, in calling the elder Mr. Palmer's attention to the profusion of diamonds worn by Mrs. Vanderheck upon the evening of Mrs. Merrill's reception. You can understand why, perhaps," she added, sarcastically, and turning to the detective.

He merely nodded in reply, but muttered under his breath, with a kind of admiration for her daring:

"Clever—clever, from the word 'go.'"

"With a wig of white hair, a few additional wrinkles, and the sedate dress of a woman of sixty, I passed as Mrs. Walton, the mother of a lunatic son. It was not such a very difficult matter after all," she added, glancing vindictively at Ray: "the chief requirement was plenty of assurance, or cheek, as you men would express it. My only fear was that the diamonds would be missed before we were admitted to the doctor's house."

"When did you take that package from my pocket?" Ray demanded, with some curiosity. "Was it when I leaned forward to assist you about your dress?"

The woman's lips curled.

"And run the risk of being detected before leaving the carriage after all my trouble? No, indeed," she scornfully returned. "My *coup de grace* was just after ringing Doctor Wesselhoff's bell, while we stood together on the steps; the package was not large, though valuable, and it was but the work of a moment to transfer it from your pocket to mine, while you stood there with your arms full."

Ray regarded her wonderingly. She must have been very dextrous, he thought, and yet he remembered now that she had turned suddenly and brushed rather rudely against him.

"And in St. Louis—" Mr. Rider began.

Mrs. Montague flushed, and a wary gleam came into her eye.

"Yes, of course," she interrupted, hastily; "I was also the Mrs. Walton, of St. Louis. It was very easy to hire an extra room under that name."

"And your agent was—who?" continued Mr. Rider.

"That does not matter," she retorted, sharply. "You have found me out. I have recklessly explained my own agency in these affairs, but you will not succeed in making me implicate any one else."

"Very well; we will question you no further upon that point now," said the detective; "but it does not take a very wise head to suspect who was your accomplice, and I imagine it will not take a great deal of hunting, either, to find him," and Mr. Rider resolved to make a bee line for the Fall River boat the moment he could get through with his business there. "And now, gentlemen," he resumed, turning to the lawyers and Ray, "I think we'll close this examination here, and I'll take my prisoner into camp."

A cry of horror burst from Mrs. Montague's blanched lips at this remark.

"You cannot mean it—you will not dare to take me to a vile jail," she exclaimed, in tones of mingled fear and anger.

"Jails were made for thieves, swindlers, and abductors," was the laconic response.

The woman sprang to her feet again, and shot a withering glance at him.

"I go to a common prison? never!" she said, fiercely, and

with all the haughtiness of which she was capable.

"The fact of your having figured as a leader in high life, madame, does not exempt you from the penalty of the law, since you have already declared yourself guilty of the crimes I have named," coolly rejoined the detective.

"Oh, I cannot—I cannot," moaned the wretched woman, wringing her hands in abject distress. Then her glance fell upon Mona, who had quietly seated herself a little in the background, after the detective had relieved her of the clothing which she had brought into the room.

"You will not let them send me to prison—you will not let them bring me to trial and sentence me to such degradation," she moaned, imploringly.

Mr. Rider regarded her with amazement and supreme contempt at this servile appeal, for so it seemed to him.

"How can you expect that Miss Richards will succor you after your heartless and wicked treatment of her?" he demanded more sharply than he had yet spoken to her.

"Because, Mr. Rider," Mona gently interposed, "she bears a name she knows I am anxious to save from all taint or reproach; because she was the wife, and I the only child, of Walter Richmond Montague Dinsmore."

The detective gave vent to a long, low whistle of surprise.

"Zounds! can that be possible?" he cried, as he turned his wondering glance upon the lawyers.

"Yes," said Mr. Corbin, "it is the truth, and, of course, it is time that it should be revealed. I have known that Mrs.

Richmond Montague and Mrs. Walter Dinsmore were one and the same person ever since the death of Mr. Dinsmore. The lady came to me immediately after that event and requested me to ascertain if he had made a will. I instituted inquiries and learned that he had tried to do so, but failed to sign it. She then revealed to me that she was the wife of Mr. Dinsmore, but that they had separated only a year after their marriage, although he had allowed her an annual income of twenty-five hundred dollars for separate maintenance. She produced her certificate and other proofs that she was his lawful wife, and authorized me to claim his fortune for her, but stipulated that she was not to appear personally in the matter, as she did not wish to be identified as Mrs. Dinsmore, after having appeared in New York society as Mrs. Montague. She absolutely refused to make her husband's niece—or supposed niece—any allowance, although I felt that it was cruel to deprive the young lady of everything when she had been reared in luxury and expected to be the sole heir, and I tried to persuade her to settle upon her the same amount that she herself had hitherto received from Mr. Dinsmore. All my arguments were without avail, however, and I was obliged to act as she required. You all know the result; Miss Mona was deprived of both fortune and home, and Mrs. Montague, as she still wished to be known, suddenly became, in truth, the rich woman she was supposed to be previously."

"Did you know of this?" Mr. Rider asked, turning to Mr. Graves.

"I knew that a woman claiming to be a Mrs. Dinsmore had secured the fortune which should have been settled upon this young lady; but I did not know that Mrs. Montague was that woman until Miss Dinsmore, as I suppose we must now call her"—with a smile at Mona—"returned from the South. Until then I also believed that she was only the niece of my friend. If I had ever suspected the truth you may be very sure that I should have fought hard to establish the fact."

"I suspected the fact when Miss Mona came to me, bringing her mother's picture, and told me her story," Mr. Corbin here remarked. "I was convinced of it after I had paid a visit to and made some inquiries of Mrs. Montague—"

"Ha!" that woman interposed as she turned angrily upon Mona, "then you did make use of that torn picture after all!"

"I took it to an artist, had it copied, then gave the pieces to Mary to be burned, as you had commanded," Mona quietly replied.

"Oh! how you have fooled me!" Mrs. Montague exclaimed, flushing hotly. "If I had only acted upon my first impressions, I should have sent you adrift at once—I should not have tolerated your presence a single hour; but you were so demure and innocent that you deceived me completely, and I never found you out until the morning after my high-tea. Then I understood your game, and resolved to so effectually clip your wings that you could never do me any mischief."

Mona started at this last revelation, and light began to break upon her mind.

"How did you find me out?" she inquired, in a low tone.

"I had a letter telling me that my seamstress, who called herself Ruth Richards, was no other than Mona Montague—the last person in all the world whom I would have wished to receive into my family—and that she was having secret meetings with Raymond Palmer."

"Who wrote that letter?" Mona demanded, with heightened color.

"I do not know—it was anonymous; but I was convinced at once that you were Mona Montague, from the fact that you were having secret interviews with Ray Palmer, for his father had told me of his interest in her. Of course I instantly came to the conclusion that you were plotting against me, and, though I did not believe that you could prove your identity, or your mother's legal marriage, I feared that something might occur to trouble me in the possession of my fortune; so I resolved to marry you to Louis and settle the matter for all time."

"Then that was why you started so suddenly for the South?" Mona said, with flashing eyes.

"That was not my only reason for going," returned Mrs. Montague, flushing. "I—I had a telegram calling me to St. Louis, and so thought the opportunity a fine one to carry out my scheme regarding you."

"And did you suppose, for one moment, that you could drive me into a marriage with a man for whom I had not the slightest affection or even respect?" Mona demanded, bending an indignant look upon the unprincipled schemer.

"I at least resolved that I would so compromise you that no one else would ever marry you," was the malicious retort, as the woman turned her vindictive glance from her to Ray.

"Nothing could really compromise me but voluntary wrong-doing," Mona answered, with quiet dignity, "and your vile scheme was but a miserable failure."

"I do not need to be twitted of the fact," Mrs. Montague

impatiently returned. "My whole life has been a failure," she went on, her face almost convulsed with pain and passion. "Oh! if I had only destroyed that marriage certificate you would never have triumphed over me like this; you would never have learned the truth about yourself."

"Oh, yes, I should," Mona composedly returned, "and even my trip to New Orleans resulted advantageously to me."

"How so?" questioned her enemy, with a start, and regarding her with a frown.

"An accident revealed to me, on the last night of our stay there, the whole truth about myself. Up to that time I was entirely ignorant of the fact that my supposed uncle was my father, for I knew nothing about the discovery of the certificate until my return from Havana."

"What do you mean?—what accident do you refer to?" Mrs. Montague asked.

"The day I was eighteen years old I asked my father some very close questions regarding my parentage, of which I had been kept very ignorant all my life. Some of them he answered, some of them he evaded, and, on the whole, my conversation with him was very unsatisfactory; for I really did not know much more about myself and my father and mother at its close than at its beginning.

"On the same day he gave me a small mirror that had once belonged to Marie Antoinette, and which, he said, had been handed down as an heirloom in my mother's family for several generations. This mirror he cautioned me never to part with; and so, when I went South with you, I packed it with my other things in my trunk. That last evening in New Orleans, while removing and repacking some clothing I dropped the book containing my mirror. When I picked it up I discovered that it contained a secret drawer in its frame. In the drawer there were some letters, a box containing two rings belonging to my mother and a full confession, written by my father upon the very day that he had presented me with the royal keepsake.

"So," Mona concluded, "you perceive that even had you destroyed the certificate proving their marriage, I should have other and sufficient proof that I was the child of Mr. and Mrs. Walter Dinsmore."

"Oh! if I had only forced the sale of all his property and gone back at once to California, I should have escaped all this and kept my fortune," groaned the unhappy woman, in deep distress.

"Really, Mrs. Dinsmore, you are showing anything but a right spirit—" Mr. Corbin began, in a tone of reproof, when she interrupted him with passionate vehemence.

"Never address me by that name," she cried. "Do you suppose I wish to be known as the widow of the man who repudiated me? Never! That was why I adopted the name of Montague, and I still wish to be known as such. Ah!—but if I have to go to—Oh, pray plead for me!" she cried, turning again to Mona; "do not let them send me to prison."

Just at that moment Mr. Palmer's wan face appeared again at the rear door of the drawing-room.

He beckoned to Ray, who immediately left the room, and Mona, who had grown very thoughtful after Mrs. Montague's last appeal, left her seat and approached the lawyers.

"Mr. Graves—Mr. Corbin," she said, in a low tone, which

only they could hear, "cannot something be done to keep this matter from becoming public? I cannot bear the thought of having my dear father's name become the subject of any scandal in connection with this woman. It would wound me very sorely to have it known that Mrs. Richmond Montague, who has figured so conspicuously in New York society, was his discarded wife; that she robbed me of my fortune, and why; that she—the woman bearing his name—was the unprincipled schemer who defrauded Mr. Justin Cutler and Mrs. Vanderheck, and robbed Mr. Palmer of valuable diamonds. I could not endure," she went on, flushing crimson, "that my name should be brought before the public in connection with Louis Hamblin and that wretched voyage from New Orleans to Havana."

"But, my dear Miss Dinsmore—" began Mr. Corbin.

"Please let me continue," Mona interposed, smiling faintly, yet betraying considerable feeling. "I think I know what you wished to remark—that she has had the benefit of all this money which she has obtained under false pretenses, and that she ought to suffer the extreme penalty of the law for her misdeeds. She cannot fail to suffer all, and more than any one could desire, in the failure of her schemes, in the discovery of her wickedness, and in the loss of the fortune of which she felt so secure. But even if she were indifferent to all this I should still beg you to consider the bitter humiliation which a public trial would entail upon me, and the reproach upon my father's hitherto unsullied name. If—if I will cause Mr. Cutler and Mrs. Vanderheck to be reimbursed for the loss which they sustained through Mrs. Montague's dishonesty, cannot you arrange some way by which a committal and a trial can be avoided?"

"I am afraid it would be defeating all law and justice," Mr. Corbin began again, and just at that moment Ray returned to the room, looking very grave and thoughtful.

Mona's face lighted as she saw him.

"Ray, come here, please, and plead for me," she said, turning her earnest face toward him; and he saw at once that her heart was very much set upon her object, whatever it might be.

Mrs. Georgie Sheldon

CHAPTER XXI

MRS. MONTAGUE TELLS HER STORY

"What is it, Mona?" Ray inquired, as he went to her side. "You may be very sure that I will second your wishes if they are wise and do not interfere in any way with your interests."

Mona briefly repeated what she had already proposed to the lawyers, and Ray immediately responded that it was also his wish and his father's that as far as they were concerned all public proceedings against Mrs. Montague should be suspended.

"Come with me to another room where we can converse more freely," he added, "for I have a proposition to make to you in my father's name. Mr. Rider," raising his voice and addressing the detective, "will you allow Mrs. Montague to remain alone with Miss Dinsmore for a little while, as I wish to confer with you upon a matter of importance?"

The detective took a swift survey of the room before answering. It was evident that he had no intention of allowing his captive to escape him now after all his previous efforts to secure her.

"Yes," he replied, "I will go with you into the hall, if that will do."

He knew that in the hall he should be able to keep his eyes upon both doors of the drawing-room, and no one could pass in and out without his knowing it, while there was no other way of egress.

The four gentlemen accordingly withdrew, thus leaving Mona and Mrs. Montague by themselves.

Mona seated herself by a window, and as far as possible from the woman, for she shrank with the greatest aversion from her, while she felt that her own presence must be oppressive and full of reproach to her.

But the woman's curiosity was for the moment greater than her anxiety or remorse, and after a brief silence, she abruptly inquired:

"How did that detective find that box of diamonds?"

"He did not find them. I accidentally discovered them," Mona replied.

"You? What were you prowling about in my room for?" crossly demanded Mrs. Montague.

"I was simply looking for a pair of scissors which I had left there the day before we went South. But why did you lock me in the room, for I suppose it was you?"

"Because I was desperate," was the defiant response. "I had just learned how you had escaped from Louis, but I had not a thought of finding you here. When I saw you in my room, however, a great fear came over me that you would yet prove my ruin. I imagined that you had just arrived in New York, and had come here to take away your things, and were perhaps searching my room for proofs of your identity. So on the impulse of the moment I locked you in, intending to make my own terms with you before I let you go."

"Did you suppose, after my experience in New Orleans, that I would trust myself with you without letting some one know where I could be found?" Mona quietly asked.

"If I had stopped to think I might have known that you would not," the woman said, sullenly. "But how did you get out of that hotel in Havana?"

"Mr. Justin Cutler assisted me."

Mrs. Montague flushed hotly at the mention of that name.

"Yes, I know, but how?" she said.

Mona briefly explained the manner of her escape, then inquired, in a voice of grave reproach:

"How could you conspire against me in such a way? How could you aid your nephew in so foul a wrong?"

"I have already told you—to make our fortunes secure," was the cool retort.

Mona shuddered. It seemed such a heartless thing to do, to plan the ruin of a homeless, unprotected girl for the sake of money.

Mrs. Montague noticed it, and smiled bitterly.

"You surely did not suppose I bore you any love, did you?" she sneered. "I have told you how I hated your mother, and it is but natural that the feeling should manifest itself against her child, especially as you both had usurped the affections of my husband."

"Such a spirit is utterly beyond my comprehension," gravely said the girl, "when your only possible reason for such hatred of a beautiful girl was that my father loved and married her."

"Well, and wasn't that enough?" hotly exclaimed Mrs. Montague. "For years Walter Dinsmore's aunt had intended that he should marry me—that was the condition upon which he was to have her fortune—and I had been reared with that expectation. Therefore, it was no light grief when I learned by accident, three weeks after he sailed for Europe, that he had married a girl who had come to New York to earn her living as a milliner. They went abroad together and registered as Mr. and Mrs. Richmond Montague. I was wild, frantic, desperate, when I discovered it; but I kept the matter to myself. I did not wish Miss Dinsmore to learn the fact, for I had a plan in my mind which I hoped might yet serve to give me the position I so coveted. I persuaded Miss Dinsmore that it would be wise to let me follow Walter to Europe, and I promised her that if such a thing were possible, I would return as his wife. Six weeks after he sailed with his bride, I also left for Europe with some friends. I kept track of the unsuspicious couple for four months, but it was not until they settled in Paris for the winter that I had an opportunity to put any of my plans into action."

"If you please, Mrs. Montague, I would rather you would not tell me any more," Mona here interrupted, with a shiver of repulsion. "My father wrote out the whole story, and so I know all about it. You accomplished your purpose and wrecked the life of a pure and beautiful woman—a loved and loving wife; but truly I believe if my mother could speak to-day she would say that she would far rather have suffered the

Mrs. Georgie Sheldon

wrong and wretchedness to which she was subjected than to have exchanged places with you."

"Do you dare to twit me of my present extremity and misery?" cried Mrs. Montague, angrily.

"Not at all; I was not thinking of these later wrongs of which you have been guilty," Mona gently returned, "but only of the ruin which you wrought in the lives of my father and mother. I cannot think that you were happy even after you had succeeded in your wretched plots."

"Happy!" repeated the woman, with great bitterness. "For two years I was the most miserable creature on earth. I will tell it, and you shall listen; you shall hear my side of the story," she went on, fiercely, as she noticed that Mona was restless under the recital. "As I said before, when they settled in Paris for the winter I began to develop my plans. I went to a skillful costumer, and provided myself with a complete disguise, then hired a room in the same house, although I took care to keep out of the sight of Walter Dinsmore and his wife. One day he went out of the city on a hunting excursion, and met with an accident—he fell and sprained his ankle, and lay in the forest for hours in great pain. He was finally found by some peasants who bore him to their cottage, and kindly cared for him. His first thought was, of course, for his wife, and he sent a messenger with a letter to her telling of his injury. I saw the man when he rode to the door. I instinctively knew there was ill news. I said I knew Mrs. Montague, and I would deliver the letter. I opened and read it, and saw that my opportunity had come. Walter Dinsmore, with many sickening protestations of love, wrote of his accident, and said it would be some time before he should be able to return to Paris, but he wished that she would take a comfortable carriage the next day, and come to him if she felt able to do so. Of course I never delivered the letter, but the next day I went to Mona Forester, and told her that her lover had deserted her; that she was no wife, for their marriage had been but a farce; that he had not even given her his real name; that he was already weary of her, and she would never see him again, for he was pledged to marry me as soon as he should return to America.

"At first she would not believe one word of it—she had the utmost confidence in the man she idolized; but as the days went by and he did not return she began to fear there was some foundation for my statements. Then a few cunning suggestions to the landlord and his wife poisoned their minds against her. They accused her of having been living in their house in an unlawful manner, and drove her out of it with anger and scorn.

"She left on the fifth day after Walter's accident, and I hired the butler of the house to go with her and make it appear as if she had eloped with him. He carried out my instructions so faithfully that their sudden flitting had every appearance of the flight of a pair of lovers. When Walter received no answer from his wife, and she did not go to him, as he requested, he became very anxious, and insisted upon returning to Paris, in spite of his injury. Immediately upon his arrival he was told that his lady had eloped with the butler of the house, and the angry landlord compelled him to quit the place also.

"I did not set eyes on him again for more than two years, when he returned at Miss Dinsmore's earnest request, for she had not long to live. He did not seem like the same man, and apparently had no interest in life. When Miss Dinsmore on her death-bed begged him to let her see the consummation of her one desire he listlessly consented, and we were married in her presence, and she died in less than a month. Then he confessed his former marriage to me, and told me that he had

Mrs. Georgie Sheldon

a child; that her home must be with us, and to escape all scandal and remark we would go to the far West. I was furious over this revelation, but I concealed the fact from him, for I loved him with all my soul, and I would have adopted a dozen children if by so doing I could have won his heart. I consented to have you in the family, provided that you should be reared as his niece, and never be told of your parentage. He replied, with exceeding bitterness, that he was not anxious that his child should grow up to hate her father for his lack of faith in her mother, and his deep injustice to her.

"We went to San Francisco to live, but I hated you even more bitterly than I had hated your mother, and every caress which I saw my husband lavish upon you was like a poisoned dagger in my heart. But he never knew it—he never knew that I had had anything to do with the tragedy of his life, until more than a year after our marriage.

"My own child—a little girl—was born about ten months after that event; but she did not live, and this only served to make me more bitter against you; for, although my husband professed to feel great sorrow that she could not have lived to be a comfort to us and a companion to you, I knew that he would never have loved her with the peculiar tenderness which he always manifested toward you.

"When your mother fled from him and Paris she left everything that he had lavished upon her save what clothing she needed and money to defray necessary expenses during the next few months; and so after my marriage I found pocketed away among some old clothing belonging to my husband the keepsakes that he had given to her and also their marriage certificate. I took possession of them, for I resolved that if you should outlive your father you should never have anything to prove that you were his child; if I could not have my husband's heart I would at least have his money.

"One day a little over a year after our marriage, on my return from a drive, I was told that a man was waiting in the library to see me. Without a suspicion of coming evil, I went at once to ascertain his errand, and was horrified to find there the butler—the man whom I had hired to act as your mother's escort to London. He had been hunting for me for three years to extort more money from me, and had finally traced me from New York to San Francisco.

"He demanded another large sum from me. It was in vain that I told him I had paid him generously for the service he had rendered me. He insisted that I must come to his terms or he would reveal everything to my husband. Of course I yielded to that threat, and paid him the sum he demanded, but I might have saved the money, for Walter Dinsmore, who had that morning started for Oakland for the day, but changed his mind and returned while I was out, was sitting in a small alcove leading out of the library, and had heard the whole conversation.

"Of course there was a terrible scene, and he obliged me to confess everything, although he had heard enough to enable him to comprehend the whole, and then he sternly repudiated me; but, scorning the scandal which would attend proceedings for a divorce, he gave me a meager stipend for separate maintenance, and told me he never wished to look upon my face again. He settled his business, sold his property, and returned to New York with you and your nurse, leaving me to my fate. He forbade me to live under the name of Dinsmore, but I would not resume my maiden name, and so adopted that of Mrs. Richmond Montague. But I still treasured that certificate and my own also, for I meant, if I should outlive him, to claim his fortune, and also kept myself pretty well posted regarding his movements.

"Shortly after our separation my only sister died, and her

Mrs. Georgie Sheldon

son, Louis, was thus left destitute, and an orphan. I believed that I could make him useful to me, so I adopted him. We have roved a great deal, for we have had to eke out my limited income by the use of our wits. My best game, though, was with the crescents which Miss Dinsmore gave me as a wedding present, and which I had duplicated several times. Early last fall we came to New York, for in spite of all the past I still loved Walter Dinsmore, and longed to be near him.

"I felt as if the fates had favored me when I heard that he had died without making his will, and I knew from the fact that you were known only as his niece, Miss Mona Montague, that you must still be in ignorance of your real relationship toward him. So it was comparatively easy for me to establish my claim to his property. I did not appear personally in the matter, for I was leading quite a brilliant career here as Mrs. Richmond Montague, and I did not wish to figure as the discarded wife of Walter Dinsmore, so no one save Mr. Corbin even suspected my identity. If Walter Dinsmore had never written that miserable confession, or if I had at once turned all his property into money and gone abroad, or to California, I need never have been brought to this. As matters stand now, however, I suppose you will claim everything," she concluded, with a sullen frown.

Mona thought that if the law had its course with her she would need but very little of the ill-gotten wealth upon which she had been flourishing so extravagantly of late. But she simply replied, in a cold, resolute tone:

"I certainly feel that I am entitled to the property which my father wished me to have."

"Indeed! then you have changed your mind since the night when you so indignantly affirmed to Louis that you did not wish to profit by so much as a dollar from the man who had so wronged your mother," sneered her companion, bitterly.

"Certainly," calmly returned Mona, "now that I know the truth. My father did my mother no willful wrong, although in his morbid grief and sensitiveness he imputed such wrong to himself, and never ceased to reproach himself for it. You alone," Mona continued, with stern denunciation, "are guilty of the ruin of their happiness and lives; you alone will have to answer for it. You have been a very wicked woman, Mrs. Montague, not only in connection with your schemes regarding them, but in your corruption of the morals of your nephew. I should suppose your conscience would never cease to reproach you for having reared him to such a life of crime. You will have to answer for that also."

Mrs. Montague shivered visibly at these words, thus betraying that she was not altogether indifferent to her accountability.

But she quickly threw off the feeling, or the outward appearance of it, and tossing her head defiantly, she remarked:

"I do not know who has made you my mentor, Miss Dinsmore; but there is one thing more that I wish you to explain to me—how came that detective to be in my house?"

"He was passing in the street, and I asked him to come in," Mona replied.

"Indeed! and where, pray, did you make the acquaintance of the high-toned Mr. Rider?" sarcastically inquired Mrs. Montague.

"In St. Louis."

"In St. Louis!" the woman repeated, astonished.

"Yes. You doubtless remember the day that I rode with you and your nephew in the street-car, when you were both disguised."

"Yes, but did you know us at that time?"

"No, I only recognized the dress you had on."

"Ah! What a fool I was ever to wear it the second time," sighed the wretched woman, regretfully.

"I knew it was very like in both color and texture the piece of goods that Mr. Palmer had once shown me. I was almost sure when I saw that it had been mended that it was the same dress that Mrs. Vanderbeck had worn when she stole the Palmer diamonds, and immediately telegraphed to have the fragment sent to me."

"And Ray Palmer had it and had kept it all that time!" interposed Mrs. Montague, with a frown. "I hunted everywhere for it."

"He sent it to me by the next mail, and I began my hunt for the dress, although at that time I did not suspect that it belonged to you," Mona continued. Then she explained how, while assisting the chambermaid about her work, she had found the garment hanging in a wardrobe, and proved by fitting the fragment to the rent that her suspicions were correct.

"You will also remember," she added, "how you chided me a little later for going out without consulting you. I had been out to seek a detective to tell him what I had discovered."

"Ha! that was how you made Mr. Rider's acquaintance?" interrupted Mrs. Montague, with a start.

"Yes. He told me he was in St. Louis on business connected with that very case. He was very much elated after hearing my story, but when he went to make his arrest he found that Mrs. Walton and her so-called son had both disappeared. I was, of course, very much disappointed, but I never dreamed—"

"That I and my hopeful nephew were the accomplished sharpers," supplemented Mrs. Montague, with a bitter laugh. "Well, Mona Dinsmore, you have been very keen. I will give you credit for that—you have beaten me; I confess that you have utterly defeated me, and your mother is amply avenged through you. No doubt, you are very triumphant over my downfall," she concluded, acrimoniously.

"Indeed, I am not," Mona returned, with a sigh. "I do not think I could triumph in the downfall of any one, and though I am filled with horror over what you have told me, I am very sorry for you."

"Sorry for me!" repeated the woman, with skeptical contempt.

"Yes, I am truly sorry for you, and for any one who has fallen so low, for I am sure you must have seasons of suffering and remorse that are very hard to bear, while as for avenging my mother, I never had such a thought; I do not believe she would wish me to entertain any such spirit. I intend to assert my rights, as my father's daughter, but not with any desire for revenge."

Mona's remarks were here suddenly cut short by the return of the four gentlemen, and Mrs. Montague eagerly and searchingly scanned their faces as they gravely resumed their seats.

Mrs. Georgie Sheldon

CHAPTER XXII

MRS. MONTAGUE'S ANNUITY

Mona, too, regarded the lawyers with some anxiety, for she felt extremely sensitive about having her father's troubles and past life become the subject of a public scandal.

Ray noticed it, and telegraphed her a gleam of hope from his tender eyes.

The proposition which he had made to the lawyers upon leaving the room was in accordance with his father's request.

Mr. Palmer had begged that all proceedings in the case of the robbery might be quashed.

"I would rather lose three times the amount that woman stole from us than to have all New York know the wretched truth," he said to Ray, after calling him from the drawing-room. "To have it known that she robbed us and then tried to fortify herself by a marriage with me! I could not bear it. I have made a fool of myself, Ray," he went on, with pitiable humility, "but I don't want everybody discussing the mortifying details of the affair. If you can prevail upon the lawyers to settle everything quietly, do so, and, of course, Rider being a private detective, and in our pay, will do as we say, and, my boy, you and I will ignore the subject, after this, for all time."

Ray grasped his father's hand in heartfelt sympathy as he replied:

"We will manage to hush the matter, never fear. I am very sure that Mona will also desire to do so, and though I should be glad to have that woman reap the full reward of her wickedness I can forego that satisfaction for the sake of saving her feelings and yours."

Then, as we know, he returned to the drawing-room where Mona called to him to come and plead for the same thing.

The lawyers were both willing, for Mona's sake, to refrain from active proceedings against Mrs. Montague if she would resign all Mr. Dinsmore's property; but Mr. Rider objected very emphatically to this plan.

"It has been a tough case," he said, somewhat obstinately, "and it is no more than fair that a man should have the glory of working it up. Money isn't everything to a person in such business—reputation is worth considerable."

They had quite a spirited argument with him; but he yielded the point at last, provided Mr. Cutler would consent, although not with a very good grace, and then they all went back to Mona and her unhappy companion.

But Mrs. Montague put a grave front upon her critical situation.

"Well, and have you decided the fate of your prisoner?" she inquired of Mr. Rider, with haughty audacity, although her face was as white as her handkerchief as she put the question.

"Well, madame," he retorted, with scant ceremony, "if it had been left with me to settle there would have been no discussion with you—you would be in the Tombs."

"Well?" she asked, impatiently, seeing there was more to be said about the matter, and turning to Mr. Corbin.

"We have decided, Mrs. Montague, that in the first place, you are to relinquish everything which you inherited from Mr. Dinsmore at the time of his death."

"Everything?" she began, interrupting him.

"Please listen to what I have to tell you, and defer your objections until later," remarked the lawyer, coldly.

"Yes, everything. You are also to give up all jewels of every description that you have in your possession to make good as far as may be the losses of those who have suffered through your dishonesty. You are then to pledge yourself to leave New York and never show yourself here again upon pain of immediate arrest, nor cause any of the revelations of this morning to be made public. Upon these conditions we have decided, for the sake of the feelings of others, to let you go free and not subject you to a trial for your crime—provided Mr. Cutler agrees to this decision."

"But—but I must have something to live on," the miserable woman said, with white lips. "I can't give up everything; the law would give me my third, and I ought to inherit much more through my child."

"The law would give you—a criminal—nothing," Mr. Graves here sternly remarked. "Let me but reveal the fact that Mr. Dinsmore wished to secure everything to his daughter, and how you defrauded her, and you would find that the law would not deal very generously with you."

"But I must have money. I could not bear poverty," reiterated the woman, tremulously.

"Mr. Graves—Mr. Corbin!" Mona here interposed, turning to them, "it surely becomes the daughter's duty to be as generous as the father, and—"

"Generous!" bitterly exclaimed Mrs. Montague.

"Yes, he was generous," Mona asserted, with cold positiveness, "for, after all the wrong of which you had been guilty, he certainly would have been justified if he had utterly renounced you and refused to make any provision for you. But since he did not, I will do what I think he would have wished, and, with the consent of these gentlemen," with a glance at Ray and the lawyers, "I will continue the same annuity that he granted to you."

"That is an exceedingly noble and liberal proposition, Miss Dinsmore," Mr. Corbin remarked, bestowing a glance of admiration upon her, "and with all my heart I honor you for it."

Mrs. Montague did not make any acknowledgment or reply. She had dropped her head upon her hands and seemed to be lost in her own unhappy reflections.

Mr. Graves and Mr. Corbin conferred together for a few moments, and then the former remarked:

"Mrs. Montague will, of course, wish to give these subjects some consideration, and meanwhile I will go to consult with Mr. Cutler regarding his interest in the matter."

He left immediately, and Mr. Corbin and Mr. Rider fell into

general conversation, while Ray and Mona withdrew to the lower end of the drawing-room, where they could talk over matters unheard.

Mr. Graves was gone about an hour, and then returned accompanied by Mr. Justin Cutler himself.

After discussing at some length the question of Mrs. Montague being brought to trial he finally agreed to concur in the decision of the others.

"For Miss Dinsmore's sake I will waive all proceedings," he remarked, "but were it not for the feelings of that young lady," he added, sternly, "I would press the matter to the extent of the law."

Mrs. Montague shuddered at his relentless tone, but Mona thanked him with a smile for the concession.

Mrs. Montague then consented to abide by the conditions made by the lawyers, and, at their command, brought forth her valuable store of jewels to have them appraised and used to indemnify those who had suffered loss through her crimes.

Ray laid out what he thought would serve to make Mr. Cutler's loss good, selected what stones he thought belonged to his own firm, and then it was decided that the real crescents should be given to Mrs. Vanderheck if she wished them, or they should be sold and the money given to her.

Mrs. Montague was then informed that she must at once surrender all deeds, bonds, bank stock, etc., which she had received from the Dinsmore estate, and would be expected to leave the city before noon of the next day.

She curtly replied that she would require only three hours,

and that she would leave the house before sunset. The house, having been purchased with Mr. Dinsmore's money, would henceforth belong to Mona, therefore she and Ray decided to remain where they were until her departure and see that everything was properly secured afterward.

Having decided that these matters should not be made public, nothing could be done with Louis Hamblin, and Mr. Rider, much against his inclination, was obliged to forego making the arrest on the Fall River boat.

Mrs. Montague hastened her preparations and left her elegant home on West Forty-ninth street in season to meet her nephew a little after the hour appointed in the morning. Mr. Corbin previous to this handed her the first payment of her annuity, and obtained an address to which it was to be sent in the future, and thus the two accomplished sharpers disappeared from New York society, which knew them no more.

The next evening Ray and Mona were talking over their plans for the future, in the cozy library in Mr. Graves' house, when the young girl remarked:

"Ray, would you not like to read the story that my father concealed in the royal mirror?"

"Yes, dear, if you wish me," her lover replied.

Mona excused herself and went to get it. When she returned she brought the ancient keepsake with her.

She explained how the secret drawer operated, showed him the two rings and the letters, then putting Mr. Dinsmore's confession into his hands, bade him read it; and this is what his eager eyes perused:

Mrs. Georgie Sheldon

"MY DEAR MONA:—You who have been the darling of my heart, the pride of my life; you have just left me, to go to your caller, after having probed my heart to its very core. I can never make you know the bitterness of spirit that I experience, as I write these lines, for the questions you have just asked me have completely unmanned me—have made a veritable coward of me when I should have boldly told you the truth, let the consequence be what it would; whether it would have touched your heart with pity and fresh love for a sorrowing and repentant man, or driven you away from me in hate and scorn such as I experience for myself. You have just told me that I have made your life a very happy one; that you love me dearly. Oh, my darling, you will never know, until I am gone, how I hug these sweet words to my soul, and exult over them with secret joy, and you will never know, either, until then, how I long and hunger to hear you call me just once by the sacred name 'father,'

"Yes, Mona, I am your father; you are my child, and yet I had not the courage to tell you so, with all the rest of the sad story, this morning, for fear I should see all the love die out of your face, and you would turn coldly from me as you learned the great wrong I once did your mother.

"I told you that your father is dead. So he is, to you, and has been for many long years; for when I brought you from England, when you were only two years old, I vowed that you should never know that I was the man who, by my cowardice and neglect, ruined your mother's life; so I adopted you as my niece, and you have always believed yourself to be the child of my only and idolized sister. But, to begin at the beginning, I first met Mona Forester one day while attending my aunt to a millinery store, where she had her bonnets and caps made. She waited upon her, and I sat and watched the beautiful girl, entranced by her loveliness and winning manner. She was a cultured lady, in spite of the fact that she was obliged to earn her living in so humble a way.

"Her parents had both died two years previously, leaving her homeless and destitute, after having been reared in the lap of luxury. I saw her often after that, we soon learned to love each other, and it was not long before she was my promised wife.

"But my first sin was in not giving her my full name. I was afraid she might be shy of me, if she knew that I was the heir of the wealthy Miss Dinsmore, and so I told her my name was Richmond Montague. About that time, my studies being completed, my aunt wanted me to go abroad for a couple of years.

"She also wished me to marry the child of an intimate friend, and take her with me. She had been planning this marriage for years and had threatened, if I disappointed her, to leave all her money to some one else.

"Now comes my second sin against your mother. If I had been loyal and true, I should have frankly told my aunt of my love for Mona Forester, and that I could never marry another woman, fortune or no fortune. But I shirked the duty—I thought something might happen before my return to give me the fortune, and then I should be free to choose for myself; so I led Miss Dinsmore to believe that on my return I would marry Miss Barton. I wanted the fortune—I loved money and the pleasure it brought, but I did not want Miss Barton for a wife. She was proud and haughty—a girl bound up in the world and fashion, and I did love sweet and amiable Mona Forester.

"Now my third sin: I was selfish. I could not bear the thought of leaving my love behind, and so I persuaded her to a secret marriage, and to go to Europe with me. I never should have done this; a man is a coward and knave who will not boldly acknowledge his wife before the world. I hated myself for my weakness, yet had not strength of purpose to do what was right. We sailed under the name of Mr. and Mrs. Richmond Montague, and Mona did not know that I had any other; but I took care that the marriage certificate was made out with my full name, so that the ceremony should be perfectly legal.

"We were very happy, for I idolized my young wife, and our life for six months was one of earth's sweetest poems. We traveled a great deal during the summer, and then settled in Paris for the winter. We had rooms in a pleasant house in a first-class locality; our meals were served in our own dining-room, and everything seemed almost as homelike as if we had been in America.

"One day I took a sudden freak that I wanted to go hunting. Mona begged me not to go; she was afraid of fire-arms, and feared some accident. But I laughed at her fears, told her that I was an expert with a gun, and went away in spite of her pleadings, little thinking I should never see my darling again. I did meet with an accident—I fell and sprained my ankle very badly, and lay for several hours in a dense forest unable to move.

"Finally some peasants found me, and took me to their cottage, but it was too late to send news of my injury to Paris that night. But the next morning early I sent the man of the house—who was going through the city on his way to visit some friends for a week, with a letter to Mona, telling her to take a carriage and come to me. She did not come, and I heard nothing from her. I could not send to her again, for there was no one in the cottage to go, and no neighbor within a mile. I was terribly anxious, and imagined a hundred things, and at the end of a week, unable to endure the suspense any longer, I insisted upon being taken back to Paris in spite of the serious condition of my foot and ankle.

"But, oh, my child, the tidings that met me there were such as to drive the strongest mind distracted. The landlord told me that my wife had fled with the butler of the house. At first I laughed in his face at anything so absurd, but when he flew into a towering passion and accused me of having brought disgrace upon his house by living there unlawfully with a woman who was not my wife, I began to think there must be some truth in his statements. In vain I denied the charge; he would not listen to me, and drove me also from his dwelling.

"I was too lame and helpless to attempt to follow Mona, but I set a detective at work to find my wife, for I still had faith in her, and thought she might be the victim of the landlord's suspicions. The detective traced her to London, and brought me word that a couple answering the description of my wife and the butler had crossed the channel on a certain date, and had since been living under the same roof in London.

"Then I cursed my wife, and said I would never trust a human being again. I was a long time getting over my lameness, but I still kept my detective on the watch, and one day he came to me with the intelligence that the butler had deserted his victim, and the lady was ill, and almost destitute.

"That Mona should want or suffer, under any circumstances, was the last thing I could wish, even though I then firmly believed that she had deserted me; while the thought that my child might even lack the necessities of life, was sufficient incentive to make me hasten at once to her relief. But I have told you, Mona, that she was dead, and I found only a weak and helpless baby to need my care. The nurse told me that the lady had wanted to go to America several weeks

Mrs. Georgie Sheldon

previously, but her physician had forbidden her to attempt to cross the ocean. She told me that a gentleman had taken the room for her and had been very kind to her, but the lady had been very unhappy and ill most of the time, since coming to the house. I questioned her closely, but evidently Mona had made a confidante of no one, and she had lived very quietly, seldom going out, and seeing no one. I could not reconcile this with the fact of her having eloped with the butler, and I realized all too late that I should have come to her the moment I learned where she was, demanded an explanation, and at least given her a chance to defend herself. My darling might have lived, if I had done so, and my child would not have been motherless.

"I was frantic with grief, and tried to drown my sorrow by constant change of scene. I traveled for two years, and then was summoned home to my aunt, who was dying. She insisted that my marriage with Miss Barton should be immediately consummated, and I, too wretched to contest the point, let them have their way. Miss Dinsmore died soon afterward, but without suspecting my previous marriage. Then I confessed the truth to my wife, and told her of the existence of my child. I saw at once that she was deeply wounded upon learning of this secret of my life, but I never suspected how exceedingly jealous and bitter she was, or that she had any previous knowledge of the fact, until a little more than a year after our marriage, when I accidentally overheard a conversation between her and the man who had been her accomplice in ruining your mother's happiness and mine. That elopement, so called, had always seemed utterly inexplicable to me until then.

"I learned that day that Margaret Barton had known of my marriage with Mona Forester almost from the first, that she had followed us abroad, and came disguised into the very house where we were living; that she had intercepted my letter, telling Mona of my accident, and made the poor child believe that I had deserted her, and that I had not really married her, but simply brought her abroad with me to be the plaything of my season of travel, after which I was pledged to marry her, Margaret Barton. She repeated this cunning tale to the landlord, and then, when he drove my darling forth into the street, she hired the butler to follow her, and thus give her departure the appearance of an elopement. It was a plot fit to emanate only from the heart and brain of a fiend, and I wormed it out of her little by little, after the departure of her tool, who had traced her to this country, hoping to get more money for keeping her secret.

"I cannot, neither do I wish to describe the scene that followed this discovery. I was like a madman for a season, when I learned how I had been duped, how my darling had been wronged and betrayed, and driven to her untimely death, and I closed my heart and my doors forever against Margaret Barton. I settled an annuity of twenty-five hundred dollars upon her, then taking you, I left San Francisco. I came to settle in New York.

"You know all the rest, my Mona, but you cannot know how I have longed to own you, my child, and dared not, fearing to alienate your love by confessing the truth. I am going to conceal this avowal in the secret drawer of the mirror, that I have given you to-day, and some time you will read this story and perhaps pity and forgive your father for the culpable cowardice and wrong-doing of his early life. That woman stole the certificate of my first marriage and all the trinkets I had given your mother; but I swear to you that Mona Forester was my lawful wife—that you are our child, and in a few days I shall make my will, so stating, and bequeath to you the bulk of my fortune. I will also in that document explain the secret of this mirror so that you will have no difficulty in finding this confession, your mother's

Mrs. Georgie Sheldon

rings, and some letters which may be a comfort to you.

"Now, my darling, this is all; but I hope you will not love me less when you learn your mother's sad story and my weakness and sin in not boldly acknowledging her as my wife before the world. Oh, if I could hear but once, your dear lips call me 'father' I could ask no greater comfort in life—it would be the sweetest music I have ever heard since I lost my other Mona; yet it cannot be. But that God may bless you, and give you a happy life, is the earnest prayer of your loving father,

"WALTER RICHMOND MONTAGUE DINSMORE."

Ray was deeply moved as he finished reading this sad tale.

"It is the saddest story I ever heard," he said, as he folded the closely written sheets and returned them to Mona, "and Mr. Dinsmore must have suffered very keenly since the discovery of the great wrong done his wife, for his whole confession betrays how sensitive and remorseful he was."

"My poor father! if he had only told me! I could not have loved him less, and it would have been such a comfort to have known of this relationship, and to have talked with him about my mother," said Mona, with tears in her beautiful eyes.

"Well, dear, we will begin our life with no concealments," said Ray, with a tender smile, "And now, when may I tell Mr. Graves that you will come to me?"

"When you will, Ray," Mona answered, flushing, but with a look of love and trust that made his heart leap with gladness.

"Then one month from to-day, dear," he said, as he bent his

lips to hers.

And so, when the roses began to bloom and all the world was in its brightest dress, there was a quiet wedding one morning in Mr. Graves' spacious drawing-room and Mona Dinsmore gave herself to the man she loved.

There were only a few tried and true friends present to witness the ceremony, but everybody was happy, and all agreed that the bride was very lovely in her simple but elegant traveling dress.

"I cannot have a large wedding or any parade with gay people about me, for my heart is still too sore over the loss of my dear father," Mona had said, with quivering lips, when they had asked her wishes regarding the wedding, and so everything had been done very simply.

It is doubtful if so young a bride was ever made the recipient of so many diamonds as fell to Mona's lot that day.

Mr. Palmer, true to his promise, had all the recovered stones reset for her, and made her a handsome gift besides. Mr. and Miss Cutler presented to her a pair of beautiful stars for the hair, and Ray put a blazing solitaire above her wedding-ring, for a guard.

After a sumptuous wedding-breakfast, the happy couple started for a trip to the Golden Gate city, while during their absence, Mr. Palmer, senior, had his residence partially remodeled and refurnished for the fair daughter to whom already his heart had gone out in tender affection.

A notice of the marriage appeared in the papers, together with a statement that "the handsome fortune left by the late Walter Dinsmore had been restored to the young lady formerly known as Miss Mona Montague, now Mrs. Raymond Palmer, who had been fraudulently deprived of it, through the craftiness of a woman calling herself Mrs. Dinsmore."

Mona did not wish anything of her father's sad story to be made public, and so, it was arranged that this was all that should be given to the reporters, to show that she was Mr. Dinsmore's heiress, and would resume her former position in the world upon her return from her bridal trip.

Other books by this author

His Heart's Queen

Mona

Mrs. Georgie Sheldon

Choose from Thousands of 1stWorldLibrary Classics By

A. M. Barnard
Ada Leverson
Adolphus William Ward
Aesop
Agatha Christie
Alexander Aaronsohn
Alexander Kielland
Alexandre Dumas
Alfred Gatty
Alfred Ollivant
Alice Duer Miller
Alice Turner Curtis
Alice Dunbar
Allen Chapman
Alleyne Ireland
Ambrose Bierce
Amelia E. Barr
Amory H. Bradford
Andrew Lang
Andrew McFarland Davis
Andy Adams
Angela Brazil
Anna Alice Chapin
Anna Sewell
Annie Besant
Annie Hamilton Donnell
Annie Payson Call
Annie Roe Carr
Annonaymous
Anton Chekhov
Archibald Lee Fletcher
Arnold Bennett
Arthur C. Benson
Arthur Conan Doyle
Arthur M. Winfield
Arthur Ransome
Arthur Schnitzler
Arthur Train
Atticus
B.H. Baden-Powell
B. M. Bower
B. C. Chatterjee
Baroness Emmuska Orczy
Baroness Orczy
Basil King
Bayard Taylor
Ben Macomber
Bertha Muzzy Bower
Bjornstjerne Bjornson

Booth Tarkington
Boyd Cable
Bram Stoker
C. Collodi
C. E. Orr
C. M. Ingleby
Carolyn Wells
Catherine Parr Traill
Charles A. Eastman
Charles Amory Beach
Charles Dickens
Charles Dudley Warner
Charles Farrar Browne
Charles Ives
Charles Kingsley
Charles Klein
Charles Hanson Towne
Charles Lathrop Pack
Charles Romyn Dake
Charles Whibley
Charles Willing Beale
Charlotte M. Braeme
Charlotte M. Yonge
Charlotte Perkins Stetson
Clair W. Hayes
Clarence Day Jr.
Clarence E. Mulford
Clemence Housman
Confucius
Coningsby Dawson
Cornelis DeWitt Wilcox
Cyril Burleigh
D. H. Lawrence
Daniel Defoe
David Garnett
Dinah Craik
Don Carlos Janes
Donald Keyhoe
Dorothy Kilner
Dougan Clark
Douglas Fairbanks
E. Nesbit
E. P. Roe
E. Phillips Oppenheim
E. S. Brooks
Earl Barnes
Edgar Rice Burroughs
Edith Van Dyne
Edith Wharton

Edward Everett Hale
Edward J. O'Biren
Edward S. Ellis
Edwin L. Arnold
Eleanor Atkins
Eleanor Hallowell Abbott
Eliot Gregory
Elizabeth Gaskell
Elizabeth McCracken
Elizabeth Von Arnim
Ellem Key
Emerson Hough
Emilie F. Carlen
Emily Bronte
Emily Dickinson
Enid Bagnold
Enilor Macartney Lane
Erasmus W. Jones
Ernie Howard Pie
Ethel May Dell
Ethel Turner
Ethel Watts Mumford
Eugene Sue
Eugenie Foa
Eugene Wood
Eustace Hale Ball
Evelyn Everett-green
Everard Cotes
F. H. Cheley
F. J. Cross
F. Marion Crawford
Fannie E. Newberry
Federick Austin Ogg
Ferdinand Ossendowski
Fergus Hume
Florence A. Kilpatrick
Fremont B. Deering
Francis Bacon
Francis Darwin
Frances Hodgson Burnett
Frances Parkinson Keyes
Frank Gee Patchin
Frank Harris
Frank Jewett Mather
Frank L. Packard
Frank V. Webster
Frederic Stewart Isham
Frederick Trevor Hill
Frederick Winslow Taylor

Friedrich Kerst
Friedrich Nietzsche
Fyodor Dostoyevsky
G.A. Henty
G.K. Chesterton
Gabrielle E. Jackson
Garrett P. Serviss
Gaston Leroux
George A. Warren
George Ade
Geroge Bernard Shaw
George Cary Eggleston
George Durston
George Ebers
George Eliot
George Gissing
George MacDonald
George Meredith
George Orwell
George Sylvester Viereck
George Tucker
George W. Cable
George Wharton James
Gertrude Atherton
Gordon Casserly
Grace E. King
Grace Gallatin
Grace Greenwood
Grant Allen
Guillermo A. Sherwell
Gulielma Zollinger
Gustav Flaubert
H. A. Cody
H. B. Irving
H. C. Bailey
H. G. Wells
H. H. Munro
H. Irving Hancock
H. R. Naylor
H. Rider Haggard
H. W. C. Davis
Haldeman Julius
Hall Caine
Hamilton Wright Mabie
Hans Christian Andersen
Harold Avery
Harold McGrath
Harriet Beecher Stowe
Harry Castlemon
Harry Coghill
Harry Houidini

Hayden Carruth
Helent Hunt Jackson
Helen Nicolay
Hendrik Conscience
Hendy David Thoreau
Henri Barbusse
Henrik Ibsen
Henry Adams
Henry Ford
Henry Frost
Henry James
Henry Jones Ford
Henry Seton Merriman
Henry W Longfellow
Herbert A. Giles
Herbert Carter
Herbert N. Casson
Herman Hesse
Hildegard G. Frey
Homer
Honore De Balzac
Horace B. Day
Horace Walpole
Horatio Alger Jr.
Howard Pyle
Howard R. Garis
Hugh Lofting
Hugh Walpole
Humphry Ward
Ian Maclaren
Inez Haynes Gillmore
Irving Bacheller
Isabel Cecilia Williams
Isabel Hornibrook
Israel Abrahams
Ivan Turgenev
J. G.Austin
J. Henri Fabre
J. M. Barrie
J. M. Walsh
J. Macdonald Oxley
J. R. Miller
J. S. Fletcher
J. S. Knowles
J. Storer Clouston
J. W. Duffield
Jack London
Jacob Abbott
James Allen
James Andrews
James Baldwin

James Branch Cabell
James DeMille
James Joyce
James Lane Allen
James Lane Allen
James Oliver Curwood
James Oppenheim
James Otis
James R. Driscoll
Jane Abbott
Jane Austen
Jane L. Stewart
Janet Aldridge
Jens Peter Jacobsen
Jerome K. Jerome
Jessie Graham Flower
John Buchan
John Burroughs
John Cournos
John F. Kennedy
John Gay
John Glasworthy
John Habberton
John Joy Bell
John Kendrick Bangs
John Milton
John Philip Sousa
John Taintor Foote
Jonas Lauritz Idemil Lie
Jonathan Swift
Joseph A. Altsheler
Joseph Carey
Joseph Conrad
Joseph E. Badger Jr
Joseph Hergesheimer
Joseph Jacobs
Jules Vernes
Julian Hawthrone
Julie A Lippmann
Justin Huntly McCarthy
Kakuzo Okakura
Karle Wilson Baker
Kate Chopin
Kenneth Grahame
Kenneth McGaffey
Kate Langley Bosher
Kate Langley Bosher
Katherine Cecil Thurston
Katherine Stokes
L. A. Abbot
L. T. Meade

L. Frank Baum
Latta Griswold
Laura Dent Crane
Laura Lee Hope
Laurence Housman
Lawrence Beasley
Leo Tolstoy
Leonid Andreyev
Lewis Carroll
Lewis Sperry Chafer
Lilian Bell
Lloyd Osbourne
Louis Hughes
Louis Joseph Vance
Louis Tracy
Louisa May Alcott
Lucy Fitch Perkins
Lucy Maud Montgomery
Luther Benson
Lydia Miller Middleton
Lyndon Orr
M. Corvus
M. H. Adams
Margaret E. Sangster
Margret Howth
Margaret Vandercook
Margaret W. Hungerford
Margret Penrose
Maria Edgeworth
Maria Thompson Daviess
Mariano Azuela
Marion Polk Angellotti
Mark Overton
Mark Twain
Mary Austin
Mary Catherine Crowley
Mary Cole
Mary Hastings Bradley
Mary Roberts Rinehart
Mary Rowlandson
M. Wollstonecraft Shelley
Maud Lindsay
Max Beerbohm
Myra Kelly
Nathaniel Hawthrone
Nicolo Machiavelli
O. F. Walton
Oscar Wilde
Owen Johnson
P.G. Wodehouse
Paul and Mabel Thorne

Paul G. Tomlinson
Paul Severing
Percy Brebner
Percy Keese Fitzhugh
Peter B. Kyne
Plato
Quincy Allen
R. Derby Holmes
R. L. Stevenson
R. S. Ball
Rabindranath Tagore
Rahul Alvares
Ralph Bonehill
Ralph Henry Barbour
Ralph Victor
Ralph Waldo Emmerson
Rene Descartes
Ray Cummings
Rex Beach
Rex E. Beach
Richard Harding Davis
Richard Jefferies
Richard Le Gallienne
Robert Barr
Robert Frost
Robert Gordon Anderson
Robert L. Drake
Robert Lansing
Robert Lynd
Robert Michael Ballantyne
Robert W. Chambers
Rosa Nouchette Carey
Rudyard Kipling
Saint Augustine
Samuel B. Allison
Samuel Hopkins Adams
Sarah Bernhardt
Sarah C. Hallowell
Selma Lagerlof
Sherwood Anderson
Sigmund Freud
Standish O'Grady
Stanley Weyman
Stella Benson
Stella M. Francis
Stephen Crane
Stewart Edward White
Stijn Streuvels
Swami Abhedananda
Swami Parmananda
T. S. Ackland

T. S. Arthur
The Princess Der Ling
Thomas A. Janvier
Thomas A Kempis
Thomas Anderton
Thomas Bailey Aldrich
Thomas Bulfinch
Thomas De Quincey
Thomas Dixon
Thomas H. Huxley
Thomas Hardy
Thomas More
Thornton W. Burgess
U. S. Grant
Upton Sinclair
Valentine Williams
Various Authors
Vaughan Kester
Victor Appleton
Victor G. Durham
Victoria Cross
Virginia Woolf
Wadsworth Camp
Walter Camp
Walter Scott
Washington Irving
Wilbur Lawton
Wilkie Collins
Willa Cather
Willard F. Baker
William Dean Howells
William le Queux
W. Makepeace Thackeray
William W. Walter
William Shakespeare
Winston Churchill
Yei Theodora Ozaki
Yogi Ramacharaka
Young E. Allison
Zane Grey

www.ingramcontent.com/pod-product-compliance
Lightning Source LLC
Chambersburg PA
CBHW030114180626
46812CB00002B/416